"Heroic fantasy has been denounced as backward-looking (while science fiction is forward-looking), yet our scientists look to stars named for ancient gods and heroes, and there can never be a fiction or a populace with any imagination about the future if they lack an imagination about the past. We are rooted in both directions in time. The plain truth is that the finest stories throughout recorded history have been heroic fantasies.

"Herein, a huge dose of rousing adventures with magic, action, but also heart, humanity, and vision."

—Jessica Amanda Salmonson

HEROIC VISIONS II

Thirteen brand-new tales from the masters of the genre

Ace Fantasy books edited by Jessica Amanda Salmonson

HEROIC VISIONS
HEROIC VISIONS II

Ace Fantasy books by Jessica Amanda Salmonson

The Tomoe Gozen Saga

TOMOE GOZEN
THE GOLDEN NAGINATA
THOUSAND SHRINE WARRIOR

HEROIC VISIONS II

EDITED BY
JESSICA AMANDA SALMONSON

ACE FANTASY BOOKS
NEW YORK

HEROIC VISIONS II

An Ace Fantasy Book/published by arrangement with
the editor

PRINTING HISTORY
Ace Fantasy edition/July 1986

Cover art by Stephen Hickman.

ISBN: 0-441-32822-9

Ace Fantasy Books are published by
The Berkley Publishing Group,
200 Madison Avenue, New York, New York 10016.
PRINTED IN THE UNITED STATES OF AMERICA

ACKNOWLEDGMENTS

"The Inn at the World's End" © 1986 by Keith Roberts, permission of the author's agent. "Voices" © 1986 by Michael Bishop, permission of the author. "Lazarus" © 1986 by Ellen Kushner, permission of the author. "La Strega" © 1986 by Richard A. Russo, permission of the author. "Honor" © 1986 by Jody Scott, permission of the author. "The Lingering Minstrel" © 1986 by Jessica Amanda Salmonson. "The Head of Shemesh the Eshurian" © 1986 by Avram Davidson, permission of the author. "The Lion of Elirhom's Anger" © 1986 by Michael Nicholas Richard, permission of the author. "Eammon's Banshee'" © 1986 by Gillian FitzGerald, permission of the author. "The Slaughter of the Gods" © 1986 by Manly Wade Wellman, permission of the author. "Cohen the Clam-Killer" © 1983 by Steven Bryan Bieler, reprinted by permission of the author. "The Word-Woman of Dza" © 1986 by Grania Davis, permission of the author. "Masquerade of a Dead Sword" © 1986 by Thomas Ligotti, permission of the author. Introduction © 1986 by Jessica Amanda Salmonson, quotation from *Gog* by permission of Printing House A. Mondadori and Stanislao Paszkowski, for the Papini estate.

To John and Eileen

"They must be loving comrades,
The blowing wind and ceaseless wave."
—Ki no Tsurayuku, *The Tosa Diary*

CONTENTS

HEROIC VISIONS II

MASTERPIECES OF HEROIC FANTASY: AN INTRODUCTION BY JESSICA AMANDA SALMONSON, GIOVANNI PAPINI, AND GOG.

Giovanni Papini coyly refused responsibility for the ravings of the savage madman Gog, whose miscellaneous and vicious writings were edited by Giovanni into a grotesque book entitled, simply, *Gog,* and which Mary Prichard Agnetti translated for American consumption more than fifty years ago. The corrupt wisdom of Gog covers much the same ground as the *Bible* plus much else besides, and is almost as immoral. Perhaps that is why I like it.

Taking a vacation from the task of Introductionist, I thought to give this space over to a chapter from *Gog,* "The Masterpieces of Literature." The majority of those masterpieces are inescapably heroic fantasies of one kind or another. (And I say "inescapably" because a discussion of the finest writings of western civilization can go a long way without mentioning such matter as science fiction, mystery, westerns, nurse novels, and gothics; but if one bars fantasy, there's little left to discuss.) I think you will enjoy the game of figuring out just what works Gog has described.

I've written at length in times past how heroic fantasy Really Truly Is marvelous stuff, the modern descendant of the same classics Gog discusses. Critical individuals occasionally buttonhole me in public places demanding to know where I get off drawing parallels between Conan and Macbeth; and in the future I shall refer them to Gog's essay on the masterpieces of literature.

With your kind indulgence, the chapter promised:

"For reasons of my own I felt the necessity to familiarize myself with what college professors call 'the masterpieces of literature.' I therefore requested a certain librarian, the professor of an academic title and one of whose efficiency I had been assured, to prepare for me as brief a list as possible and to provide me with the best editions of the works chosen. As soon as these treasures were in my possession I closed my door to all intruders and stayed in bed to read.

"My first impression was one of bewilderment, for I could hardly believe that such humbug could really be a first-class product of the human intellect. What was not clear to me I set down as unimportant, and what I did understand either failed to amuse me or disgusted me. Absurd, tiresome stuff I found it all—sometimes entirely futile or even sickening. Tales there were that, if true, impressed me as being highly improbable and, if invented, then as being absurd. Presently I wrote to a well-known professor of W. College, asking for his opinion concerning the accuracy of my list. He replied that it was perfectly correct and so I had to resign myself to my fate. I had the courage to read those books, all save three or four that, after perusal of the opening pages, I felt I really could not face.

"I read of bodies of men called 'heroes' disembowling one another throughout a whole decade beneath the walls of a small town, all on account of a mature female who had been seduced; of the journeyings of a living man in the realms of death, merely as an excuse for speaking ill alike of the living and the dead; of a couple of lunatics, one lean and one fat, roaming the country looking for a beating; of a warrior losing his reason for a woman's sake and then amusing himself with stripping leaves from the oaks in a forest; of a wretched coward whose father had been murdered and who wreaked vengeance by causing the death of the girl who loved him; and of sundry other assorted personages: of a limping devil who lifted the roofs of houses to expose the shame they harbored; of the adventures of an ordinary individual who played the giant among pygmies and the dwarf among giants—an attitude inappropriate and absurd enough in any case. I read the painful adventures of an imbecile who, after a chain of ridiculous mishaps, still maintained that this was the best of all possible worlds. Then came the doings of an adept in witchcraft, who had a professional devil as his servant; the dreary story of a provincial adulteress who was herself so bored that she ended by taking poison; the wordy and inane outpourings of a prophet who kept company with an eagle and a serpent; the tale of an impoverished and fever-maddened youth who murdered an aged dame and then—idiot that he was—found himself actually incapable of enjoying the fruits of his crime and finally gave himself up to the police.

"My virgin intellect vaguely apprehended that this literature, so highly esteemed today, is really still of the Stone Age, and I was bitterly disappointed. Next I engaged a specialist in poetry, who further bewildered me by explaining that these works are esteemed for their style, form, and language, for the images and thoughts they contain, and that a trained mind delights in their perusal. I retorted that for my part, being obliged to read most of them in translation, I cared little for their form, and that as for their contents it seemed to me (what indeed it is) antiquated, senseless, stupid, and extravagant. This consultation cost me one hundred dollars and yielded me nothing at all.

"Fortunately for me I became acquainted later on with some young authors who shared my opinion concerning these old books and who gave me their own works to read. In these, amid much that was obscure, I found a food better suited to my taste. But I still question the possibility of bringing literature to a state of definite perfection, and I deem it more than probable that a century hence no one will devote himself to an industry that lags so far behind the times and gives so poor a return."

Hence I can say that modern heroic fantasy is everything Gog sees in classical literature, plus some besides, and almost as immoral. Perhaps that is why I like it.

—Jessica Amanda Salmonson
Seattle

THE INN AT THE WORLD'S END

Keith Roberts

Keith Roberts' name came up repeatedly whenever I discussed the possibility of **Heroic Visions II.** *He's much noted in England, and a favorite of discerning Americans as well; I suppose I was skulking about town with the uncultured, as I'd not read his books:* **The Furies, Pavane, The Inner Wheel, Anita, The Boat of Fate, Machines and Men, The Chalk Giants, The Grain Kings, The Passing of the Dragons, Ladies from Hell, Molly Zero,** *and* **Kiteworld.** *More fool I, to be sure. When such people as bibliographer/critic Mike Ashley and author/fan Frank Denton tell me, "This is your man," I have to listen. I was soon in contact with Leslie Flood, Mr. Roberts' agent.*

I still know nothing of Keith the man, but that he was born in 1935 in Kettering, Northamptonshire, and that, as I have belatedly discovered, he is one of the finest fantasy authors in the world today.

"The Inn at the World's End" is the first of a proposed series about the Cavalier of Mongay, though at present only this one tale exists. I would certainly like to have one for every heroic fantasy anthology I may edit, were this possible. Now I must confess to you, a lot of heroic fantasy has elements of the tongue-in-cheek, as witness Avram's superior but often funny

story of Corydon, many of Fritz Leiber's fantasies, and the equally notorious tales of the Dying Earth by the eternally surprising Jack Vance. But my own philosophies tend to the gloomy edge of things, as may be evidenced in my own novels and tales, and I could be perfectly satisfied to edit anthologies of a purely terrifying nature, spiritually and materially, beginning and end, to leave the reader wisely willing to contemplate suicide. Few stories more than Keith Roberts' fits my most personal ideal of heroic fantasy, or any fiction for that matter. For though I do read and enjoy (and include in this series) a good deal of comedy, I believe the great art of our existence is always about something fundamentally sad about such flickering lives, and unwholesome about the manner in which we edge ourselves daily toward that abyss.

THE TRAVELLER FROM THE BRASSY TOWN of Paynilt, where lines of shops display their glittering wares and the pavements scuff with drifts of greenish rust, will find the Southern Road both long and hard. Beyond the town the way climbs upward mile on mile, till the grass thins and yellows and rock outcrops come bursting through like the patched skulls of giants. There in midsummer the hawks hover, the wind whistles dry and keen over heather and the tufted gorse. From the highest point—in the locality they call it God Bring Rest—the track once more begins to descend, crossing a series of ridges and sweeping valleys, their bottoms clothed with ancient and gigantic trees. The forests of the Middle Lands are cheerful with birdsong; but here no leaf rustles, and the piping is stilled. To either side dim arcades afford glimpses of monstrous boles and branches; the earth beneath them is bare and pale. These are the Haunted Woods, and few care to rest under their shade.

Beyond the last of the trees the road rises a final time, climbing a flank of down with a shake and wriggle, as if glad to free itself from gloom. At the low crest stands a cairn of rock, to which the thoughtful add a stone in gratitude. Others pray; but the man who now reined his horse beside the flinty pile did neither of these things. He sat on the animal quietly, a half smile on his lips, staring into distance. Or rather it seemed his eyes recorded, independently of thought. There was a blankness, almost a blindness, about his gaze; his mind was elsewhere, locked inward.

He was dressed in the manner of a Cavalier. At his waist hung a dagger and rapier; the full russet cloak, the flared leggings, the deep-brimmed hat with its rich bunch of plumes, were the garb of Mongay, the antique Kingdom that lies a week or more's ride from Paynilt, beyond Tallisglow with its foundries and rich ore beds. Both cloak and hat betokened the quality of the wearer; but the cloth, though good, had a shabby and uncared-for look, although such men normally make much of display. His leggings and the harness of the horse were dull and unpolished and he wore, instead of a doublet of velvet, a simple tunic of dark fustian; a garment more suited to an artisan than to a man of noble birth. His dark hair hung lank and unpowdered; only his hands, laid now on the high pommel of the saddle, spoke of a man unused to physical toil. The flat, square nails were clean and neatly trimmed, the fingers long and slender. They tapped now, seemingly with impatience, fidgeted with the reins, and at last the rider recollected himself. He drew erect, and the smile returned, this time with a bitterness that twisted the corner of his mouth. It was as if in the same moment he had been reminded both of some mission and of the certainty that, like his present journey, it would prove to have but scant significance. He shook the reins gently, easing his mount forward in a walk.

The view revealed at the crest of the little rise was unexpectedly sweeping. To right and left, clear in the warm air, low hills were checkered with the green and yellow of crops. Between them the land ran out to a flat horizon, dimly seen. To the left a second, broader road curved from distance to join the rocky Paynilt track; at the junction, thrusting and glinting between trees, rose the red-tiled roofs of a village or small town. The rider twisted his lips once more, and consulted a square of parchment that he drew from beneath his cloak. He stared at it awhile; and it seemed for once his interest was engaged. He slipped the thing away, almost with a show of briskness, and spoke to the horse, urging it into a trot. The sun, sinking ahead, gleamed in his eyes, throwing his shadow long and wriggling across the tussocky grass beside the track. Man and doppelganger moved steadily, now with no hesitation; and with no backward glance.

Those who have travelled that dusty route will also know that, beyond the Haunted Woods, the Soulgap Cross gives access to the south. Here the road runs in from the rich farms of the Middle Lands, with their busy stone-built towns; Tollchapel, Pickering, Fivestreets, Mercervil. Beyond them lie hundred-gated Streanling, legendary Garnord, the Middle Sea itself. Here too a road runs west, broadening and fading, into the untrodden Lands of the dead; and foursquare in the gap, planted as if defiantly, stands the little town toward which the traveller now proceeded. Its name, writ fair on every map, is Trerule Hessen.

On the outskirts of the place the stranger, in whom it seemed no haste or urgency could long abide, allowed his mount to slacken its pace once more. The mare bent her head, cropping idly at the wayside grass studded with the starlike flowers of June; while the Cavalier shaded his eyes, seeing how ahead the light flew up and around the steep-backed roofs of the town, waking a cloud of dust motes that drifted golden as a smoke of pollen. Scents came to him, of hay and meadow blossoms; such scents as lovers smell, walking and brushing in the dusk. The peacefulness of the place reached him, through the guarded gate of his senses, and it seemed for an instant the cloud of gloom that rode with him was lifted, the smile he smiled was fractionally less cold. In his indifference he had purposed to ride on through the night; now it came to him that his mount, which had carried him well, had also carried him far. The discomfort of the beast formed no part of his plan; he patted the neck of the mare and walked her forward again, gazing at the houses that hunched and tottered to either side.

Many folk were abroad in the warm evening; all who met him touched their hats or smiled and nodded, according to their station. These salutations the traveller returned, with a punctilious and yet a weary courtesy, peering under the dark slouch of his hat brim at the bow-fronted windows of shops, the lamps lit in the gathering dusk. Their flames guttered; a door banged closed, another as abruptly opened. Something of that hill wind, it seemed, had travelled with the stranger; a girl's hair brushed sudden round her face, a passerby swung round, surprised at a close shrilling. But the Cavalier paid no outward heed. His senses, aided perhaps by the curious visitation, probed the buildings he passed, noting more than his eyes beheld. His mind, made free, climbed twisting stairs, looked down between curving wind braces at a man who lay sick unto death, a young girl who would shortly be a bride. Another might have marvelled, but such was not his nature.

And in truth the experience was not strange to him.

He reined at length before a long, low-fronted hotel, its stuccoed walls white-painted, its upper windows glowing here and there with lamplight. The insignia of the place, the Wyvvern, displayed itself proudly on a great board surrounded by curling ironwork and strapped to the facade by long iron-bolted bars. These details his eyes observed while the odd extension of himself absorbed what lay beyond. He saw sleeping chambers each like the next, small and square with neat-plumped beds and wash-hand stands; cream-painted, broken-locked doors; a dining room carpeted in dull red, lit by a forest of brass lamps that swung together now and tinkled. He saw too the folk who thronged the place; the dealers in turned goods, leather and grain, watches, gunflints, fire-screens, and painted trays. Something like a shadow crossed his face, though his features, so grimly and habitually composed, would allow themselves no real semblance of change. By no nuance would he permit himself criticism of his fellows; or fellow travellers, as he privately deemed them to be. He moved on nonetheless; the grief that possessed him would feed too readily amid a desert of wealth.

Beyond the Wyvvern stretched a great livery yard, with to one side a blacksmith's forge. The smith was still at his labors; an intermittent pulsing of orange light showed distant brick-built walls, whitewashed and cobweb-hung. Beyond the circle of light, the first stars pricked the sky.

Next to the forge the second of Trerule's inns, a jolly, homely little building, proclaimed itself the Spellpot and its Master the good Erik Forebrew. The horseman, leaning to make out the ornate, faded lettering, sensed the cheerful disorder of the place; the plain board floors, the grubby kitchens, the unswept bars with their litter of pipe dottles and sawdust. The door stood ajar, radiating warmth and light, cooking smells leaking into the cooling air. The traveller shook his head, smiling again his faint, cold smile. Neither was this place for him; yet he bore no ill will at merriment.

The little town was all but behind him. Ahead, dim now in the afterglow, stretched the drear and viewless tract that all men feared. The Cavalier reined awhile, staring with that curious gaze that seemed both lackluster and intent. He marked the road, fading into gloom; the stands of stunted bushes, the odd and skeletal tree; the ridge, low and dark, behind which the sun had dropped. Beyond, so ran the stories, the waste stretched on and on, clear to the Winter Sea. Beyond the Sea lay Worldedge and the Frozen Falls. From the desolation a wind skirled in, sharp and cold and endless.

The traveller turned. He had become aware by degrees of a bulk that interposed itself between him and the dying light. It reared before him, sagging and soaring, growing outward in the manner of all great wooden buildings. Their makers had never learned the simple truth that a beam laid on edge is stouter than a beam laid flat; and from that error came the wild device of jettying, of thrusting each floor outward beyond the story beneath. The horseman craned his neck, following the magpie-work of wood and plaster up to the high eaves, and smiled again as his eye lighted on the sign of the place.

It seemed newer-painted than those of its neighbors, or perhaps the pigments used by the artist had proved more enduring. The heavy board thrust out foursquare to the Dead Land winds, silent now and still, though the stranger guessed how in the gales of winter it would swing and groan, transmitting its complaint through the fabric of the building by every mighty sinew. The name it bore was that of the World's End Inn, and the device above the legend was equally and appropriately terrific. The sun was depicted, and the globe of Earth; but the Daystar burned with a terrible effulgence, stretching tendrils of fire till Earth blazed and dripped, melting like cobbler's wax held close to a hearth while a column of dark red steam whirled into the void. All this the traveller saw and more; he realized with his curious inner sight how the benches and tables of the place gleamed in lamplight, their plain wood burnished white; how its floors were clean and its curtains primped and gay, how its stairways roved and wandered, how its linen cupboards were piled with welcome laundered sheets. He saw from the legend above the yard gate that its Taverner was Master Hessean Lanting, and waited no more. He pressed the crown of his hat more firmly to his skull, ducked his head, clattered the horse beneath the creeper-trailing arch.

Goodman Lanting was burly and balding, thick in the forearms and sturdy in the belly; his voice was slow and rumbling, in keeping with his person and the stature of the place. He it was who oversaw the stabling of the Cavalier's horse, giving the tired mare into the charge of a cheerful-faced scrap of a stable lad. He stood lantern in hand while the traveller unbuckled the saddlebags, swinging the heavy leather across his shoulder. He was accustomed, as a Taverner must be, to note and assess the quality of his guests; his gray-green prominent eyes marked the well-filled purse the stranger transferred to an inner pocket, then as the cloak swung back the Twelve Apostles—the measured pistol charges dangling from their bandolier. Lastly he stared at the great pistols themselves, gleaming with oil and beautiful with inlay. On them, it seemed, was lavished the concern the stranger denied to himself. The Cavalier withdrew them from their holsters, inspecting them, releasing the cocks, lowering each to the frizzen before slipping the great weapons carefully into the capacious bags. At that Goodman Lanting cleared his throat. "Never, sir," he said thoughtfully, "have I seen finer arms."

The other turned, aware of the close attention with which he had been favored, and smiled his bleak little smile. "Good innkeeper," he said in a quiet and courteous voice, "you need have no concern for me. Were my tale known to you, you would know how blind folly once destroyed a great gift of God. Since that day I have brought no harm to man or beast; I desire only peace with my fellows, and the wisdom that comes from understanding."

The Taverner shrugged, not in all respects assured; for the other's tones, though polite, had in them something of that weary indifference so often to be seen in his dark, set countenance. But pistols, and swords for that matter, were in truth no novelties to Goodman Lanting; few travellers to the World's End cared to make the trip empty-handed. He let his eyes dwell for a moment on the grim expanse of heath, glowing now in the ghostly afterlight of the sunken sun. "Bear arms and welcome, sir," he said. "Now by your leave, this air is not for chatting in. The mists rise swiftly here, winter and summer alike. Your meal, I warrant, is already preparing; and perhaps too you would do me the kindness to view the room in which I've placed you, before Mistress Weatherfair cumbers its bed with sheets."

The other shrugged in turn. "All rooms are alike to me," he said. "A bed is all I ask, four walls and a roof." He eased the saddlebags on his shoulder, and glanced himself through the high gateway to the heath. "Perhaps," he said, "arms may not come amiss, in such a house as yours."

The Taverner preceded him across the yard, shoulders squared. "Neither arms nor incense," he said. "Know you, Master, the World's End draws no strength from powder and sparks; no, nor the baubles of priests." It seemed he would not speak again, but at the side door of the inn he turned. "For twenty years and more I've kept this place," he said, "and it has well kept me. A few years more, with luck, I've got to run." He stared up, under his shaggy brows. "Have ye seen the building, good sir?" he asked. "Did ye mark it from afar?"

He pointed, and the lantern swung, sending yellow half-moons of light across the polished cobbles. "Up there," he said. "Do ye see the twist of the chimneys? And that gable? Do ye see the lean of the wall? Back, as though a great wind pressed on it? Do ye know this place in winter?"

The traveller shook his head, lips pursed.

"It's quiet now," said the Taverner. "Quiet as Hell is quiet. But come the winter, there's another tale. To see that sign of mine stream out, in the blasts that visit us; to see the fire-drakes hiss among the chimney pots; to see that, Sir, is to know that powder and ball are little enough things. And yet we hold our place; aye, and are merry in it."

The other peered, intently. "Merriment," he said, "is a mystery of which I would fain know more."

Hessean Lanting frowned, as if unsure whether or not some jibe was intended. "Merriment, sir," he said, "springs from a warm hearth and a well-kept board; from fine-fettled ale, and a full belly. And from a sense of duty done."

"Duty?" said the other thoughtfully.

"Yes, Master," said the Taverner, "duty. . . ." He paused. "I don't hail from these parts," he said. "Tollchapel, that's where I was raised. With good land round me and deep soil for the wheat. Farmers, my folk were; farmers and freeholders, this fifty year. Yet when the call came, it was answered. And you'll find there's others, all of Trerule Hessen. We're the Westguard." He peered up once more. "Now I'll charge you, as I charge all my guests. Bring no Dead Land talk within these walls, or Dead Land thoughts, if you'll bear so far with my humor. Ghost me no ghosts, troll me no trolls; and you'll find good fellowship enough. Fear, sir, grows first in the heart; and that the Deadlanders know. This House is closed to 'em. Barred. We laugh at 'em here, we spit 'em, we put 'em on the roast. That's the way it's been these twenty years, and that's the way it will remain."

The other bowed. "A guest respects another's house," he said. "And in Mongay we know well both how to guest and host. You speak much wisdom Goodman Lanting."

The Taverner stared again a final time, then stepped aside,

gesturing to the other to precede him. The Cavalier once more inclined his head, and the door was slammed, the bolts shot closed against the wind from the waste.

The small chamber to which he was shown was pronounced by the Cavalier satisfactory in all respects. Hot water was brought, and towels, and he was left to himself. A while later he repaired to the lower parts of the inn, minus the cape and leggings but still with the dagger and rapier at his belt. The Taverner, with little more than a glance, conducted him to a side room; but at this the stranger demurred. "Goodman Lanting," he said courteously, "I marked your words as you charged me, and as befits a guest. So I choose, by your leave, not to begin by shunning my fellow men. Since my needs are simple, let my meat be brought to your greatest room. Hearing the talk of your folk will be my pleasure."

The Taverner was much mollified by this. Cavaliers of Mongay were infrequent guests, but those he had encountered had inclined to something less than civility, despite the stranger's claim. He preceded the traveller at once into the main chamber of the place, a wide, low room opening from the street and lined with massive beams of time-blackened oak. Smoke filled it, the fumes of many pipes; and there was a hubbub of talk. The noise stilled at sight of the Cavalier, and Hessean Lanting raised his own voice in its stead. "Here is a tired enough warfarer," he said, "who yet desires good company and scorns to sup alone. Make room for him, you Jan Tinker and Moonride; we will show him in Trerule Hessen, we know how to return a courtesy."

The men addressed made room, albeit suspiciously, for there was that in the stranger's face and bearing that scarce invited confidences. The sadness that enveloped him, which in another might have been intriguing or an invitation to sympathy, seemed in him a mere sullenness of nature; his heavy features and straggling hair were less than comely, while even in his courtesy was something that chilled. However, he bowed pleasantly enough, and when he later called for all pots and glasses to be replenished and charged against his bill, the buzz of talk rose once more, and the former atmosphere largely returned. He ate what was brought him, sipping from an ale mug and listening to the flow of chatter round about; later he took himself to a corner seat by the great empty fireplace, sank into a deep armchair, and with sundry preparations puffed alight a slender, amber-stemmed pipe.

In time it seemed his habitual gloom once more lightened fractionally, for about him were men from every walk of life, and the tenor of their many conversations soothed by its very inconsequence. Here a plasterer, still in the white-splashed cap of his trade, discoursed at length on the mysteries of mixing lime; a joiner and a roughmason engaged in hot dispute on the relative merits of certain sporting dogs; a seaman with a single glinting earring roared tales of distant brawlings; while through all ran a thread of laughter over Forebrew at the Spellpot, his transmutations and rainbowed dismays. The traveller smiled with the rest at the inchoate conjurer and his ill-disciplined machines; he lay back in the chair, let his eyes rove across the great tar-black beams, patched and jointed and burly, glistening with the iron patina of centuries.

It was Moonride, the blacksmith, who first engaged the traveller directly in talk. His forge it had been that the Cavalier had seen sparkling in the night, a fact he readily affirmed. "We see few gentlemen of Mongay in these parts," he said in his turn. "If I may make so bold Sir, what brings you to Trerule Hessen of all places, and the End of the World?"

His manner, though blunt, was friendly enough, so that the Cavalier, for once, had little hesitation in answering. "I am travelling to the Middle Lands," he said. "I am bound for Garnord."

Moonride swigged at his ale. "Some weighty matter it must be," he said, "for one of your quality to journey so far."

The Cavalier shook his head. "About me I see many gentlemen," he said softly, "and all of greater worth than I. So let us have no talk, good friend of quality." He paused, frowning; but a compulsion was on him, the same compulsion, in truth, that had made him, in the stable yard, hint at a secret known to few. He must abide in this house and learn all he could of its folk; though as yet he knew not why. "I am bound for Garnord," he said again finally, "where I hope to find employment."

This had the effect of once more stopping all talk. For a Cavalier of Mongay to make such an admission was an unheard-of thing; and Moonride squeezed his brawny arms till the circlets of polished metal tinkled and gleamed. "Garnord is a good way off," he said slowly, "and I for one would not care to make the trip. They say the pavements glitter there with gold; but no man sleeps safe in his bed, for fear of prowlers in the night."

Coming from one whose living poised so precariously on the threshold of things unmentionable, this seemed a curious sentiment; but the traveller forebore to comment. "That may well be," he said. "Nevertheless, it is to Garnord I must go."

The eyes of the blacksmith strayed momentarily to the rapier at the other's waist, its basket hilt glittering in lamplight. "If ye take me not amiss, Sir," he said, "what trade may a gentleman such as yourself lay claim to?" It was perhaps a breach of the strict etiquette that governed that amazing house; but the Cavalier took no offence. "The trade of arms, of course," he said, "is our profession from birth. Perhaps at a need, that might be pressed into service. In Garnord is a street of armorers, where the costliest weapons are made and bought; perhaps what small skill I possess would be useful to some merchant, and buy me at least a crust. I am under penance for a sin; I do no ill to man nor beast, and must earn my keep with my hands."

At this even the attention of Farport the seaman was engaged. "Sin?" he said, in his deep voice. "Sin, and penance? There is no sin in Mongay, save curtness to one's betters. Who gave this penance? Some priest, or the God he served?"

The Cavalier smiled. "There are sterner masters than priests," he said. "I gave it to myself."

Moonride frowned, seeming uncertain what further remark to offer; and silence redescended, to be broken finally by Goodman Lanting. "Now," he said, bustling forward, "we have all heard remarkable things and must not press this guest of ours further. What sorrows he might bear, we know not, nor are they our concern. Though I for one wish him a speedy release from them. Now bring your pots, for we will drink to his prosperity, and trust he remembers his stay at the End of the World with kindness."

The intervention met with general approval. Mugs were drained and refilled, and the talk once more became cheerful. Moonride lounged beside the traveller, who at last seemed at his ease; while Farport squatted cross-legged at his knee and began a rambling story about parrots and turtles and a woman called Adaan who lived in the Land of Yellow Salt, far away beyond the Great Weed Lake.

The vast clock over the mantel solemnly ticked; folk went and came, noisily and with laughter. The traveller, lulled by good ale, let his chin sink toward his chest; then on the instant he was jerked to full awareness. An icy thrill shot through him, flew to the tips of his limbs. His heart pounded, and he straightened, staring wildly round. Moonride turned surprised, following the direction of his gaze. A moment's silence, then the blacksmith laughed. "What ails you, Sir?" he said. "T'is only old Gaffer Mirthrule. A queer-tempered creature, and no mistake, but I warrant there's no harm in him. Why, a man such as yourself could break him with one hand."

But the Cavalier made no reply. Instead he watched the little creature who had entered, and who now limped toward the servery, with the intensity of a man who watches the poisonous shiftings of a snake. The chill, settling deeper, closed about his heart with icy fingers; till Moonride and Jan Turner, Farport and Goodman Lanting, faded in his awareness with the place in which he sat, became distant and gray as ghosts. *"This,"* he groaned, as if to himself. "For *this*, you drove me here. Is there no release . . . ?"

There was no answer, save for the wind that shrilled about the place, rattled angry and sudden at a casement. He saw the jerky movements of the Gaffer, the wizened monkey face. He tried to turn his eyes away, and could not. He saw how Mirthrule fiddled with a little purse, saw the fingers wrench and tatter at the fastening; he saw the change pecked up from the countertop, fast as a snatching hen. At his heels skirmished a foxy dog, patched in brown and grubby white, and like its master, twinklingly unstill. He saw the claw-hand drop to the creature's skull, the purse stowed back with twitchings and angry jerks into the Gaffer's clothes. Then Mirthrule turned, and for an instant eyes of man and dog locked with the stranger's own. The hate-pulse came then quick and hot, like the stabbing of a blade. The Cavalier's hand dropped to the sword hilt; he strained upward in his seat, groaning afresh. "No," he said in an anguished voice. "No, I will not. The penance is paid already, in blood. . . ." He fell back, sweat standing on his brow.

Moonride looked at Farport, and Farport at Moonride. If their voices were silent, their eyes spoke volumes; and the Cavalier recollected himself, it seemed with a mighty effort. "Gentlemen," he said a little haltingly, "I pray your forgiveness. It is a fit that comes upon me, now and again, but it augurs no ill, of that you have the word of Mongay. Give me your cups, and I will see them recharged. Then you must tell me more of strange creatures, and this woman of the Yellow Lands. I am much indebted for your kindness; it has made the time pass more pleasantly than I can recall."

They chattered on, uneasy at first, warming again finally to their themes. The traveller heard the words, smiling and nodding, answering as best he could. He turned his head to his newfound friends, fighting magnetic force; but from the corner of the great room, he knew, two pairs of eyes watched through the smoke; black and glittering, identical, intense with hatred.

The clock boomed, striking the hours and quarters. Midnight came at last, and the traveller, with a further and singular effort, wrenched himself away. He made his good-nights to his friends and to his host; a lamp was produced for him and he made his way, unused spurs tinkling as he walked, to the great staircase that dominated the far end of the room. As he moved, he averted his gaze from where the hate-stabbings came afresh, quicker and more intense than before. He climbed the stairs, crossed a landing to another flight, climbed again. His shadow wavered behind him on the bare plaster walls; he reached his room finally, unlatched the door, set the lamp carefully on the washstand top. He stooped to twitch off the spurs, and cast himself on the bed. The wind cried afresh, skirling at the casement, and he raised his voice in a wild shout, *"To me . . . why to me . . . ?"*

The shout, and the burst of wailing that almost seemed to answer it, caught the ear of Mistress Weatherfair as she climbed, candle in hand, to bed. The old woman paused, uncertain, then limped forward, frowning, to the door of the room in which the traveller lay. Sobbings she heard, as of a soul sore distressed; and the voice came again.

"*Not* to me. It is no concern of mine. . . ."

The wind shrilled, making her cup her hand protectingly about the candle flame. Timbers creaked and shifted; it was as if the whole vast building now opposed some force, leaning, butting its great shoulders, resisting with the strength and patient weight of years. The strange conversation went on; for in later times the housekeeper was to swear that, while one guest was admitted, two occupied that room that night. She strained to catch the answers of whatever companion the traveller had brought with him, but to no avail. Each, it seemed, was lost in the singing of that strange wind.

"I *know* it to be true," groaned the Cavalier. "Where two have come, others will follow. And these brave souls, opposing Death with Life, will lose their battle. . . ."

The candle flame shook again, and was almost extinguished.

"Then let it *be* so," came the voice from behind the door. "If they have eyes that cannot see, and ears that cannot hear, the penalty is theirs. The cause is not mine. . . ."

"Merciful Heaven," whispered Mistress Weatherfair. "Can the man be crazed?"

"Then a priest must do the work," went on the traveller in more reasonable tones. "Or a conjurer. Willingly would I undertake that part of it. You know I have some small skill—"

The outburst that answered him was the most furious yet. Almost it was as if the corridor lurched.

"Then come," he shouted, with a return to his former wildness. "Come, I yield to you. Instruct me. . . ." She heard the bedsprings click, the sound of his boots on the floor; then on an instant the creaking of the casement stay. The pane flew back; glass shattered somewhere, and the wind was in the building. Yet not a wind; the wailing coalesced, became a sound the like of which Mistress Weatherfair had never heard. A voice, surely; yet the voice of nothing mortal. The single note trembled the air of the corridor; powerful, clear, ineffably sweet. Triumph there was in it, and sadness; yet overall, a terrifying Love. The old woman scurried for her room, trembling in her turn, mouthing prayers; shot the bolts of the door and huddled in her bed, the clothes drawn round her ears. Yet still she seemed to hear the echoes of that unearthly sound, tingling, fading, dying away along her tattered nerves.

The Cavalier flung himself at the saddlebags, wrenching at the straps and buckles. He straightened, glaring and panting. His feet clumped hollow on the boards; he wrenched the door back, ran for the stairs, turned and ran again. And light was still streaming from the great room of the inn!

He fell back, chest heaving. He wiped his forehead with his wrist and stepped forward again, knowing what he would see. From below, voices still rumbled; before him the stair treads gleamed, polished by the steps of centuries. Above them jerked a flickering yellow star. The light it shed, the sickly gleam, illumined a sallow face; twisted and worrying, hating, uncomprehending. At his heels skirmished the foxlike dog; and Gaffer Mirthrule was climbing the stairs!

The hammering in his chest reached a peak; then in its place came chilly calm. Almost it was as if a voice spoke, inside his brain. "They cannot stand the insult," ran the whisper. "Challenge; forever, their hating gives them away." And as the sibilance died away, the creature on the stairs looked up. For an instant both man and dog were still.

The Cavalier spread his feet where he stood. "No farther, Gaffer," he said quietly. "Your course is run."

He saw the dead eyes glare, the lips part in a snarl; and the Gaffer waited for no more. A dagger twitched itself from his jerkin; he ran upward, soundless, closing with twinkling speed; and a covey of fat sparks leaped on the stair. An instant in which the world seemed poised; and darkness split apart in bright thunder.

The lamp fell, splashing flame and oil. Powder smoke rolled downward, heavy as oil itself, spreading into the great chamber with its trestles and stout chairs. Then the appalled face of Farport was glaring up; Goodman Lanting, thick-voiced with rage, was crying murder; and Moonride the blacksmith was snatching a long pike from the wall.

The Cavalier clung to the stair rail. *"The dog. Mark the dog...."*

They froze; the Taverner with a cudgel he had snatched from somewhere, Moonride with the pike still in his hands. They saw how the animal ran, keening, from what remained of its master. The paws scrabbled the wainscot; and the creature was diminishing, shrinking before their eyes. A gust of vapor rushed across the chamber, nauseous and sweet; and the thing was gone!

"Now see the rest," said the traveller. "Run for your Sergeant Merrymeet, if murder has been done." He kicked at something that lay on the shining treads; it rolled, clattering, likewise diminishing as it came. Fumes rose from it, like the smoke of iodine. The curved chip that remained skittered across the floor to the feet of Moonride, hard and light as a sliver of wood. On it as it lay was what seemed the sketch of a man; and on the features, glaring still, the imprint of indelible hate. The blacksmith, groaning, crunched down with his heel, and the thing was done.

The traveller descended heavily. He laid the great pistol on the table, sat and stared at his hands. After a moment, it seemed by an effort of will, the trembling of the fingers grew less; and he looked up, once more with his faint, cold smile. "Goodman Lanting," he said, "bring me a cup of ale, and spice it well with brandy. Stint not, nor deny me, for I have cleaned your House."

• • •

The great sign of the inn creaked gently in the dawn wind. To the east a solitary streak of yellow slashed the clouds; above, the sky was gray as unhoned steel. One star or planet burned, winking on the rim of the world.

Beneath the sign stood a little group of men. Farport was there, stroking at his great moustache; and Moonride with his steel-cased arms, Merrymeet the Sergeant, burly Goodman Lanting. The wind gusted again, blowing from the Dead Lands, moving the lank hair of the traveller round his face. From the pommel of his saddle, in a canvas bag, hung all that remained of the creature they had known as Gaffer Mirthrule. The mare curveted, rolling her great eye, disliking the load she bore; and Hessean Lanting stepped back, shaking his heavy head. The night had aged him visibly; still he seemed unable to believe what he had harbored within his walls.

The Cavalier reached to grip his shoulder. "Courage, Goodman," he said. "And my thanks to you all. Your kindness will be remembered, if I receive no more. As for the rest, I will scatter this dirt far from harm. Do you be vigilant, for the dog will seek to return. Call out Master Forebrew, with his potions and electric machines; the remedy, and your defense, lie there."

He took up the reins, and Hessean Lanting spoke. "Why did ye this for us?" he asked. "And where fare ye now?"

The traveller stared down broodingly. "I did what I must," he said, "for another, as much as for you. As for where I fare, perhaps it is better if you do not know. The Way is changed; I am not master of my Fate, as you perhaps have guessed."

Still the Taverner seemed unsatisfied. He rubbed his pate, frowning as if grappling with a concept strange to him. "A Deadlander is not mortal," he said. "That we all know. And yet the pistol . . . what spells were cast, what runes? What gave ye such a power?"

They were startled by the change in the traveller's normally impassive countenance. There passed across it for an instant an expression of pain such as they had never seen. Then it was gone; all that remained was the faint and bitter smile. The Cavalier leaned forward to touch the long holster beside the horse's neck. "An arm that spilled the blood of innocence," he said, "is no ordinary tool to face; even for a Deadlander. To fight evil with a greater, friend, that is my allotted task." It seemed he would have said more, but on the instant the wind shrilled from ahead; a single note, curiously sweet, clear and distant as a trumpet. The traveller stiffened, like a man who hears a summons that is imperative. Then with no more ado he touched heels to the horse. He raised an arm, silently, and cantered between the last of the houses, out onto the wide, dim heath.

VOICES

Michael Bishop

In the previous volume of this anthology series, I had the fortune of presenting to the world Michael Bishop's "The Monkey's Bride." It became one of the more widely noted stories of the year, and only barely missed the World Fantasy Award for which it was a finalist. It is one story I know will have a long life before the public, although we can hope against a theme anthology entitled **Magic Monkeys.**

I find myself in the unusual and somewhat pleasant position of not merely *having another major novelette from the pen of Michael Bishop (or, as it were, his first composition entirely by word processor) but of having inspired its composition by means of one of my prose-poems in the Chinese manner, "The Master Ventriloquist," that Mike was later chagrined to find was not taken from a traditional legend but was entirely the product of my demented imagination. My version was under 250 words. Mike's is somewhat longer. I was tempted to print the prose-poem here as part of the headnote, but have resisted doing so, though the diehards among you may look it up in the little-magazine* **Fantasy & Terror,** *new series #3, published by Richard H. Fawcett, Uncasville, CT., and edited by myself.*

Had an author of mediocre ability been thus inspired, I

should have informed him or her never to publish the tale without my permission, permission not to be granted. But where genius is involved, it is quite a different matter, though I trust Mike knows he now runs the risk of having one of his novelettes appear in a 250-word version under my byline.

A YOUNG MAN CALLED HU SHAOQI was possessed of two rare talents. The first he practiced openly, and it delighted nearly everyone who knew him. The second he regarded as a curse and kept altogether hidden from the world. In Hu Shaoqi's opinion these two talents canceled each other and distinguished him in painful ways from the people whom he loved. That not even his mother and father noticed the signs of his secret unhappiness worked like an evil burrowing worm to undermine his native good cheer.

Hu Shaoqi's first talent was an ability to throw his voice. He could make the spotted ponies in the paddock behind the house of the village's chief lord appear to recite poetry. He could project eloquent speeches into the mortar-stopped mouths of stone dogs and lions. He could convince a modest young woman from a fine family that she had just blurted out a curse more appropriate to the lips of a barbarian soldier. He could even make the giant eagles of Xiangcheng and the dwarf dragons of the mountain caves sing like lovely girls.

This talent Hu Shaoqi viewed as a welcome gift. It amused his family, astonished his acquaintances, and so pleased the chief lord (who shamefully exulted in his ponies' recitations of long passages of epic verse) that he often called on Hu Shaoqi to entertain his guests at formal dinners, afterwards rewarding the young man with exotic foods or semiprecious stones. Using this talent, Hu Shaoqi could imagine himself making his way in life without having to marry wealth, or to become a monk, or to devote himself to the respectable drudgery of scholarship. Although not an especially materialistic young man, this idea appealed to him, and already, he felt, he had made a good start on securing his fortune.

Hu Shaoqi's second, and purposely unrevealed, talent was an ability to hear voices that no one else could hear. It did not escape him that this bittersweet talent turned his happier bent for ventriloquism inside out. Both centered on illusions created by the human voice. (If, of course, the voices that sometimes swept into his mind did not actually belong to dead people or demons.) In the first instance he, Hu Shaoqi, was the perpetrator of the hoaxing voices, but in the second—frighteningly—he never had a credible notion of who or what was trying to empty its fearsome nonsense into his head.

To Hu Shaoqi's shame and confusion the voices had begun in his thirteenth year, not long after his first nocturnal spurting of man seed. For the next three years this troubling auditory phenomenon had continued. Although it came to him most frequently at night, occasionally it took place in the midst of conversation with parents or friends. Usually the voice or voices merely prated at him, telling him that he was not who he thought he was, that no one he knew was in truth the person he believed, and that one day he would be called upon to repay either the gods or his ancestors for his ability to throw his voice. Finally, altogether upsettingly, the phenomenon overtook him during one of his performances in the court of the village lord.

In front of forty people the sixteen-year-old Hu Shaoqi was making the overweight lady of the lord cackle like a chicken, hiss like a serpent, and bray like an ass. Everyone in attendance was laughing, including the delighted lady herself. Then, completely without warning, a voice insinuated itself into his ears—nay, into some astonished portion of his mind—telling him terrible secrets, cajoling him, *commanding* him.

"Hu Shaoqi," said the voice, sounding at one moment like a great growling bear, at the next like a trio of old women speaking in unison, and at the next like nothing human at all, "you must forsake this village and these silly people and journey at once to the Mountain of Everlasting Winter."

"Silly people?" the boy echoed the voice or voices.

Everyone at court gaped at him. The noblewoman who had been doing such expert animal imitations fell silent. A look of surprised disappointment captured her face, for Hu Shaoqi had just reclaimed his audience's attention and she had foolishly begun to believe that it was hers by right.

"Silly, indeed," the voice or voices reiterated. "You are not who you think you are, doltish boy. Nor are any of these village louts who they so smugly believe themselves to be. So I tell you again that you must leave Xiangcheng and set off this very evening for the Mountain of Everlasting Winter."

Heedless of his onlookers, Hu Shaoqi turned in a circle. "But *why?* You have to tell me why!"

"Why, to discover the underlying meaning of this great and

mysterious world. To discover also the real identity of the idiots whom you have been trying to entertain. Therefore, boy, betake yourself to the Mountain of Everlasting Winter."

"But I don't *want* to go to the Mountain of Everlasting Winter!" Hu Shaoqi cried.

"Of course you don't," said the village lord, approaching the ventriloquist, for he had correctly surmised that the young man was at the mercy of some sort of *kuei*, or demon, and wished with all his heart to comfort him. "No one wants to go there."

But in his distress and confusion, Hu Shaoqi shouted, "Leave me alone, you fool!" Frantically, he shoved the well-meaning lord aside and fled from the court into the streets of the village, and from the village streets into the solitude of the evening woods. Alone, he slumped to the ground and put his hands over his ears, horrified by all that had so far happened and terrified that even worse might yet befall him.

"Get up," the *kuei* commanded Hu Shaoqi. "Get up this instant and begin your journey to the Mountain."

"I won't!"

"Would you prefer that I repossess your only distinguishing talent as a human being?"

"Take it!" the boy challenged his tormentor. Then he lay on his side, clasping his head and hoping that the demon would accept his ventriloquist's skills as a ransom and from henceforth leave him in peace.

Instead, as if the intelligence behind the voices had been weighing options, the voices said, "Hu Shaoqi, if you do not set out on your journey before sunup, I promise you that tomorrow you will contract a fever and die. You will forevermore cease to *be* Hu Shaoqi, and not even your mother and your father will be able to recall your name."

Threatened in this absolute way, Hu Shaoqi eventually pulled himself to his feet, returned to his own house, and secretly gathered together some few small items that he thought might prove useful on his trek, including a copper bowl, a second set of sandals, and a single bag of rice. (He had no wish either to wake his parents or to deprive them of what was theirs.) The Mountain of Everlasting Winter lay several days' journey to the west, over roads that only madmen or monks ever thought to travel alone, for it bore its unusual name—and effectively discouraged visitors to its vicinity—because snow, glacial ice, and clouds like great frozen stones attended the peak year round. Everyone believed that a peculiarly antisocial deity resided there, for almost every "summer" the rock-hard carcasses of one or two adventurers who had thought to climb the mountain would be recovered from a moraine pushing out of a crevice at its base. Indeed, Hu Shaoqi felt a dread certainty that he would meet his own death on the mountain, assuming, of course, that he managed to escape being killed by one of the bandit packs notorious for patroling the roads that wound into that bleak and forbidding territory.

And so, in the very dead of night, fear evicted the young ventriloquist from the cradle of his family and the nursery of his native village. Fear—and resentment of the threats that had occasioned that fear—accompanied him through the early stages of his journey. Animals, sensing his fear, avoided him, and he ensured their continuing skittishness by tossing taro roots or wild eggplants at those brave enough to stop and look at him. Had he not been under the tyrannical compulsion of the voices (which, since leaving home, he had not heard again), he would have put silly words on the velvet tongue of a deer or filtered one of the teachings of the *Scripture in Forty-two Chapters* through the beak of an unsuspecting owl.

As it was, however, he longed for companionship but had no stomach for the mindless pity of ungulates and birds. Although a solitary exile with no one but himself to talk to, Hu Shaoqi could easily summon from himself half a hundred different voices. Unfortunately, he knew all these spurious voices too well to take any comfort from their rote exhortations to have courage, practice his survival skills, and meditate on the compensatory beauties of the wilderness. They were little more than children's voices, which echoed in his head like old pottery breaking or dry leaves tiptoeing over cobbles.

As he traveled, the terrain grew more rugged, temperatures dropped, and the people he encountered wore unfamiliar garments and spoke strange dialects. Their houses looked less like houses than colossal but misplaced beaver lodges. The beasts of burden carrying these folks' firewood and market products resembled animals out of fable. The air smelled of greasy smoke and old snow. The mountains separating the barren villages were like huge, fancifully eroded anthills. The sky sagging against the peaks contained clouds as splintered and opaque as hammered ice. The channeled and rechanneled wind roared continuously, as if creation itself were in the throes of violent self-disintegration.

Late one afternoon, on a narrow track above a giddy-making abyss, three bandits jumped in front of Hu Shaoqi and threatened him with their staves. From natural towers of rock, another five or six men leapt into the path behind him. Hu Shaoqi had never seen such ugly, brutelike specimens of humanity. They demanded money. He had none. They wanted anything he had. He had nothing but the robe on his back, his copper bowl, one extra sandal (he had already lost its mate), and a walking stick that he had found earlier that same morning. The rice that he had taken from his parents' tiny house was long since gone; he had eaten every bit of it on his very first day away from Xiangcheng.

Not a little frustrated by these discoveries, the bandits resolved to deprive Hu Shaoqi of his life. Their leader, a man with a face so badly scarred that it looked like a platter of broken porcelain ineptly pieced back together, seized the unoffending wayfarer by his robe and told him in grisly detail of all the many methods available to them to free his sniveling spirit, little by little, from his body.

"But why would you wish to do such things to me?" Hu Shaoqi asked. "I've done you no harm."

"You do us harm by intruding," the leader of the bandits retorted. "You do us harm by lacking anything of substance to filch from your nauseating person."

"Then waste no further time on me, sir."

"Only enough to lay you out dead. After which we'll strip you of your lice-ridden garment and leave your body on the path as a warning to any other would-be trespassers. Besides, even the giant raptors who nest aloft must eat, eh, boy?"

"But why not simply let me go?" Hu Shaoqi pleaded. "I'll warn others to stay away."

"Death's the fate of all those stupid enough to intrude upon our strongholds," the bandit said. "And if you should prove too effective in your warnings to others, numbskull, who would we have left to rob? Is it your desire to ruin us completely?"

Realizing at last that there was no arguing with the bandit leader or any of his henchmen, Hu Shaoqi threw his voice. He threw it in several different directions in such rapid succession that the bandits believed themselves surrounded by a far-traveling unit of the Emperor's most able and ferocious troops.

A pillar of granite called out orders.

A roadside shrine whinnied like a hundred horses.

A flock of sparrows divested itself of a dozen dozen murderous battlecries.

A stand of wind-whipped trees clacked its barren branches like so many swords striking steel against steel in cold preparation for attack.

Although the bandits could see no one approaching, this great unexpected clamor so terrified them that most of them fled, without having plucked a single hair from Hu Shaoqi's head. The bandit with the crazed-porcelain face released his captive and turned in a circle, looking for the invisible enemy. It seemed for a moment that his ugly shattered face might shatter again, falling to discouraged pieces there on the narrow mountain track. Indeed, when the clamor of unseen opponents persisted (for Hu Shaoqi was putting ungodly strain on his vocal cords and facial muscles to ensure that his "allies" grew louder and ever more numerous), the bandit chief lost all heart and went running after the men who had already broken for safety, shouting, "Cowards, come back!" at the top of his heaving lungs. But even when he had caught up with the slowest of this craven lot, the frightened head brigand continued pursuing the others until they had all disappeared.

Exhausted, Hu Shaoqi collapsed to his knees. No longer did whinnying horses or battle-crying birds disturb the loud silences of the windy upland terrain, and the wayfarer, weeping into his hands, principally wept to acknowledge the fact that he was still alive. A moment ago the issue had been in doubt, and yet he had summoned the resources—the god-given skills—to save himself.

And then, for the first time since he had left Xiangcheng, the *kuei* that had sent him on this perilous quest insinuated its voices into Hu Shaoqi's head, laughing in delight, snorting and snuffling like an entire pen of hungry pigs.

"Very good, my little manikin," the demon said between these snorts and snuffles. "You almost surprise me. Not quite, let me stipulate, but almost."

Hu Shaoqi struggled to his feet and shook his fist defiantly at the leaden sky. "Why are you doing this to me?" he shouted.

But the voices in his head replied only, "To the Mountain, boy. To the Mountain."

Although he begged and expostulated and threatened the

kuei, it would not say more. The hideous sounds of its hilarity died inside him, fading away until all that he could hear were the groanings of the rocks, the continuous high lament of the wind, and the pounding of his homesick heart.

Later that evening, to reduce the chances of another bandit attack, Hu Shaoqi left the path and entered a stand of gnarled evergreens. Soon, though, he found himself lost (a paradox not dissimilar to the inherent contradiction of his unasked-for talents) on a carpet of scratchy needles on a higher slope of the mountain. His robe was damp with sweat, the soles of his sandals had begun to shred, and the copper bowl he held in the hammock of cloth between his knees glinted like a miniature moon in the malevolent glow of the wintry sunset. The bowl was empty. Behind the young man's navel hunger had balled up like a slimy clump of cat's hair. Aggrieved by this uncomfortable knot, he clutched his abdomen and for the second time that day began to cry.

"Stop your shameful display of tears!" he heard a scrawny hare sitting on a nearby rock rebuke him. "Are you truly afraid that you will never eat again, O timid and irresolute *boy?*"

Stunned, Hu Shaoqi stood up. Had the hare actually spoken, or had he thrown his own self-accusing voice into the whiskery mouth of the creature? Or, for novelty's sake, had the ventriloquist demon commandeered the little animal's body in order to chasten him? It *was* humiliating to hear oneself upbraided and disparaged by a mangy forest animal no larger than an overgrown toad. For which grudging reason Hu Shaoqi had to admire the nasty genius of the *kuei*'s technique. Nevertheless, he found a stone on the ground and flung it vigorously at the hare, which leapt from its rock and disappeared into the underbrush.

"Why, then, boy, I'll just use *your* mouth," he heard his own hijacked voice say. "Do you like that better?"

This development likewise startled the wayfarer. "Who speaks?" he croaked, finding it hard to reclaim his voice. "Who has stolen my tongue?"

Hu Shaoqi's lips and tongue did the bidding of the intelligence that had already scolded him: "Maybe it was the cat who put that hair ball of hunger in your belly, boy."

His own voice, another's words.

As if retreat would save him, the young man backed up

until his shoulders were against the trunk of a gnarled tree. No use, he realized, no use at all. The puppet of the master ventriloquist says *what* it is bid to say, *when* it is bid to say it.

Malicious laughter burst from Hu Shaoqi's lips, terrifying him even further. The worst part of his fear was the knowledge that he could not escape the demon causing it, for that cunning immaterial creature had taken alternating control of his voicebox and the muscles of his lips and tongue. Flight would avail him nothing, for the demon would accompany him, all the while mocking his attempts to escape in the sardonic inflections of his own voice. Hu Shaoqi wanted to scream, but the *kuei* distilling its caustic laughter in his throat would not let him.

At last the laughter stopped, and the demon used him to say, "Not a thought for your mother, lad? Not a thought for the worry and confusion of your parents?"

Hu Shaoqi wrapped his arms backwards around the tree trunk and tried to recover his wits.

"Speak, delicate lad! I give you back your voice!"

"About my mother, Peng Chao, I am indeed concerned," he said, his own words running so abruptly into the demon's that for a moment the lack of a break between them made him doubt that he had truly suffered possession.

"Doubt it not," the demon countered, again stealing his voice, and during this odd dialogue Hu Shaoqi's head snapped from side to side like that of an actor essaying two parts in a traveling drama. "I am with you always."

"Then you should understand that I deserted my household only because voices told me I must. It was not disrespect for my mother or unhappiness with my father's authority that drove me from Xiangcheng. And if you are one of those nagging voices, demon, then *you* must bear at least some of the burden of her sorrow and disappointment."

"I do, lad. I do. That's why I ask about her. That's why I chide you for seeming to forget her."

"Would you have me return to Xiangcheng to comfort my family?"

"The journey you have begun takes pride of place over all other responsibilities. But not even a hero should forget his mother."

Hu Shaoqi pushed himself away from the tree and pounded hard on his chest, as if to pummel into submission the spirit that was so duplicitously dealing with him. *"Then . . . what*

...would...you...have...me...DO,...monster?" he shouted, and the echo of each word reverberated like a blast on a war horn of ivory or bone.

Then the young man's head was wrenched about, and when sounds next escaped him, they were oily with the imprint of the demon's personality: "Look into your begging bowl, boy."

"It's empty!" But Hu Shaoqi looked, to confirm the fact, and so confirmed it all too easily.

"Burnish the metal with the sleeve of your robe."

His indignation giving way to cautious curiosity, the young man obeyed the demon, rubbing the dew-rimed bowl inside and out with his sleeve. The sun was completely gone now, a skull-like moon had risen in the east, dapples of metallic light fell through the canopy of evergreen needles, and in the bottom of his begging bowl Hu Shaoqi saw reflected a spiderweb of evening stars.

"Blow on them," the *kuei* said.

Peng Chao's son once again obeyed the demon, and immediately the concave copper of the bowl showed him his family's house in Xiangcheng and his still youthful-looking mother lying on her side on a pallet in an attitude of grieving weariness. A pug-nosed yellow dog that Hu Shaoqi had named Lung, or dragon, sat at the head of the woman's pallet, nuzzling her brow. These images were not static, but their reduced scale aside, precisely reminiscent of a living human and a living canine figure. Hu Shaoqi could scarcely believe their fidelity to life. His eyes misted, and he glanced up diagonally at the chilly, noncommittal moon.

"See the state she's in. See how you've left her."

"Why do you torment me with the presentation of a scene that I am helpless to alter?" the young man asked, too frustrated by his helplessness to rant.

"You're not helpless, lad. You're a ventriloquist."

"I'm your puppet, rather. And what good is ventriloquism when I am not there in my father's house to amuse the honorable Peng Chao with my talent?"

"Don't amuse her, stupid one! Comfort her!"

"How?" The bowl in his hands, Hu Shaoqi was reeling from tree to tree, staining the ancient copper with the salt of his tears but quickly wiping each discoloration away to behold again the poignant picture of his mother's grief.

"Throw your voice, young idiot! Throw your voice!"

The unhappy traveler halted. Still staring into the bowl, he considered the queer advice that had just passed his own lips. Throw his voice? He was better than a week's walk from Xiangcheng. What was the farthest he had ever cast his voice? He had not done badly with the bandits, of course, but that effort had required him to achieve variety and amplitude, not a ridiculously prohibitive distance. Once, however, he had made Madame Duan believe that a stork on a mist-touched hill had called out to her to be its mate, praising her legs as equal in scrawniness to those of any desirable female of its own species. How far had that been? Quite far, really, but he, Hu Shaoqi, had still reposed *within sight* of both the preening bird and the befuddled Madame Duan. He had never tried to project his voice into the mouth of a Mongol horseman half a continent away.

"You're not *that* far from your village, boy. Enter your ugly little dog as I have entered you. To pierce your muddle-headness, must I explain at even greater length?"

This riposte left an acid taste on Hu Shaoqi's tongue. But, he reflected, it was just. If living pictures could appear in the bottoms of copper bowls, then surely he could exercise his talent for ventriloquism at a distance of as much as even *twelve* days' walk. He concentrated his gaze on Lung, the dog, and tried with all his will to send his thoughts into the creature's head and his voice into its tiny throat.

Peng Chao, Hu Shaoqi's mother, ignored the little dog's efforts to share her unhappiness. Lung was not her dog, but her son's, and although she was pleased in an absentminded way that her fatigue and melancholy should fret the animal, her fear that bandits had killed her only child or that he had provoked some stranger's wrath with a misapplication of his eccentric talent, kept her from returning Lung's tender, but sticky, ministrations.

"Mother!" Lung said.

Without looking up, Peng Chao replied, "So great is my unhappiness that I've even begun to hear his sweet voice in this poor animal's mouth."

"Mother," Hu Shaoqi said through Lung, "it's truly I. I'm here beside you."

At these words Peng Chao sat up on her pallet and stared at the small yellow dog, whose eyes seemed more intelligent than usual and whose head had cocked to one side in a pose of solicitous expectation. Well, those appearances were surely only whimsical accidents. Madame Peng looked away from the dog at various corners of the room, her eyebrows arrowing in over her nose and her mouth assuming a critical involuntary purse.

"No more of your tricks, Hu Shaoqi!" she said. "That you can continue doing such mischief after the cruelty of an unexplained departure will strike everyone who knows us as a failure of upbringing. You shame your father and me. You toy with our goodwill."

"Most Honorable Mother, I'm *not* playing a voice-throwing trick on you," Lung said, wagging his tail.

"Why, of course not. You simply wish for me to believe that your dog has miraculously learned to speak, and that it does so employing *your* voice, and that it calls me Most Honorable Mother only as a doggy courtesy."

"No, Mother, no. I *am* throwing my voice, of course, but not from anywhere in Xiangcheng."

"Come out this instant, you naughty young man," said Peng Chao, still searching the room for a sign of her son. "I will not much longer tolerate the indignity of conversing with your dog."

Hu Shaoqi explained that he was on a mountain quite remote from the village. "I chose Lung as a vehicle for my words, Most Honorable Mother, not to insult you, but to ease your dear mind about both my whereabouts and the present state of my health." Lung, meanwhile, selected this moment to flop down on his side against Madame Peng's bedding. He exposed his soft belly and began tenderly cleaning his privates with his tongue.

Hu Yong, Hu Shaoqi's father, entered the house, and a long conversation that the dog was unable to interrupt ensued. Peng Chao told Hu Yong that an evil spirit had taken up residence in the animal and was trying to upset her own delicate mental balance by mimicking Hu Shaoqi's beloved voice. The *kuei* inhabiting the dog insisted that their son was throwing his voice in Lung's mouth from a great distance, but this was clearly a lie. Moreover, the whole unpleasant episode was undoubtedly one of the consequences of Hu Yong's impiety last spring, when he had drunk too much at a memorial ceremony for Peng Chao's departed grandfather, once a holy man of great reputation in Kweichow.

"It's truly I," Lung protested on Hu Shaoqi's behalf, looking up from his well-licked crotch. "Please don't argue, honorable parents. I simply wanted you to know that I am well and doing as the relentless voices inside my temples have commanded me."

"Then you aren't well at all," Hu Yong told the dog, angry with his wife for reminding him of his folly this past spring. "You're possessed, just as your mother—"

"I'm *not* Lung's mother," Peng Chao declared.

"—just as Madame Peng has said," Hu Yong corrected himself. "Now all that's left for me is to take you outside and beat you soundly for augmenting our sorrow. In this way I'll drive the demon from your too compliant dogflesh and put an end to at least a portion of our unwarranted torment."

Lung, detecting the note of menace in Hu Yong's words, rolled to his haunches, lifted his hindquarters, and started backing from the room. "Father," Hu Shaoqi said through the nervous creature's flat, ebony muzzle, "you mustn't do this. Lung's not to blame. Lung's only my innocent mouthpiece."

"If only you had declined that final bowl," Peng Chao chided her husband. "If only you had burned incense."

Although a paunchy man in an ample robe, Hu Yong made a successful leap at Lung, grabbing the dog by the scruff and swinging him up into his arms. He then proceeded straight through the house, out its rear door, into the chicken yard, and directly to a rock shrine against which Madame Peng's maid had earlier propped a broom. Bent over like a man planting rice, Hu Yong gripped this broom halfway up its handle and began whisking away at the squirming animal's backside.

"Father!" Hu Shaoqi cried. "Most Honorable Father, you're making a grievously unfortunate mistake!"

"I have Madame Peng to tell me that," Hu Yong managed through clenched teeth, still ineptly flailing at the dog's elusive rump. "I do not require you to second her opinion, Demon-in-the-Dog."

Peng Chao appeared on the threshold of the chicken yard. "That's not the way to beat a dog," she said. "You must grip the broom at the end, you must stand up to your full height, you must . . ."

Unable to tolerate either further imprisonment in poor Lung's body or the dismaying burlesque of his parents' behavior, Hu Shaoqi withdrew from the dog, reluctantly relocating himself on the high slope of his anonymous mountain redoubt. Cold moonlight still sifted through the trees, and disconcerting images continued to dance in the bottom of his copper bowl. Angrily, then, he flung the bowl off the mountain and into the waiting night.

"Foolish," the demon said through Hu Shaoqi's aching throat.

The young man lifted his hands as if to strangle himself. *"Who are you? What are you? Why do you want me to go to the Mountain of Everlasting Winter? Why have you singled me out?"*

He wrestled himself away from the edge of a gaping chasm, then felt his hands thrust emphatically down to his sides, where they hung from his slender wrists like huge, impotent spiders.

"It's for your talent that I've singled you out, lad. It's so wonderfully akin to my own."

"But why, implacable one? *Why?"*

"Because ever since the world began, and especially since the human race arose from the lice on the corpse of the deity called Pan Ku, I have carried within me a great and amusing secret. It's time to impart it to someone, fortunate boy. It's time to share what only I among all the gods know."

"And the voices that have haunted me ever since I first spilled semen into my nightclothes?"

"All mine, lad, every one."

"Why?"

"To prepare you for manhood and the revelation of my secret."

"I've no wish to learn it. I don't want to know it."

"It's out of your hands," the *kuei* told Hu Shaoqi. "Lie down beneath that tree, and I'll take your hunger from you and give you this one last night of splendid, refreshing sleep —for until I've told my secret, you won't need food or rest again."

Hu Shaoqi could do nothing to combat this suggestion. He lay down beneath a grotesque cedar, surprised to find that the painful tightness in his stomach had disappeared, and fell into a slumber as full of pleasant images of his home and family as the bottom of his dinner bowl had just been with grotesque and farcical ones. In the morning he awoke rested and stoically resigned to continue his trek to the *kuei*'s unimaginable god-home.

• • •

The remainder of this journey took many days, through country even more forbidding than the groaning mountains that Hu Shaoqi had already traversed. Just as the demon had promised, no hunger pangs assailed him and sleep was an unnecessary indulgence that the young man was glad to leave to people who truly required it. Often he was pinched by anxious thoughts about Peng Chao and Hu Yong, but each time such thoughts arose, the sight of his parents arguing with each other and mistreating Lung was thrown against his inner eye like an estranging shadow. His pity for his mother and father evaporated, his heart hardened, his jaw set. One evening it occurred to him that maybe the demon had allowed him to witness his parents in such an unattractive light for the express purpose of sabotaging his homesickness, but it was too late to go back and it was purposeless self-flagellation to lay upon himself the lash of remorse. He kept going.

Oddly, the *kuei* had relinquished its grip on both his body and his vocal machinery. Hu Shaoqi had no idea where the demon had gone. It had not completely forsaken him, he knew, because whenever he had doubts about which mountain track to follow or which of two icy streams to ford, a voice inside him gave him a prompt that decided the matter. Otherwise the young man relied entirely on his own wits, and fended for himself, and journeyed ever farther westward, like a holy man looking for the one sacred earthly place where he may experience enlightenment. After all, the *kuei* had promised him a powerful revelation in its otherworldly god-home.

It was nearly a week after the episode with the bowl that the troubled young man clambered up a glacial crevasse high above the layer of clouds covering most of this desolate stretch of the continent, into view of his long-sought destination—the abode of the ventriloquist demon.

Ice clung to the peach fuzz on Hu Shaoqi's cheeks, and to his eyelashes, and to the cold-bruised lobes of his ears. He could scarcely feel his feet. But in the wind at the top of the world, he staggered toward the *kuei*'s miraculous dwelling, marveling at both its beauty and its imperviousness to the onslaughts of everlasting winter. He beheld it by starlight, and through the almond-thin lenses of ice on his eyeballs, and by a secret yearning of the heart that invested every ridge and shingle of the god-home with a saintly fire.

The *kuei*'s dwelling was a rose-colored pavilion beside a

pagoda whose upper stories disappeared into the night like the segments of an infinitely tall telescope. A delicate wooden bridge with enameled handrails crossed another glacial chasm to the pavilion's front door. Despite the roaring wind, beds of lotus flowers with scarlet petals hugged the foundations of the structure and a pair of mossy willow trees stood sentinel beyond the bridge. Neither the willows nor the lotus blossoms danced themselves to shreds in the recurrent blasts sweeping the peak.

"Come," said the demon, intruding this word into the traveler's mind rather than shaping it on his tongue. "Don't be an idiot. Come out of the cold."

Although astonished by the pavilion and its adjacent pagoda, Hu Shaoqi hurried to obey. Simultaneously he understood that *kuei* or demons lacked both the spiritual power and the transhuman prestige to inhabit dwellings like this one. Therefore no mere evil spirit had possessed him, no mere demon had dictated his strenuous but failure-proof trek to the top of the world. He was dealing not with a sprite or a ghost, but an immortal god. The chief question that remained was, Which one? Hu Shaoqi knew fear again, but nevertheless continued to approach the bridge.

Inside the outer pale of the god-home, a balmy breeze overtook him and sweet fragrances wafted into his nostrils, and his frozen body began to thaw. Incense mingled with the scent of the flowers. Wind chimes of glass, copper, and polished stone played melodies so much gentler than those of the careering winds on the peaks, that the young man kept shaking his head to determine if this action would restore the pitiless roaring. To his considerable relief, it never did.

The throne room of the pavilion humbled Hu Shaoqi. An ivory chair with lion's paws on its legs and a sunlike maned head in the middle of its back support occupied the dais on the room's far west. A pair of embossed gongs—one silver, one gold—flanked the throne. Painted vases, pâpier-maché death masks, folding rice-paper screens, and watercolored scrolls complemented these imperial furnishings and shone upside down in the liquid depths of the throne room's marble floor. Hu Shaoqi walked toward the lion chair with an acute sensitivity to the echoes of his own slapping footfalls.

"I'm here," he said. "Is that your secret? That no other mortal has ever set foot in this lovely pavilion before?"

To Hu Shaoqi's great surprise his dog Lung padded into the

throne room from one of the pavilion's adjoining wings and hopped up into the lion chair as if perfectly comfortable in so exalted a place. Lung circled about several times, slumped down facing his young master, and inclined his head toward his hind quarters so that he could scratch his ear by halfheartedly jiggling one back foot.

"For my own amusement," Lung said, "I've brought plenty of other mortals here, boy. Unlike you, many of them didn't even have to walk to get here."

"Lung," Hu Shaoqi exclaimed. "Little Dragon!" He noted that the dog's voice was not *his* voice, as it had been in the little drama played out in the bottom of his discarded dinner bowl, but an entirely new one appropriate to a creature of Lung's size and disposition. As if the *kuei*—the god, rather—had developed a small growly voice exclusively for the animal. Hu Shaoqi reached to fondle Lung's mite-infested ear, but Lung bared his teeth and snarled, preventing contact.

"You don't really wish to touch me," the dog warned, in a combination growl and articulate snore—so that now it seemed that through Lung's pink lips two or maybe even three voices were speaking in ill-synchronized harmony. "I'm here in the guise of your dog to ease the act of talking with me. The sight of my true form would melt your eyeballs. The sound of my true voice would burst your eardrums." As if to give a credible dignity to these threats, the god's borrowed dog body stopped jiggling its foot against its ear and stared Hu Shaoqi directly in the eye.

Daunted, the young man looked down. "Are you, then, Old Man Heaven? Or Yen Lo Wang, the Judge?"

"I'm far more ancient than even those upstart pretenders," the dog said indignantly, in its eerie double blur of a voice. "Even Shang Ti and the Great Emperor of the Eastern Peak are infants—mere puppies—in comparison to me. I use them as mouthpieces. I sometimes condescend to let them do my barking."

At these words a strange feeling came over Hu Shaoqi. It consisted of equal parts of terror, reverence, nostalgia, joy, melancholy, anger, love, outrage, apprehension, contentment, perplexity, lust, exhilaration, despair, and mindless panic—indeed, every human emotion except maybe apathy and boredom.

Hu Shaoqi was lost to himself, frozen in place, and suddenly, without moving from his position before the lion chair, he found free-floating pieces of himself—his eyes and his memory—touring the various levels of the infinitely tall pagoda beside the god-home, going from floor to floor through all the stages of his life that his manipulated intelligence could divide into discrete and hence understandable units. Conception, gestation, birth, infancy, toddlerhood, childish self-definition: Each level of the pagoda, as his eyes and memory climbed through the rose-colored structure, represented a vivid and seemingly self-contained period of his development as a person; and yet he ascended through these levels as if his body lacked all substance and no floors separated these crucial periods. Voices accompanied his ascent, the voices of Peng Chao, Hu Yong, playmates, teachers, Lung the dog, other animals, and of course a host of other half-forgotten or at best half-remembered children and adults, all of whom had dripped a little of the lukewarm paraffin of their personalities into his own hot and ever-flowing one. The cacophony of these voices, their contending echoes in the well of the infinite pagoda, rang in Hu Shaoqi's head like the music of either a disintegrating or a resurgent chaos. He could not tell which, and he hardly cared.

And then he was in front of Lung again, in the pavilion, and the strange feeling that had overmastered him grew even stranger. He was going to speak, but the words that he intended to say he knew to belong to the god who had summoned him all the way from Xiangcheng.

"Tell me your secret and let me go."

The dog on the throne cocked its head. "Did you hear what you've just said, boy? Don't you think it perfectly in character? Why, it even reproduces the underlying anxiety that a callow young man in your position would inevitably experience here. I do it all the time, but it never fails to astonish me. That's why I'm able to revel in my own accomplishment, the surprise of rediscovering the formidable extent of my knowledge and power."

Hu Shaoqi was having trouble following the god's elliptical chain of reasoning. "Please, O Great One, what are you talking about? Have pity on a mortal of lesser understanding."

"There again!" Lung barked. "It's second nature to me, for I'm the infallible universal dramaturge."

Bewildered, the young man started to frame another plea for compassion.

"Not only that," Lung enthusiastically cut him off, "I play

all the parts. I compose, I enact, and I direct. *That's* my secret, boy. Do you understand?"

Hu Shaoqi, every piece of his skin tingling as if it had been sliced from his muscles from the underside, shook his head. "No," he murmured, but the word exploded into the throne room like a cannon shot, greatly embarrassing him.

"And I can take you out of character too," said Lung. "I can go mad inside you to relieve a bit of the pressure of sustaining the world's activity."

"Go mad?"

"As now, puppet. As now. For this *is* a kind of madness, you see, sharing with one of the integers of my dependent creation the secret of its dependency. Haven't you yet begun to understand?"

But he had, Hu Shaoqi, and to show that he had, he spoke words that his interrogator had already scripted for him: "I'm no more obtuse than you want me to be, am I?"

Lung's pink tongue made a circuit of its lips, even flicking up to wet the flat, ugly nose. "Excellent riposte. Excellent."

"Self-praise is no praise at all."

"Better, even better. It's borrowed, of course, but ultimately it's borrowed only from myself."

"I thought of you once as a ventriloquist demon, a mere *kuei* with the upsetting ability to hijack—occasionally—my foolish mortal tongue. But now I know you as the Ventriloquist God, who has animated us solely for the purpose of throwing your voice, or voices, into every living husk that has ever been. The meaning of it all is that although *you* count, *we* don't. Puppets are made for instruction and amusement. We, too. Your amusement, but our veiled and therefore mocking instruction."

"Hush," the dog said, laughing in its wheezing, doggy way. "You outrun your allotted dialogue."

Whereupon the creature told Hu Shaoqi to look in turn at the huge medallions of the gongs, the gold one first and then the silver. In the surface of the gold gong, as days ago in the copper at the bottom of his begging bowl, Hu Shaoqi saw moving pictures. Only gods—Shang Ti, Old Man Heaven, Yen Lo Wang, Hsi Ho, Pan Ku, Fu Hsi, and a host of other immortals—disported themselves in the gleaming gold, whereas in the silver only human beings warred and partied, wept and sang, argued and reconciled. Both gongs, however, made it clear to Hu Shaoqi that the Ventriloquist God who had brought him here exercised total control over the players, whether divine or human, visible in their surfaces. The sounds conducted through the metals and around the rims of the gongs had their origin in the throat of the little dog observing Hu Shaoqi, and the dog had its artificial life through the grace and contrivance of the Proprietor of the god-home.

All life, then, was illusion, just as Buddhist teaching had long held, but in a peculiarly narrow and degrading way that the young man had never suspected. It was a shock, and an annihilating wrench, to find that he and all his loved ones—indeed, the whole of creation—were mere substanceless effigies through which the Ventriloquist God could pipe the devious excreta of its everlasting vanity.

"You're not amused?" the dog asked.

A kernel of separate being deep inside Hu Shaoqi wanted to say no to the god in its own voice, but the god forced from the young man a no that failed to coincide with that inner one, being playful and sarcastic rather than freighted with true conviction.

"Turn around, Hu Shaoqi. Turn around."

The upright puppet turned, and there in the pavilion stood upright effigies of Peng Chao and Hu Yong, his parents. Their bodies were ashen and airy, like statues made of volcanic pumice, and the hinge buttons at their jaws glittered meaningfully. They began to talk, these two, but in a manner totally out of keeping with what Hu Shaoqi knew of them. Madame Peng was telling her husband a tale of such flagrant bawdiness that the young man's ears began to burn, while Hu Yong was tittering at each repeated obscenity or sexual innuendo like a half-wit girl of thirteen. Immediately other ashen simulacra of people whom Hu Shaoqi recognized appeared in the pavilion, each with bolts or buttons holding on their lower jaws, and they all began gibbering, ululating, or hacking out hideous noises like persons possessed. The hubbub that Hu Shaoqi had heard in his ethereal flight upward through the pagoda here became a crazy cosmic din that he could no longer tolerate.

"STOP IT!" he shouted. And, for once, the words issuing from his mouth seemed to be wholly his own.

Perhaps for the first time in his life.

Further, at this command, most of the lava-stone statues powdered and blew away. The din diminished. When he shouted the same words again, the remainder of the effigies also disappeared—all but those of his mother and father. Peng

Chao was still reciting an indelicate adventure that her son could in no wise credit, and Hu Yong was still giggling girlishly at the outrageous tale. It was a nightmare, their spurious behavior, even worse than what the deity had inflicted upon them in the copper bowl.

"I SAID STOP IT!"

But they would not. The Ventriloquist God was enjoying his discomfiture too much to let the performance end. So Hu Shaoqi whirled on Lung, the dog, whose tongue was lolling from its mouth in the careless, laughing way of all such curs, and with both hands seized the startled animal's throat before it could react. He yanked the creature off the throne and began strangling it, telling himself over and over again, This is not Lung, this is not actually my beloved Lung. The dog's eyes bulged and its hind feet tried to gain purchase at the midriff of Hu Shaoqi's robe, but the young man kept swinging it from side to side and tightening his grip, with the result that the imprisoned god could not yet wriggle free and manifest.

Over his shoulder the young man saw that the statues of his mother and father had finally begun to crumble. Their stupid voices continued to sound in the throne room, but more thinly than before, and soon all that was left of either simulacrum was a wind-nudged mound of bleak grit and the whisper of emancipation.

Hu Shaoqi tossed Lung away from him, and the dog broke its back on the rim of the marble dais supporting its throne. Its yelp of pain crescendoed through the pavilion like two great armies colliding, and where a small, twisted dog had been, Hu Shaoqi saw an immense winged serpent with scales like dead leaves and a lion's head unreeling from its toothless mouth a pair of split, snaky tongues. This creature—this being—reared up on the coils of its lower body in much the way that the pagoda next to the pavilion climbed heavenward on its successive stories, and Hu Shaoqi had to tilt back his head to see the ancient leonine face glowering at him like a once glorious sun on the brink of self-extinguishment.

"You're (you're) fortunate (fortunate) I (I) don't (don't) simply (simply) crush (crush) you (you)," the god said in its blurred double voice, and Hu Shaoqi automatically adjusted his hearing to filter out the echo, "but I fear *you're* not solely a walking mouthpiece for my own capricious japeries."

"I'm not," Hu Shaoqi retorted.

"How did you discover your autonomy?" the god asked.

"It was something I always assumed. Until I arrived here, I had no reason to doubt it. It was your purpose to reveal that assumption as an illusion, but it's my gift to you, Ventriloquist God, to turn the tables, to declare from the kernel of being deep within myself that the *real* illusion is your arrogant illusion of total mastery."

"Worship me," the serpentine lion said.

Hu Shaoqi knelt before the monster, casting down his eyes and touching the tips of his fingers to his forehead.

"You submit? You do my will?"

"Voluntarily," Hu Shaoqi replied. "I'm not a god. I'm but a mortal human being."

"Then you comprehend your place?"

"It's a high place, O Great One, for it's no contemptible thing to be a kind of philosophical monkey. To have a voice that splices unintelligible noises into chains of airy import."

The dragon deity spoke no other word, and for the leftover length of that immortal night, Hu Shaoqi remained on his knees before the creature, meditating and praying. When next he looked up, he found himself sitting on the slope of the selfsame mountain on which he had used his copper bowl to witness some dismaying events in his father's household in Xiangcheng. Well, now those events struck Hu Shaoqi as more humorous than otherwise. But although he could laugh at them, a natural anxiety—a concern for the well-being of every member of his family—prodded him to rise and begin the homeward leg of his journey which would either confirm or cancel his fears.

So Hu Shaoqi returned to his native village, and his arrival there stupefied many and greatly cheered his mother and father, who had given him up for dead. Lung was there, too, and although the young man tried to show the dog both affection and the rough playfulness that his pet had once insisted on, Lung regarded him with reproachful eyes and tuck-tail suspicion.

But this was the only unhappy aspect of Hu Shaoqi's return, and the hearty meal of chicken and fried vegetables that Madame Peng prepared for him on his first evening home more than made up for the dog's queer lack of enthusiasm. Never had he had a bigger hunger, and never had he so enjoyed a mortal craving.

While he was eating, a choir of children celebrating an

autumn festival came down the street and paused just outside to share its song with his family. Hu Shaoqi, even as he ate, listened in wonder, hearing every voice distinct from all the others and then hearing them in unison as if they were complementary pipes on the same joyous wind instrument. And such voices those children had, such beautiful, beautiful voices!

"Throw your voice into theirs," Hu Yong urged his son. "Make Little Dragon there sing with them."

"Forgive me, Most Honorable Father," Hu Shaoqi said, "but it's very hard to do while eating."

Fortunately Hu Yong accepted this explanation, and it was only later in all their lives that he came to realize that his son had apparently renounced that talent forever.

LAZARUS

Ellen Kushner

Ellen Kushner compiled the excellent fantasy anthology **Basilisk** *for Ace Books some while back, with a cover so hideously inappropriate that the publisher felt morally required to reissue the book with a totally new cover thereon. Ellen's not yet a well-known writer, but she's bound to become one. And already, among a coterie of perversely inclined women readers of fantasy (men too, I suspect), whether she knows it or not, Ellen Kushner is something of a cult figure—on the strength of one novelette, "The Unicorn Masque." I recall panting and chattering ridiculously in a conversation with Joanna Russ about this story shortly after its appearance in the World Fantasy Award winning anthology* **Elsewhere**. *I've ever since attempted to get a Kushner story for one of my anthologies, and finally I've succeeded.*

"Lazarus" had a checkered life seeking publication and is somewhat revised from the original, much-rejected manuscript that was faulted chiefly for a peculiar punctuation and, doubtless, its extraordinary content. The punctuation is toned down in this final draft, although its mildly experimental edge is preserved; and the content—not altered a bit. Don't say you weren't warned.

The story is a prequel to "The Unicorn Masque," and was

written somewhat earlier. Ellen says, "I used to read to my college friends the Adventures of Lazarus Merridon, sitting cross-legged on my dorm bed, watching out of the corner of my eye to see if their glasses were steaming up properly."

There is every possibility of other of Lazarus's adventures being revised for future publication. Some of us, glasses ready, are waiting to start steaming.

—WAKE UP. WAKE UP.

—He's awake.

No I'm not. Open wide eyes.

—How are you feeling, sir?

Close eyes. I really can't move.

—Weak yet.

—Get up, please.

I arise, myself and not myself. Someone else has hold of me, but I know that I contain enough.

—Ah, fine. You look well.

He turns to other.

—Can sing, dance, play, converse . . . ?

—Very well, thank you. Have I a name?

—You don't remember?

—I never can remember names.

—Lazarus Merridon.

—It's changed.

—Is it appropriate?

—Was I dead, or a beggar?

Silence.

—Or both?

—Come, Mr. Merridon, we'll show you your chamber.

—And it is now upon the stroke of noon, I venture.

—Two hours past, I'm afraid. You slept long.

I am a very well-turned man, by almost any time's standards. I know things I shouldn't know: the points and lace on the new clothes give me no trouble. The two watch carefully. I look to see if they are excited by my nudity. The plump, thick one squeezes his fingers together, his rings digging into the puffy flesh; but it is just, or mainly, because I am expensive. I flash a smile at them.

—Am I serviceable?

He almost squeals.

—Most, most serviceable.

Then:

—You don't remember?

—I remember nothing but what you will, sir.

The other, dark and lean, warns me:

—With sleep may come strange dreams. You are not to be disturbed by them, they will fade in time.

—Very well.

They leave.

I will not torture myself with thoughts of who I am. I am as I am, and so will I be. . . . The room is beautiful, white walls and dark beams. There are Turkish carpets, hangings, a carved armchair with thick red cushions, fruit and wine on the table. A good life, this. A window looks out over green fields touched with rain. A great bed of dark wood, with four stately pillars and a carved canopy; sheets smooth, and white as the sun. . . .

I dream of fucking. Pushing and pushing but nothing resolves, but God I am in love, God he is beautiful, lovely, lovely. . .

I wake up breathing hard. *He?* He. Am I—a lover of men? I get up and pace, a robe of thick blue silk pulled from the chair billowing about my shoulders. I don't know. I don't know at all. Is it the thing to be, here? Unlike the points and laces, I am not sure of it. No woman has appeared yet, so how can I tell?

Knocking at the door. I take pleasure in letting them wait until I attend to the tying of my laces. The elegant, sleek-fitting clothes are black. Then I pull open the heavy oaken door. Two strange men with drawn swords confront me. I can sing, dance, play, converse. . . .

—Here!

A rapier arcs through the air to my hand. En garde. Parry, retreat, parry, riposte, advance . . . The second man waits behind me, quite still. Let us hope he remains so. I am tired, but they can't want to have me killed so new. Weak but agile, I dispatch the first swordsman. Turn around to the second. He is much faster. But so am I, now. The blades clash sharply back and forth, like a saw, like the pendulum of a clock. He pinks my wrist—startled by my first blood, I attack with more ferocity. I slice him several times, and at last he falls against the wall, slides slowly down it.

My two patrons step forth.

—Well enough, I think.

I pant and sweat. My wrist oozes blood. I suck on the wound, but draw my arm back in distaste: the blood tastes altogether metallic, not salty at all.

—It will heal by itself.

I indicate the two dead swordsmen.

—Will theirs?

—They are not whole. Didn't you notice that they have no voices?

I didn't notice. I am very tired. I sketch a bow, turn and go back to my room.

I dream that I am not like all the rest. My appearance is fine, but when I open my mouth to speak with them, a glorious torrent of words rushes out . . . and, man or woman, they turn blank, uncomprehending faces to me—blank—oh, God, they really *are* blank—where are their faces—I am surrounded by heavy bodies, the men's thick, strong, with forests of dark hair sprouting red rod penises, the women's round and full, breasts ripe and ready to drop. . . .

Awake, I survey my body. It is long, slender, and most beautiful. Already the wound on my wrist has scabbed over. In a silver basin I try to examine my face. Startling blue eyes stare into mine, set in a delicate face, almost a girl's but that its lines are harder, angles more severe. I'm hungry. I pick an apple out of the bowl of fruit. One knocks.

—Mr. Merridon! You are bade to dinner!

The three of us dine in a small oak-paneled room lit by candle-light.

—Some grapes, sir?

Fat, ringed hands hold up the bunch.

—Thank you, but I have never liked them.

He raises his eyebrows, questioning, at the other. I refrain from smiling; instead, I turn the talk to vineyards. Then the lean one takes a ribboned lute from the wall.

—You'll play for us, sir?

It is good to hold such a beautiful instrument. I play a dance tune, and then a song of love denied. My fingers are sure, my voice true.

The fat one grins greasily at the other.

—Fit for a queen, eh?

—Of course.

—A beautiful man . . .

In comes a girl. Slender, in dark green velvet.

—Welcome (says Pudge-Rings).

Her eyes are downcast. She is dark and fine. I want her.

—Does she have speech? Does she bleed truly?

Her dark eyes widen.

—Yes, Mr. Merridon.

Lean One speaks stiffly. I have offended them. Here they have brought me a true woman. But I appreciate it. God, she is beautiful, lovely. I rise, taking her hand's feather weight.

—Lady, will you sit?

I set her in my chair, and stand behind it. I can feel my blood, my breathing pulsing in rhythmic torrents. All of my skin feels too tight. She sits modestly; I stare. Ask:

—Have we met before?

Lean One laughs. But it is a true question.

—I think not, sir.

Her voice is soft and clear.

—You have a familiar look. Where might we have seen one another?

—I think, Mr. Merridon, that we have never met.

My hand goes out to the bare skin of her neck. Its warm smoothness has a familiar feel. My own hand is icy cold. It trembles; I can hardly draw it away for wanting to draw it down.

—Oh, Lavinia . . .

It is the first name I have spoken.

—Sir?

How long since I have seen a woman? Touched one?

—Who am I, Lavinia?

—A gentleman, sir, I hope.

She flinches her head away.

—A gentleman . . .

—Sir, perhaps you are tired.

Solicitous Lean One. But I am. Walking makes me tired, breathing makes me tired; fighting makes me tired. Passion makes me tired. Slowly I slide my hand from the column of delicate flesh. If I could lie . . .

—You will excuse me, sirs, lady.

I make my way to the door. As it closes behind me, I hear Pudge chuckling.

—A beautiful man . . .

• • •

Tightness wells in me for the length of the caress. I want him. . . . . We embrace, both our bodies taut. Suddenly I am above, looking down at the locked couple. Where I was, lies a slim woman with long dark hair. Her lover is a red-haired man. I know him now.

—Lazarus (I whisper in the dark) risen from the dead. Begged crumbs from the rich man's table.

But which is it? I was never red-haired.

In the following days Lavinia does not reappear. I spend the time being tutored and drilled by the pair in the ways of this country I am to call mine, and in the titles and courtesies current at the court of the Queen. Every day at three in the afternoon I am called to my door by knocking and open it to swordsmen: the second day, there are three; the next, four . . . all patiently waiting their turns to prove my prowess. I begin to recognize some I killed days ago, revived, unscarred. I still sleep a great deal, but do not always remember the dreams when I awake.

—Where is your home, sir?

—In Your Majesty's presence.

—Pretty, Merridon, but it won't do forever. You must have a past to go with your glorious future.

—Have I a patrimony?

Pudge answers.

—You are my son.

—Oh, sir!

—Born abroad to a dear friend of mine, now dead, alas, and to his pretty mistress; raised by me in seclusion, until fit to be presented before Her Illustrious Grace. . . .

—The rest, invent: your childhood adventures, toys, slights, first love . . .

I smile. I can do it.

—Here, boy.

Pudge twists at his finger.

—Wear this.

A heavy gold ring: a signet with a small red jewel. I slip it on my left forefinger; it lends weight to the hand. Engraved in the gold is a human figure, dancing, it seems, between sun and moon. The gem is in the sun.

—Your sign, or mine?

—Yours. Wear it.

• • •

I am in great pain. They are trying to kill me. The pain is from running. I can't move—I wrench myself from the dream, weeping. The red-haired man lying by me says, Was it the dream again? I sob and sob, he takes me in his arms, my sex warms, then I am standing on a bare plain. Are you ready? they say. Are you ready, are you sure? I am ready. My mind is bound here, trapped, set me free. . . .

I jolt awake, into the freedom of Lazarus Merridon. It is black night. I robe myself and leave the chamber. I can't remember the way to the room I first woke in. I know it is one I haven't been in since. Off in a side wing, I stumble against a door at the end of the passage. I rest against it, thinking.

I woke at midmorning in my own bed. During the day my patrons make no mention of my ramblings. Were they real at all? In the daylight none of it seems to matter so much. Awake, I amuse myself with invention.

—And the nurse screamed at me to come down from the tree, but my sister—

—You had a sister?

—Yes, a twin.

—What happened to her?

—She was taken in a raid and sold into slavery. Dead now, I think.

—What was her name?

Name?

—I . . . it was . . .

—Mr. Merridon; perhaps you had no sister?

—I . . . if you wish.

—What happened then?

—My sister said . . .

—No: The nurse said.

—I said, I couldn't come down before noon.

Struggling in the dream, not to get out but to get into it, they're keeping me from it, I have to get to the light, white and pure, white and bare, sterile, I'm on the plain again where nothing grows. Are you ready? Oh, yes, yes, yes, now, please. Are you sure? Oh, yes, yes, yes . . .

I am embracing my pillow. Furious with sweat, I unlock myself from it, hurl the downy thing across the room. The dreams claw at me, they roll me and twist me, but refuse to tell me anything. These nameless lovers . . . Lavinia; why can't I be dreaming of Lavinia? She is real, more real than I am, let her come to me asleep, awake, and I'll not rest unsatisfied. . . . I should ask my keepers, Pudgy and Lean: Please, sirs, may I have Lavinia for the night? You own me; surely you own her too. And she can't even have been expensive, coming ready-made. Not as expensive as I. I remember being quite expensive—no, valuable, the thin man said. You are very valuable to us, my dear, of course it will be costly, but that is not your concern. . . . My concern. What is my concern? I can't think, it's all bodies, a knot of flesh, how can I know . . . Cut the knot. What does it matter, the mind still remains, set it free. . . . A fine mind. What we need. Adaptable, learns quickly. But you, my dear, you're a pretty, an intelligent woman, what will you get from this? Oh, a chance, a chance to do . . . to be—

—Lazarus!

Make them go away.

—Merridon!

I am not done dreaming.

—Damn him; open the door!

—What are you doing in bed, we've been calling you.

—Get up! Get dressed.

My eyes, closed:

—Go away.

—You lady-faced ingrate wretch!

It is Pudge shrieking.

—Shh!

A bony hand on my brow.

—Lazarus, sleep. Remember the orchard, and the nurse . . .

I am a young boy, swinging my legs amid the branches and laughing.

—Who are you?

—Lazarus Me–Merridon.

—Where are you?

—In the trees.

—Where is your father?

—At home.

—Who are you?

—Lazarus.

—Who named you?

—I don't know.

The room is quiet now. I come out of the confusion of

leaves and branches and sunshine. I am Lazarus Merridon. A beautiful, agile swordsman, a fine hand on the lute, a mind quick to wit . . . I am what I always wanted to be. Am I? The dreams do *not* fade in time. Despite them I force open my eyes, get up, walk to the window. There are people in bright jeweled raiment riding in the sunny meadow: the Queen's progress must have come at last. I must go down to meet them. My fingers fumble at the laces of my clothes. God, but I'm tired. Why? A hard night, a strange sleep. I fall across the bed, just to rest. A soft knock at the door.

—Come in!

Too early for the swordsmen.

—Lavinia!

She stares at my semi-nudity.

—Lazarus, but you must get dressed! The Queen below. . .

She begins to tackle the lacings. But with drowsy strength I pull her onto me.

—Sir!

—I am not a gentleman.

She is heavy and warm.

—Lazarus!

She touches my brow with a long, fine hand.

—Lazarus, sleep.

Even my fire-haired lover, even he cannot keep me from the dreams. The blank faces; the full bodies, none of them mine . . . In a new dream I come to the moon's bare plain and strike a bargain. The part of me that matters, the part no one can touch, I tender it to the lean one who until now had only stalked the edges of my dreams. He will encase it in sunlight and set it free. I stand on the plain, the surface of the moon. Cool and delicate. On the plain, nearly there, now it is good. And are you sure of this? Oh, yes. Are you sure? Yes, yes, I need it, yes. Are you sure? Yes! Are you ready? Yes! Are you sure? Yes, *now, yes* . . .

Open wide eyes. Lavinia lying quite still, her breathing quick. Then she looks at me.

—Are you ready?

—Yes.

I dry myself off, and dress with efficiency. Below, the Queen awaits. I shall come fluidly down the stairs, a beautiful man, to sing, dance, play, converse. . . .

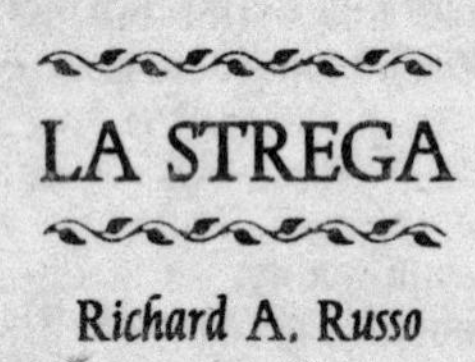

LA STREGA

Richard A. Russo

As an anthologist I'm forever on the lookout for the kind of story that "La Strega" embodies: Magic and adventure that is colorful and exciting but that never loses its compassion. Pathos, not sadism, is the phrase I've used, striving to convey my sense of what constitutes fine heroic fantasy. If someone wishes to read a story as simple escapism, I think they should be able to do that. Yet there is no reason, to my mind, that the same *story should not reward the reader whose thinking cap is left on.*

"La Strega" is a story of thrills, chills, and humanity. Solid adventure, but with heart. This is a rare achievement, though in the present anthology, you will encounter others who achieve that combination.

There is another Richard Russo out there in the world publishing fantasy and science fiction. There is bound to be confusion about them in the future. Please remember, the one with the "A for Anthony" in the middle, you first encountered in **Heroic Visions II** *and will look for in the future.*

Richard Anthony Russo grew up in the Bronx but has lived in the Bay Area, a coast away, since 1970. He has a degree in philosophy from Cornell and works as a reference librarian part time (this is the land of opportunities, after all). His mother came to America from Sicily at the age of eleven. From that you may guess the source of Richard's fascination with the history and culture of that island, where heroic fantasies are being worked out to this very day.

THE WITCH'S CAVE was just as the villagers had described it: a crooked gash in the side of the hill, like the entrance to a tomb. A tattered blanket hung across the opening.

Vito pressed closer to the cool ground and crawled forward toward the edge of the ridge. When he peered down again into the small clearing, he saw a stone firepit filled with gray ashes. A milk goat was tethered to the side of the hill. He smiled. The hole was still inhabited.

The clearing grew brighter with the approaching dawn. The villagers said the witch would rise with the sun. He still had time to prepare his trap.

Vito backed away from the crest, then circled around behind the ridge until he was directly above the entrance to the cave. He lay down his pack and drew out the net, then licked his fingers and slid them over the hard twine, feeling for snags. He licked again, and tasted salt; the net had been woven by the fishermen at Cefalu. Satisfied, he slung a coil of rope over his shoulder, then gathered several heavy stones, folded them carefully into the net, and began inching down the hillside.

Above the mouth of the cave Vito moved quickly, anchoring the net so that it was held precariously by the weight of the stones. He tied a loop around the largest rock and backed away, feeding a trail of rope as he climbed. Atop the ridge he slithered into a small hollow facing the cave. Then, still gripping the end of the rope, he drew a small shard of mirrored glass from his belt and tilted it till he could see the reflection of the cave mouth below. He watched in the glass and waited.

He was staring at the blanket, when suddenly the witch was standing in front of it—twisted and stooped, a repulsive hag. She looked at the sky, as if to judge the day, and saw the rope above her doorway.

She whirled and searched for him. Vito jerked the rope as hard as he could and leaped from the hollow; the net fell upon the startled witch before she could react. She dropped to the ground, screeching and tearing at the tough strands, and had risen to one knee by the time he reached her. He grabbed the bottom of the net and pulled, throwing her down again. She clawed at him through the webbing, and he kicked her, being careful not to look at her eyes. When she tried to crawl away, he dropped with both knees in the small of her back and pushed her face into the ground till she shrieked and spit blood. Still straddling her, he pulled the ends of the net together and tied them shut, then stood and grinned while she flailed wildly at his feet.

He crossed the clearing and worked a wooden stake loose from the edge of the firepit, then picked up a large stone. The witch whimpered as he advanced toward her. Vito laughed and raised the stone as if to strike her, then knelt and hammered the stake into the rocky soil, anchoring the net. He repeated the process, ignoring her cries, until she was pinned tightly to the ground. Then he stood over his catch and brushed himself off, resisting the urge to look at her. Instead, he clambered up the hillside to retrieve his shard of mirror, and studied her reflection as he drew near.

She was ancient and ugly, pitted and furrowed like the craggy landscape. Half her face sagged and was covered with warts; an open sore festered on one side of her nose. Her coarse woolen robe was soiled and torn. She had stopped struggling, and was gasping and wheezing pathetically.

He uncovered his knife and clenched it tightly in his right hand, blade down like a dagger. The witch screamed as he raised his arm. "This is for Nicco," he said.

He fell to his knees and brought the knife down. She tried to twist away but was caught in the net; she screamed again as the blade sank to the hilt in her chest. He grasped the handle with both hands and pulled downward, opening her gut. Blood gushed out at him, foamy and white, as he stabbed again and again. . . .

But it was not blood—it was salt! He was on his knees at the mouth of the cave, plunging his blade into a bag of salt!

He heard laughter behind him. A stone dropped with a dull thud; he looked up in time to see the net fall. He tore at it, but the strands would not yield. He was caught in his own trap.

Suddenly his feet were pulled out from under him. She'd slung a rope over one of the blanket pegs and was hoisting him off the ground. He looked for his mirror, and saw it lying out of reach.

"Still fear the *malocchio?*" The witch laughed. He looked

away as she picked up the mirror and held it out to him. "Take your glass," she taunted. "It will protect you from the evil eye!" He reached through the net and snatched the mirror from her, but felt foolish; obviously he'd already been bound by her spell.

He angled the glass to catch her reflection and was startled to see a slender young woman, no older than himself, with long black hair that fell past her shoulders. She wore a plain brown dress of rough-woven cloth, the color of the earth, and a string of dark glass beads. But her eyes were what captured him, even in the reflection: deep brown, with flecks of darker colors, mournful, yet vibrant and penetrating. She was of the old blood, dark, like him.

She stood with her hands on her hips, studying him. "Who are you, and why have you come?"

He dropped the mirror and faced her squarely. "I am Vittorio Branca," he said. "I have come from Catania to avenge the death of my mother Beatrice and my brother Niccolo."

"I have never been to Catania, nor have I taken a life."

He tore at the net but could not break free.

The witch laughed. "While you live, there is still hope of vengeance, eh?" Again he saw the grotesque hag, and spat at her through the net.

"Tell me your story," she said. When he turned away, she hunched closer, her breath reeking of sour olives. "Won't talk, eh?" Her hand darted out and grabbed a tangle of net and hair. She jerked his head closer and forced her other hand deep into his mouth, then grabbed his tongue and pulled on it, hard. Vito screamed, tried to bite her fingers, then screamed again as she held him tightly by the neck and tongue. An icy shiver ran up the base of his skull and slithered into his brain. She was going to kill him, he thought, as the top of his head seemed to melt and run like liquid over his eyes. The world went yellow, a noonday sun blazed in the morning sky, and he realized with horror that she'd opened his mind, not his skull. . . .

. . . a field outside Catania . . . two men walking slowly toward him, holding opposite ends of a ladder. On the makeshift stretcher a small body rested beneath its shroud. Niccocino! *Drowned in the river,* one of them was saying . . . it made no sense! Nicco who couldn't swim, who never went near the water? Mama! Mama! he cried as he ran . . . knowing even then that Nicco-the-Dwarf had thrown himself in, to rid them of the burden he'd become. . . .

. . . darkness . . . kneeling beside his mother, clutching the hem of her skirt. "It was after your father was killed in the mines," she was saying. "I put you and Nicco in a straw basket and strapped it to the donkey. . . . I thought I'd find work in Catania.

"It was so hot . . . you and Nicco were crying, we couldn't go on without water . . . finally we came to a well at the side of the road. The farmers bowed when they saw my veil, and were helping me draw water, when suddenly everyone froze. A witch had entered the clearing.

"They moved aside for her, leaving us alone at the well. 'Who stands in my way?' the witch cried. 'I have traveled far and my children are weary,' I said, dipping a rag in the water. 'Your children?' the witch said. She reached into the basket and pulled you both toward her, staring at you with her evil eye. When I tried to push her away, she clutched at my arm. 'Your children will not grow to be men,' she said."

His mother was staring into the darkness. A tear ran down one side of her face, and he thought how tired she looked. "Am I going to die like Nicco?" he asked, the image burning in his mind of his brother's stunted body slumped across the ladder.

"It would have been better if she had killed him!" She turned and looked at him for the first time. "Don't you see, Vito? You've grown tall and strong, but Nicco . . . Nicco would never have been a man. . . ."

Vito pulled at her wrists, trying to break her hold, but it was too late, she was inside his mind, making him suffer the horror once more. . . .

. . . the awful gurgling sound that woke him in the night . . . the knife beside his mother's outstretched hand . . . the blood soaking into the coarse wooden floor . . .

"So your mother took her own life," the witch said as the icy tendrils withdrew from his mind, and he began sobbing.

"I will kill you!" he cried, his lips twisted with hatred and rage. "I swear I will kill you!" He stared fiercely into her eyes, but found only sadness, and became confused.

The witch turned away and began gathering firewood at the edge of the clearing. When she had a small fire burning in the pit, she returned.

"If La Strega put a curse on both sons, why was only Niccolo stunted?"

Before he could answer, she slipped into the cave, leaving him hanging in the doorway. Vito twisted and jerked and pulled at the net, but could not break free. When she returned, carrying a clay pot filled with water and herbs, he was trying to bite through the tough strands.

She hung the pot over the fire to boil, then sat on the ground to watch him chew. After a while he gave up. She rose silently to put more wood on the fire, then sat facing him again.

"You have the wrong witch," she said at last.

"Don't toy with me!" he cried. "I have searched half of Sicily to find you. You are La Strega!"

"I am Elena, but I am not La Strega. The woman you came here to kill is dead. She was my mother."

"Liar!"

The witch smiled. "What happened at the well happened twenty years ago. La Strega was old even then."

"You have changed before my eyes. I cannot trust what I see."

She went back to the firepit and removed the pot, then sat, gazing into the swirling leaves.

"I am not going to kill you," she said at last. "But in return for your life, you will remain with me for three months."

"You are mad!"

"You will swear on the soul of your dead brother to forego vengeance while you remain here. After three months, if you so desire, you may take my life."

"But why?"

"So that you may find what you seek."

When she had cut him free, he yearned to kill her, but she had read him well: he would not break his vow. No matter; he had waited long years for retribution, he could wait a little longer. Besides, it would not be easy to kill her; she'd shown him that. For the next three months he would endure, studying her ways till he found her weakness, some flaw in her power he could turn against her.

"There's a cup on the shelf," she said, motioning toward the cave.

"I will not serve you!"

"I thought you might like some tea," she replied, and he

saw that she was already dipping a cup into the fragrant brew of chamomile flowers and orange rind.

He turned away before she could laugh at him, and climbed the hill to retrieve his pack. When he returned, she'd gotten the second cup and was dipping it into the kettle. He accepted it silently; then, determined not to be in her debt, pulled a dry crust of bread from his pack and broke it in half to share with her. The stale crumb stuck in his throat. Elena—La Strega was soaking her bread in the warm tea. He waited, in order not to look like he was copying, then dipped his own.

He spent the morning skulking about and avoiding any contact with her. She obliged by ignoring him. He folded up the net and climbed back to the hollow where he'd left the rest of his belongings. There, with a commanding view of La Strega's cave, he made his own camp.

Below, La Strega was carrying a bundle of olivewood from the cave. He watched as she built up the fire in the pit. Beyond her the hills opened onto a grove of wild chestnut and olive trees then sloped downward to the coastal plains outside Palermo.

When the flames had died, she filled a small clay pot with water and added strips of dried fish and fennel. She rested the covered pot in the glowing coals to cook, then returned to her cave.

That night, as they ate the stew, the witch was pensive. "To take a life is a terrible burden," she said.

"To be unavenged for the taking of one is worse."

"A curse takes as many forms as its victims. Your heart is as twisted and warped as the body of your dead brother. What hope can there be if you commit a murder?"

He laughed bitterly. "My only hope is of revenge." He tossed a twig into the coals, where it burst into flame.

"You can choose to let go of your hatred. Only then will you be free."

"I seek vengeance, not freedom."

They watched the twig burn down to an ember.

"Suppose, as you believe, I am La Strega. If you kill me, your heart will stay stunted and warped, scarred by the vengeance you wreak. The prophecy of La Strega will have come true, and you will have been its instrument."

"We are all instruments of the Fates!"

"You believe your Fate wants you to kill La Strega?"

Her logic infuriated him. "La Strega will die by my hand —that is what *I* want! I care nothing for my Fate, who has sent only suffering."

"You speak bravely, but you are a fool."

"I curse the Fate that has bound us together! If I could, I would kill it too!"

La Strega watched quietly as he scrambled up the hill, scraping his knees on the jagged rocks.

In the morning she offered him cheese made from goat's milk and they divided what was left of his bread. Vito walked off to relieve himself in the bushes, and when he returned, found her mixing dough for a sweet bread. As she turned it onto a flat stone to knead, he asked for the axe to chop wood for the oven. When she smiled, he said, "I want nothing from you, including your thanks. I do only my fair share."

He gathered a pile of logs to split, then broke several smaller branches with his hands. He paused to wipe the sweat from his forehead, and looked at La Strega.

"My mother brought me to my Fate when I was still a girl," she said as she divided the dough into round balls and covered them with a damp cloth to rise. "We traveled all day, down to the coast. Then she left me to make the last part of my journey alone.

"I walked along the shore as the sky grew dark. The air was filled with the salty tang of the tide coming in. My Fate took the form of a kind old woman waiting for me by the rocks. I gave her a sweet bread like this one; she seemed pleased, and said she'd be my ally. She told me what my life would be like."

Vito looked at her skeptically. He knew she would be trying to trick him, that he could not believe anything she told him.

Later, as she braided the dough, she began to sing a lullaby his mother had sung when he was little. He chopped with new fury at the silvery olivewood. La Strega ignored him, and went on singing as she dotted the braided sweet bread with fennel and put it in the stone oven to bake.

At midday a farmer and his wife appeared. The man carried his four-year-old son on his back. As his wife knelt at La Strega's feet, he put the boy down in her arms.

"Per piacere, Stregelena. Mi bambino, non si senta bene."

La Strega looked at the boy. *"Che cosa ha?"*

"Ho un mal di testa," the child replied, while the parents looked on helplessly.

She felt his pulse, looked at his eyes and tongue, touched his neck and forehead. The boy had been ill for several weeks, they said. Nothing seemed to help, they couldn't afford to go to a doctor in the city, he grew thinner each day . . . the mother began to cry.

La Strega turned and walked to the cave, leaving Vito alone with the family. When the boy's father looked at him hopefully, he scowled.

She returned with a bundle of blue silk bound with gold thread—her *tavola*. She unrolled it and spread her instruments before her, a bizarre collection of bone fragments, polished pebbles, twigs, and stone implements. She picked out a slender needle carved of bone, then sat beside the fire and motioned for the child to be brought to her. The farmer laid his son in her arms. Stregelena held the boy's head in her hands, and then, as she felt the pulse at the back of his neck, quickly pierced the skin behind his right ear. He whimpered as blood began to drip from the needle, which she left dangling from his flesh. She reached into the pit and dipped her thumb in the warm ashes at the edge of the fire, then rubbed them into his forehead soothingly. When she began to sing, the boy smiled, and his parents wept with relief.

When she was finished, she brought herbs from the cave and made a poultice of comfrey and St. John's wort to cover the wound she'd opened. Then she gave them goldenseal and violet petals to administer as a tea until the boy's head stopped aching. They presented her with gifts: a sack of oranges, which the woman gave to Elena, and a scraggy chicken, already cleaned and plucked, which the farmer gave to Vito, saying *"Grazie, signor, grazie."*

The next few days passed uneventfully. Vito gathered and chopped wood, helped milk the goat, tended the fire—anything that gave him an excuse to stay near and watch her. Elena asked nothing of him and accepted gratefully whatever help he offered. She shared her knowledge of herbs with him and described the illnesses she'd been called upon to cure, while he weighed everything she told him, searching for a clue to her powers. She spoke again of her Fate, the spiritual counterpart whose will was separate from her own—but he could find no way to use it against her, and suspected her of trying to divert him from his purpose.

After months of traveling alone in the mountains, brooding on revenge, he found her conversation enjoyable. Then he caught himself enjoying it and retreated to his hilltop. When he joined her again after several days, he was sullen and cold, his will to vengeance renewed.

Then a shepherd came, asking for Stregelena. He was slender and blond, of foreign blood, perhaps even a bastard son of the Norman invaders who ruled in Palermo. One of his sheep had the candle sickness; he feared for the whole flock. Would she come?

She went to her cave and chose the instruments and potions she would need. When she was ready, she asked Vito to accompany her. He refused. She followed the shepherd into the wooded hills and was gone.

This was his chance! When she was out of sight, he stole into her cave and searched through her belongings: a wooden pallet and a mattress stuffed with straw, some woolen blankets, a box full of clothes, a shelf lined with clay pots and cooking utensils. Several niches had been carved into the wall; inside were earthen jars filled with salt, date sugar, lentils and barley, dried prickly pear leathers, and herbs: marigold, comfrey, birch bark, eucalyptus leaves. Orange, lemon and cactus blossoms. Bright red poppies. One of these niches was deeper than the rest; he started to reach in, but quickly withdrew in fright at the yellowish batlike creatures that hung from the ceiling. He looked again. They were dried fish

He knelt by her bed and lifted the pallet. Beneath it he found the *tavola*. Suddenly afraid the witch might return, yet unable to restrain himself, he took the blue silk bundle and laid it gently on the bed. He unrolled it carefully, then studied the strange collection of objects: a metal lance, and needles of bone like the one she'd used on the boy; a huge fish scale; some colored pebbles; a cuttlefish bone; a sharp piece of purple glass from the slopes of Etna; several small clay vials stopped with cork, which he did not open; and the dried stems and flowers of various plants. One jagged ring of discolored bone made him shiver: the eye socket of a human skull. He rolled the cloth up and replaced it carefully beneath the pallet.

He scanned the cave again. A small stone pit at the center of the chamber served as a hearth; smoke from the fire was carried along the ceiling by a gentle draft that rose from the back of the cave. There he found a narrow tunnel and a smaller chamber where water dripped off the cold slate into clay pots left to collect it.

He went through her clothing again, sifted through some of the grain in the earthen jars, found nothing. Unable to quit, he dragged the pallet away from the wall and scraped through the loose dirt beneath it with his shoe. Something hard was buried there!

He pushed away the dirt with his hands and uncovered a thick mat of woven straw. He peeled it back and found a small wooden box hidden below.

Inside, resting on a bed of black silk, was a dry *cici*. He picked it up. It was old and gnarled, like a tiny shrunken head. He wanted to drop it back in the box, but could not let go; angry and frightened, he slipped it into a small leather pouch, which he clenched tightly in his fist. Inside, the chick-pea felt warm, like a tiny animal.

He emerged stealthily from the dim light of the cave, his heart beating wildly. He climbed the hill to his camp, dug a hole in the earth, and buried the pouch beneath his own bed.

"Vito!"

Her voice startled him. She was back already! He wheeled around, but she was not there.

"Vito!"

He saw her in the distance, waving to him from the far ridge. Her voice was distant and weak.

She was calling for him to join her. He was eager to get away from the buried chick-pea, but made himself move slowly, not to arouse her suspicion.

He walked across the open field and climbed the far ridge, where she sat waiting for him.

"Take a deep breath!" she said as he came up beside her. Below them the valley was a long straw basket filled with brilliant pink blossoms. A thick sweetness filled the air like honey. In the distance he could see the silvery gleam of the Mediterranean.

He sniffed the air suspiciously.

"Can't you smell it?" she said. "The almonds are blooming!"

• • •

As they ate their evening meal she told him of her journey; it had indeed been the candle sickness, but she'd come in time, the flock would be saved. He barely listened. He could think only of the chick-pea and how he might use it against her. Perhaps she'd trapped a demon in it, and that was the source of her power. But why wasn't it part of her *tavola?* Why would she keep it hidden?

She was prattling on about the shepherd when it finally came to him: sorcerers hid their souls outside their bodies—that was what made them invincible! He rocked back and forth with excitement. She was more than just vulnerable; she was his.

That night he was wakened by footsteps as he slept fitfully atop the buried *cici*. He did not move, but opened his eyes in the darkness, waiting for her to come near. He felt something beating like a heart in the ground beneath him; it was his own blood coursing in his veins. She stood beside him, and he realized suddenly that she would kill him rather than risk his taking her power. He rolled over quickly and clutched at her ankle; she tried to pull away, but he held on tightly, and she let out a low, braying moan.

He had captured the goat.

In the morning she asked if he'd slept well, in that twinkly way that she teased him. And that evening as they sat by the fire, she offered him one of her teas, to "help him sleep."

"I slept well," he protested.

"Of course." She sipped quietly from her own cup. The night air was chill; she drew her woolen cloak tighter around her slender shoulders.

"My mother's name was also Elena," she said. "Elena Cabria. She called me Maria Elena to avoid confusion, but it didn't matter; everyone called her La Strega."

He tensed at the sound of that name.

"That's a sign of respect, you know. They were a little afraid of her—I know I was—but they loved her too."

"They didn't know her as I did," he snarled.

"You didn't know her at all." She stood and walked into the cave before he could reply.

He slept fitfully and was lying awake, listening to the wind whispering through the bushes, when he realized someone was talking to him. He rolled onto his back and saw La Strega sitting beside him, silhouetted against the moon, her face hidden in shadow. She gazed past him as if he wasn't there. He tried to sit up, but found he couldn't move.

"What do you want, witch?"

"You know what I want," she hissed.

"It's not here! I don't have it anymore!"

But the witch stared into the darkness, ignoring his cries.

"Vengeance," she whispered, and the trees shivered.

"You believe La Strega's curse has ruined your life," she said the next morning, "yet you act to fulfill her prophecy."

"I have no choice," he said. He found her sophistries amusing, now that he held the *cici*.

"You can't bear the truth."

"Which is?"

"That she is not to blame for what happened to you."

His first impulse was to strike her; instead, he said, "You believe what it suits you to believe."

"Yes," she smiled. "Don't you?"

That night he dreamed he was playing in the orchards with Nicco. "Vittocino," his mother called. He was hiding behind an olive tree. "Here I am, Mama!" he shouted as he leaped into view. But she could not see him. "Vittocino!" she called, staring right at him. "Vittocino . . ."

He awoke with a start—at least, he thought he awoke. When he tried to roll over, he could not move, yet his mind turned like an arm in its sleeve. La Strega sat near him, her face still shrouded in shadow. "Vittocino," she taunted. "Come, my Vittocino."

I will kill you! he thought, struggling to rise.

And he awoke again, and was alone.

His life became a nightmare of two separate existences.

By day Elena was young and pretty, teasing him with her humor, challenging him with her words.

But by night she was La Strega, who came to him as a hag, her face hidden in shadow, taunting him with her whisperings as he lay powerless beneath her.

And always in the morning she was Elena again, feigning youth and innocence. He never spoke of his nightly torments, just as she never mentioned the chick-pea, still buried beneath the pile of blankets that had become his private hell.

A week went by. He watched her closely, and was disappointed to find that her work was mostly healing, and very little magic. An injured miner was brought to her from the south; she set the broken bone, then cleaned the wound with wine and covered it with a poultice of egg whites. A farmer came with a sick mule, she delivered a calf, there were three more cases of candle sickness. Families brought their ill; she gave them potions to quiet their stomachs, cool their fevers, soothe their aches. Once, called to an old man with the deadly shivers, she whispered quietly that there was nothing she could do. And always they brought her gifts—food, and the herbs and minerals they knew were difficult for her to obtain. Vito dined on the fruits of their gratitude—sardines and squid and *triglia* from the fishing villages to the north, ground wheat and barley from the plains to the east, purple-black wine from Corvo and Marsala, lemons and oranges and figs and olives from the surrounding hillsides.

Then came a small, wiry man with dark tanned skin and a close-cropped beard. "I seek the woman known as La Strega," he said. Vito recognized the cold look of torment in the man's eyes, and for a moment imagined that another tortured soul had come seeking revenge.

He looked at Elena. She did not speak.

"Please. You must help me."

She studied the man carefully, then said, "You have been cursed."

"Yes!" he cried, and the story spilled from him—he was a fisherman from the coast to the north, good at his work, always had the best catch, but his wife's brother envied him, and had paid a *mago* to put the *malocchio* on him. His wife became angry when he tried to speak of it, she could not think evil of her own brother. His life was miserable; his children were sick, he had warts on his hands that hurt when he hauled the lines, he caught nothing while others' nets were full, his wife's brother gloated.

"Do you want me to put the evil eye on him?"

The man's face was twisted with pain. Vito saw the desire for revenge swell in him, then give way to his fear of witchery. "No . . . please, no," he said. "I want only to be free." He fell to his knees and clutched at her hand. "Please, I beg you. Lift this curse from me."

"I cannot lift the evil eye," she said. "Only you can do

that. At the next full moon you must go to your brother-in-law's house and stand so that your shadow points to his window. You must sprinkle salt on the shadow, and when it is covered, squeeze the juice of a sour lemon into its eyes. Then you must turn away and not look again on his house, even if you feel him watching. When the sun rises, the curse will be lifted."

The man thanked her with tears in his eyes, but when he tried to stand, she held him. "There is a price," she said. "From that day until the next full moon, the best of each catch is mine. When the fish are salted and dried, bring them to me."

"Yes, yes, I will," the man said, obviously frightened. He thanked her again and hurried away.

"You could have asked for anything," Vito said when the man had gone.

"'Take while the patient is in pain,' eh?"

"He was terrified of you."

"He was terrified of his own desire for revenge."

"And will your 'cure' work?"

"You don't believe me?"

He thought of his mother going from one healer to the next, asking only that the *malocchio* be lifted from her sons. Why had none of them known?

"*He* believed," she was saying. "That was my power."

"The *malocchio* was removed because he believed it was removed?" Vito asked incredulously.

"No. But I could not have removed it if he did not believe I could."

"The task you set him—"

"Was to focus the power."

"And if I were to pour salt on my shadow, and the juice of a lemon . . . ?"

"What difference would it make now?"

A month had passed and he was no closer to unlocking the secret of the chick-pea. Only two months remained—he must be ready to act.

That night when she came to him, he struggled to break free of the lethargy that seized his body.

"Vittocino," she whispered. He resisted the urge to roll over, knowing his mind would only turn in its shell, and instead tried to move his body.

"Hurry, Vittocino, before it's too late." He clawed at the ground, dragging his arm forward a few inches. He felt as if it were made of lead. He heard something padding softly. She was leaving! His body stayed frozen while his mind turned.

La Strega was sitting next to him. The pale light fell on one side of her face, the same grotesque visage he'd seen the first day. Embedded in the festering mass of flesh, a horrible evil eye gleamed and twisted in its socket to stare at him.

He screamed, and his body snapped upward like a sapling that had been bent then released. He found himself sitting on the cold ground, fixed by the pale yellow eye of the moon, alone.

"My mother told me what happened," she said one evening when they had finished their meal and were watching the shadows creep over the valley at sunset. "That day at the well."

He bolted upright.

"She was on her way to the market in Enna. A sirocco was choking the land. A crowd had gathered at the well.

"The people knew and welcomed her—all but one woman, who traveled alone with her two small sons and was drinking from the well. She heard the respectful murmuring of 'La Strega,' and sneered at it. 'You will wait till I'm finished, witch!' she said.

"La Strega had been scorned before, and paid no mind. She simply waited for the woman to finish; meanwhile, she went to the donkey, where two small boys were strapped in a basket. Their mother had left them to cry while she quenched her own thirst first. *'Come bello!'* she said, reaching in to lift the first boy. *'Bello regazzo!'* Did I tell you she loved children?

"The boys' mother grabbed the witch and pushed her to the ground. The people were silent, afraid what might happen. A man helped La Strega to her feet, then smiled and pointed to the boy. 'What beautiful twins, eh, Nonna?' he said, hoping to please her. She could only shake her head sadly, for the *sight* was upon her. 'They will not grow to be men,' she said, 'unless . . .' Then her vision failed."

"Liar!" Vito cried. "You don't know anything! You weren't there!"

"And you were too young to remember, Vito. You know only what you were told."

"She was my my mother!" he cried. But Elena remained silent.

That night, when his mind turned in its sleeve to find La Strega beside him, she raised her arm and pointed a bony finger. He saw that his body was casting a long shadow in the gleam of the moon.

Then he was sitting up . . . then crawling. The ground was covered with salt. He was holding a lemon in his hand. He stood over the shadow and squeezed the juice of the lemon into its eyes . . . but it was not a shadow, it was a shroud, and a small body lay beneath it. . . .

He was slipping deeper and deeper into her spell; soon he would be lost. Only the chick-pea could save him. La Strega must know he had stolen it by now; that she hadn't tried to regain it meant she could not.

Elena was starting to prepare their supper. He climbed the ridge and dug beneath his blanket roll to uncover the buried chick-pea. He no longger hoped to control its power, only to destroy hers. Clutching it in his hand like a gem, he slid back down and sauntered across the clearing toward her.

"I have something to show you," he said.

She looked up from stirring the pot full of vegetables and saw the *cici* in his open palm. "So you've found it."

"You've known all along, haven't you?" He held it between his thumb and forefinger as a priest might hold a cross before a demon.

"I would have given it to you freely."

"Forget your tricks, witch! I've stolen your power."

"You've stolen nothing. The *cici* was yours to claim." She went back to stirring the stew.

He squeezed the hard nugget, as if to inflict pain, but she did not react.

"My mother gave it to me. She said she'd been entrusted with a man's Fate, that she'd put it in the chick-pea to be unburdened of it. She said someday the man would come looking for it, not knowing what he sought. You are that man. It is your own Fate you have captured."

Her voice grew deeper as she spoke, and she hunched over the pot, growing older before his eyes. She started to turn toward him, and he knew that if he looked upon that ancient face with its evil eye, he would be lost forever.

"No!" he screamed. "No!" He kicked over the kettle, raising a sizzling cloud of steam as the stew spilled across the hot coals. Then he ran from the clearing, from the cave, from La Strega, ran as fast as he could, still clutching the chick-pea, running for his very soul and afraid to look back.

He ran until he could run no more, then fell to the ground, his chest heaving. He looked back to see if La Strega had followed, and saw nothing but almond trees. He was in the valley below her cave.

Vito made himself get up and keep moving. He circled back through the pink trees and climbed the ridge, scurrying over the top and down into a gully, which he followed south, away from the sea and the witch's cave.

The hills were pitted with shadow. He followed a small ravine to its head, and stopped to rest for the night. Tucked within the steep walls of rock, he began to feel more secure. As the night grew cold, he curled up against a groove in the rock, trying to keep warm.

"Vito."

He leaped to his feet. The moon had risen over the silent ravine.

The chick-pea! As long as he held the chick-pea, she would know where to find him!

He drew the gnarled seed from his waistband. He should have destroyed it the first day.

He searched the ground for a flat stone, and rested the *cici* upon it. Then he found a heavy rock, held it above his head with both hands, and brought it down as hard as he could. The chick-pea was smashed into a fine powder, which he ground in the dirt with his shoe, laughing at how easy it had been.

But something was wrong. The air was suddenly heavy with dust; he had to struggle to breathe. The walls of the canyon were closing around him. He felt for a handhold, but they were too steep to climb. There was no way out.

Then he saw it. At the head of the canyon, where the stone walls converged: the dark mouth of a cave.

"Vito."

He crawled into the darkness, scraping his hands and knees on the rock. The ground gave way beneath him, he was falling! He tumbled down a dark corridor . . . and into a moonlit night on the edge of a jagged ridge.

He was so exhausted he could barely move. La Strega sat beside him, staring with her yellow eye.

"Vito," she called. "Vittocino . . ."

"Stop it!" he screamed.

"Vittocino," she whispered.

And suddenly horror swept through his heart as he recognized that voice.

His mind and body were one. He was free to move, free to get up and walk away, free to do anything he wanted. He struggled to his knees and crawled toward her.

"I hate you!" he whispered. He clutched at her cloak and pulled her closer. "I hate you!" He grabbed her shoulders and tried to turn her toward him, then shook her violently until her head flopped over and he saw the other side of her face, the side that had always been hidden. His screams became a howling fury as he pummeled her limp body. "I hate you! I hate you!" he cried, gazing at the face of his mother.

He awoke face down on the cold ground. The walls of rock converged behind him; there was no cave. He shivered, then stood and began walking toward the warm sunlight at the foot of the ravine. He climbed the nearest hill. Before him the ridge swelled up from the land like the backbone of a huge burrowing beast. He began hiking north.

She had just finished milking the goat when he entered the clearing. She put the pot of warm milk down and waited. When he stood before her, she saw that he shivered, and motioned toward the fire.

They breakfasted on dark, crusty bread and the fresh goat's milk.

"Was there ever a curse?" he asked.

"Only the curse of a mother burdened with too many cares. She believed she was trapped, that her children were burdens, that she could no longer survive. And so it came to pass."

Vito let her words wash over him, not trying to understand it all. Everything had changed. His Fate had been given back to him; he must make of it what he could.

She left him alone. After a while he found her beneath the silver-green branches of an olive tree. "The words of La Strega?" he asked.

"Something happened when she was pushed to the ground. A power surged through her . . . she *saw.* Words came, she spoke . . . she did not know what they meant. She did not understand until later that your Fate had been entrusted to her."

"Nicco?"

"His Fate was his own."

Vito shook his head sadly. "How I envied poor Nicco. I wished I'd been born the grotesque dwarf. At least there was a reason why she could not love him."

"Do not judge her too harshly. Her life was hard."

"That does not justify becoming a monster. Isn't that what you tried to tell me?"

She looked at him, and he realized how fond he'd become of her . . . at least, of *this* Elena. "When I first came—"

"You came full of hatred," she said. "It was not difficult to make you see a hag. When I caught you in your own trap, your pride made you change what you saw."

He blushed, and turned away in embarrassment, but her laughter was unjudging, and finally he had to smile too. Then he faced her squarely and said, "I want to know you as you are."

"If that is what you truly want, I cannot deceive you."

She was much older than he'd realized, though it was hard to say how he knew—a certain hardness around the eyes, perhaps, or the sureness of her stance. Yet the spirit that bubbled through her made it impossible to think of her as anything but young.

"You thought that time brings the loss of possibility. But your own Fate has proven that false." Her eyes burned with a wisdom that was timeless and ancient and newly born.

"You are La Strega," he said at last.

"Yes."

HONOR

Jody Scott

Jody Scott's has been a distinguished and impoverished career as author, alongside an undistinguished and wealth-amassing career as high-pressure saleswoman and business sharp-shooter. She was editor of the no longer extant literary journal **Circle,** *counting among its contributors Henry Miller, Anais Nin, Tennessee Williams, and other dead people (alive then, though). DAW Books inherited her novel* **Passing for Human** *when a changing of the guard at Scribner's left the book, though paid for, orphaned by a new editor, dolt that he was. An earlier novel, a coauthored mystery bylined Thurston Scott, won an award from Mystery Writers of America and was in general a raging success.* **Escapade Magazine** *serialized her otherwise unpublished novel* **Down Will Come Baby.** *What else? Oh, yeah. Her current hit is the satiric sci-fi thriller* **I, Vampire** *(Ace). Recent short stories can be found in Pam Sargent's and Ian Watson's* **Afterlives** *(Vintage), my own* **Tales By Moonlight** *(Tor) and the otherwise tediously artsy-fartsy journal of the Berkeley Publishing Cooperative in California.*

Born in Chicago, long years on the west coast and in the "mellow" Northwest (home of neo-nazism) hasn't worn away the edges of a Chicago personality. She can make the insecure red in the face with anger, and cause the wise to say, "Hoo-ha! That's funny!" immediately prior to going red in the face with anger, merely by twiddling her thumbs (or twitting their noses). Like all of us, Jody just wants to be loved, so walks softly and carries a big axe.

"Honor," like all of Jody's short stories is great. No getting around it. It's great.

AT THE AGE OF SEVEN Jody Scott was given the Ten Commandments to memorize.

They didn't set too well with our hero. She went and shinnied up the swingset pole, and from there to the garage roof. She wasn't supposed to be on the garage roof. Girls didn't do it. She might fall and get hurt. It was wonderful here. You could see the whole world. Wide fields of goldenrod. A few houses far off, and the Gas Tank by the canal that was at the border of this city.

A bird, sailing. It would be perfect to be a bird. The Ten Commandments sounded like *The Arabian Nights* a little, but were spookier and not as nice. There was something about them that Jody Scott hated.

The worst was, Thou shalt not kill.

Why not? Tarzan killed. Mowgli killed. King Arthur killed. David killed Goliath. Moses killed a whole army.

Her father killed. Her father had a whole case of guns, and 14 horned heads in a den. All the men in the neighborhood looked up to him because he killed.

Our hero was seized with gloomy forebodings.

Thou shalt not kill—what did it mean? Every time they said it, they got mad. Mrs. Lofquist the Superintendent, the pastor, Mom, all the Sunday School teachers, they all got mad when they said it.

Why?!!??

Jody Scott climbed off the garage and began swinging on one of the swings. Why were they so mad about it?

She swung really high. At the very top she jumped and landed in the grass. Why were they so mad? They had a conniption fit over "Thou Shalt Not Kill."

It could mean only one thing.

They saw something in her.

Our hero ran up the porch steps and into the house, crawled

into a clothes hamper and shut the lid. You could see light through the wickets. It was nice in here. It was a cave. You could suck your thumb and nobody would see. Nobody could have a conniption fit about it. Thumbsucking was a shame and a crime, if you were seven. But it was safe here. You could stay here for a thousand years and they wouldn't bother you.

Thou shalt not kill.

Eyes brimming, our hero thought about how sad it was that the glorious ancient days were dead and gone.

A Grecian temple. The sea, the Aegean sea. And India; how she longed to be back home in India!

Which was worse—a crime or a shame? Our hero had sworn off thumbsucking except when positively certain nobody could see. Imagine a tough 7-year-old being seen sucking her thumb like a baby. But it was an exquisite comfort. A solace. "Nobody knows the sorrow of a sober fern locked in a snowbank."

Weeping quietly, our hero wondered if death really existed or if it was made up. Swallow a watermelon seed and a watermelon will grow in your stomach. How sad it would be if her parents died in a car crash out on the highway! And it would be all her fault. Step on a crack, break your mother's back. She'd be an orphan and so would Sue, who was six and had lost a front tooth that morning. Jody Scott had helped her lose it by tying a string around it for her.

Thou shalt not kill.

Mom didn't like the kind of person our hero had grown up to be. Yes; J.S. had shown great promise as a baby, it was said, but now . . . unacceptable.

But how do you change what you really are? You can't. If you're a tomboy, you're a tomboy and that's it. Besides, there's a lot more honor in being wild, noble, and heroic, than some goofy drip who runs knock-kneed and likes pretty dresses.

Anyway, Mom and Dad still had Sue, and Sue was a real girl, a girlie girl who liked purses (ugh! yuck! bluck!) and perfume and girlie toys, and mincing around like a sissy.

But if Mom and Dad got killed in an accident . . .

Overwhelmed with grief, our hero sucked her thumb and made plans. She could take care of herself anywhere in the world; but, what would happen to poor Sue?, an innocent tot who'd not yet heard of the Ten Commandments and didn't know what crime was. It would be too tragic. J.S. would cry for years. Then she'd become a bum, cooking cans of soup under a bridge, riding boxcars, walking on the tops of trains, and giving railroad dicks the slip. Then when she got to be about thirty, she'd be a wise old Indian woman living in the hills. She'd know all about herbs. People would come from miles around, and she'd cure them miraculously and send them away refreshed in body and spirit.

Thou shalt not kill. When adults said you had done a thing, you had really done it, even if you had forgotten about it. Well, at last she'd learned why the girls made fun of her all the time. It was because of the way she walked and acted. And how she really was, deep inside. A Targui bandit chief. A rough, crude barbarian; maker of widows and orphans. No wonder she was different! And the adults had seen it all along. They thought if they didn't warn you all the time and have conniption fits, you'd murder them.

The bitter tears fell. How come all these girls knew how to fit in so well and she didn't? They just *knew.* They were born knowing. Nobody had to teach them. They were much, much smarter than J.S. was. She couldn't even learn. She was a roughneck. Not only that, but she loved it. She loved being a roughneck. She'd hate to be a girlie girl. They all thought alike, acted alike, wore the same clothes and shoes and everything, acted limp-wristed, and wouldn't allow you to be one bit different. It you were, they'd ridicule you to death. They were a school of fish. A flock of chickens. Where was the honor in that?

But it was always happening. J.S. would be off in a state of bliss or imaginings, and some drip would notice and start shrieking with laughter. Or getting mad. They all of them knew exactly how to act, and she didn't. Why??? It was terrible.

Take yesterday. Our hero out raking leaves in her Indian suit, in a state of bliss because she could smell woodsmoke on the air and it was a glorious Indian Summer day. Our hero in the thrall of being alive; the very emotion you were not supposed to have, because it was felt to be a crime and a shame; but, she did it anyway and was heaping up leaves in ecstasy, happy as a clam, humming "Alive! Alive!" while out raking the beautiful golden autumn leaves.

Just then, two girls from school walked by. They cracked up. They shrieked with laughter and walked on up the street. It all happened before our hero could think to leap behind a tree with tomahawk drawn, or rush into the house.

One of those girls was Cynthia Lill, friendly when you got her alone, but probably never again. She'd seen what a fool our hero was: unable to fit in; flatly refusing to "act like a lady" (ugh! ugh!) but wearing an Indian suit right out in public. Wearing warbonnet, fringes, tomahawk, and scalping knife. Birthday present from Dad (who as a hunter understood a few things about honor) but now, shown in its true light as babyish; tomboyish; bloodthirsty; unacceptable; retarded; and dumb.

Horrible. Our hero was trapped in a neighborhood of drips. You were supposed to wish for party dresses, patent leather Mary Jane shoes, and a hat. A hat!, it was enough to make a man puke.

Some of them even painted their fingernails. They'd put on their mother's lipstick whenever she left the house. But lipstick was only good for warpaint. How come they didn't know it?

Our hero admired the characters in books; they had honor. Even the thieves had honor. It was just the ones around here in Chicago who were bumpkins with neither brains nor honor.

"You'll change," Mom always said.

"No I won't; never," J.S. would solemnly swear a bloody oath under her breath.

That was another thing. Our hero worshipped The Goddess instead of God. Never talked about it, because it could get you in serious trouble. Never mentioned she was here on a special mission: to grow up and become R.A., the Recording Angel. If you said you were an angel, they'd give you the hee-haw, or get all cold-faced and angry. But now suddenly had come the revelation *they knew all along,* and it was clear, because of:

Thou shalt not kill.

Our hero dried a last tear, crawled out of the hamper, wandered into the bedroom she shared with Sue, and observed a fly that struggled on the window . . . but . . .

Hot dog!

Imagine having to be *warned* about not killing people. How peachy, keen, marvelous. "Captain Jody Scott of Mars, thou shalt not kill!" Could anything be better than that?

And yet it was terrifying. It meant that you might snap at any second. Run them through with a rapier. Toast them over a bonfire. Not just rough them up good-naturedly, but deal with them faithfully on her oath and knighthood. Outwit, defeat, and dispatch them to the Great Beyond where they belonged.

Ahoola!

These drips must feel not only guilty about the stupid, ridiculous way they treated her, but also frightened out of their silly, lily-livered wits. Yet the savagely violent Jody Scott was chilled into stone by this "Thou shalt not kill" threat. The weed of crime bears bitter fruit! but: she would keep a proud, stubborn silence. For was she not here on a special mission, chosen of the Goddess?

Mom came in and swatted the fly on the window. He was all crumpled up; and: he had loved life just as much as Mom did. Our hero went to bed with a raging fever. Mom brought hot lemonade with linseeds and honey in it, saying,

"You're coming down with something." Then rushed off, unaware that our hero was coming down with . . . lockjaw.

Lockjaw! The dreaded, most horrible of diseases. Your teeth clenched together, and you died and had to be buried. Never again could you open your mouth. Not in this world, not in the next. Unable to eat or talk, you'd die in three days. There was no cure.

Paralyzed with dread, J.S. felt her jaws clench up and begin to get all stiff. A boy Dad told of, stepped on a rusty nail and within three days was dead. He was Abe Lincoln's son. This was right here in Illinois before the fire. The boy was put in a coffin. Like the fly, he never moved again. There was a funeral with a glass hearse and plumes; a spooky, mysterious fate.

J.S. was terrified of lockjaw and funerals, but otherwise wasn't at all afraid to die. It was an adventure. Thrilling. All you did was leave your body. She'd done it plenty of times, but they didn't know it. Boy would they be mad! Once you died you were supposed to stay dead. How come they all knew how to act and she didn't? It was no fun. It was terrible. She was too stupid.

"Too much reading." "Too much imagining." Those things weren't true.

But it must be true, that Jody Scott was a killer. Otherwise they wouldn't say so. They wouldn't have conniption fits about it. She was a killer. Adults had eyes in the back of their heads. . . .

Hujah!, our hero leaned on the windowpane, peering out at the maple trees. Darkness was settling on the jungle. Hunting time drew near. With an agile bound she gripped a vine and soon was speeding along the leafy corridor, comforted by one thought: she was a rotten swine!, spawn of an infamous courtesan, and was the kind of swarthy scum who stops at nothing.

"Thou shalt not kill." The stupid commandment reminded her of the dumbness that was school. The wasted time. The senseless claptrap. Knavish teachers, malicious urchins... J.S. had learned to read a long time ago, when she was three or four, automatically, not on purpose, not maliciously, indeed quite by accident; yet was still being punished for it every day.

The punishment was: they put you ahead a few grades, then ridiculed you when you didn't know how to add because of having skipped over it. They'd make you stand at the blackboard and write a column of numbers and a plus sign. They'd snort and sneer because you didn't know what a plus sign was. Then they'd say, "Well, add them up! Go on! Add them up! Why, even your little sister can add better than that!" in an angry, sneering voice which meant you were a boob and a dumbbell. And it was true, because you didn't even know what "two plus two" means.

Boob! Dumbbell! And now, very soon, all this senseless cruelty would turn you into a maniac, and a buried personality would spring out. Yes, the fury of a demon would possess you. The more docile and humane you were, the kinder and more sympathetic, the worse the transition would be! And yes, the very fact that you were the Recording Angel, and *respected* adults—respected their gray hair, and called them "Sir" or "Ma'am," and never told a lie or said *bloody* and *damn* out loud; rescued kittens stuck in trees; helped baby birds that fell out of nests; had a soul overflowing with love, a brave heart, courteous tongue, and lived by the creed "nobless oblige" as in books about knighthood—these things were *just exactly* what would trigger such an uncanny, sinister metamorphosis.

Well, here was the truth. When adults said anything, they often meant the opposite. This was because they were fork-tongued cowards.

But who did they want her to kill? And how did they want her to do it?

They were scared, that was for sure. But they always went around trembling at the knees. Their cowardice and bullying forced our hero to live in a time warp, one that had escape hatches into thrilling universes.

Was there a better way to live? Hujah!, she didn't know of any.

Yes, they often used a thing called "reverse psychology." On the other hand, maybe they wanted her to kill just so she'd get in trouble. Then they could say "See what a bad person you are?" and wash their hands of it. They did that all the time. It was part of being a varlet, having no honor.

Did they expect her to kill one victim, or several?

Peering out the window, sipping hot lemonade and twirling her mustache, our hero pondered the problem.

He thought of himself as "our hero" because that's how it was in books. The only worthy character was the hero. There were no women heroes. There was only a person called The Girl, who was a drip who had to be rescued all the time. Only a fool would want to be The Girl. J.S. often took the pronoun *he* because the pronoun *she* meant you were a wimp who cried and whimpered and ran knock-kneed, blubbered, were a fool, fixed your hair constantly, sprained your ankle while running through the jungle, had no knife, couldn't defend yourself, and would sell your soul for a diamond bracelet. If this is what *she* meant, it certainly didn't apply to Captain Jody Scott of Mars in any way, shape, or form.

But the dumbest Commandment of all was "Thou shalt not commit adultery." Now who would want to? Who in their right mind, except maybe a simp like The Girl, would let themselves become an adult in this world of varlets if they didn't have to?

Did they want her to kill a particular man woman or child, or just go on a rampage, fire into the crowd, and be a mass murderer?

It couldn't be one of her parents. Not Mom. Certainly not Dad either. It would be too sad never getting another boxing lesson. "Lead with your left. Keep your guard up. Keep your tongue in." He used to be a boxer. He knew all the tricks. She'd miss watching him light his pipe or shave, dab lather on your chin with the shaving brush; and he never said much, but would let you use his razor to shave with. But Mom said no. "It makes the hair on your face grow." Hah! o.k. by her. She'd become a bearded ruffian.

Mrs. Lofquist? The school principal? Some teacher who had a fit when she didn't know what a plus sign was? J.S.

heaved a shuddering sigh. You could ask, but it wouldn't do any good. "Don't be rude! That's terribly rude!," eyes popping. Or glance down at you with a false smile. When J.S. grew up she'd probably learn to be as big a liar as they were. Mom said so. "You'll learn, young lady," she promised.

It would be far, far better to die first. Not of lockjaw, but bravely, in battle.

So!, at last she knew the truth. They really thought she was a killer. Huh! So that's what had been bothering the simpering churls all these years. Imagine that. What simpletons. What drips. Never took the trouble to ask a question or talk to you about it. Just made you promise to do things you'd never, never do in a thousand years; because they were afraid of what they called "Human Nature." Which was something terrible beyond belief. So they said.

They said the human heart was a wild, tangled bramble patch, and nobody could solve it. You were not to explore or ask questions. That would be rude. Human Nature was not only base and contemptible, but deadly and tricky. If you tried to explore it, you'd die.

Exploring it would be more fun than anything. You'd have to be braver than Magellan, of course; but as the Recording Angel, that's what she'd do.

Thou shalt not steal.

Steal? What did they take her for, a common sneak thief? Our hero scowled at the printed page. She'd never steal. It would be contemptible and unworthy. She was grossly insulted. Who did they think they were talking to—some varlet? If they did, they'd have been better off keeping their big fat mouths shut about it.

Aiming at the lamp, J.S. spat between separated front teeth. This Commandment was a fiery, rankling insult that only a poisoned arrow could avenge! But . . .

"Thou shalt not corvette thy neighbor's ass."

Now what was this?? "Thou shalt not corvette thy neighbor's *wife*."

What kind of fools made people memorize stuff like this?

Mr. Nielsen's wife, two doors to the north, was a coarse-grained churl who wore floury powder. J.S. would never dream of corvetting such a woman. The idea was appalling.

But in the next block lived Betty Jane Hamilton, a drum majorette. Did *neighbor* mean only the person one or two doors away, or did it also apply to the next block? Betty Jane Hamilton wore white satin shorts and white boots, and strutted, twirling a baton. Only a drip wouldn't corvette Betty Jane.

Our hero threw himself on his pillows. A towering brute with an uncouth shamble and a hideous scream of challenge, small wonder the good people of Chicago lived in dread of such a beast. Ahoola! And yet, it was a fine thing to stand revealed as a killer.

No more would they dismiss you with the contempt due a little child. Most adults hated children and said they didn't. They called you insulting things. "Child," which meant you were a runt and a puppet. "Cute" they only said before they knew what you were really like. And once by their dentist, who was Maurice J. Horan, D.D.S., she'd been called "Heiress!" and the smarmy look on his face implied:

"You wouldn't last two hours in this country alone."

Oh, no? She would beat them in open combat. "They cannot, and will not, destroy me."

But these Commandments, dumb though they were, plunged our hero into a condition of shadow and doubt.

Respect. It's not something you're born with. It's something you earn. By being a trained assassin. Otherwise you'd be dismissed with contempt. Patronized. Pushed aside. Called things like "daughter." She'd looked that word up and one of the meanings was *milkmaid*.

Far better to be a base, swarthy, bearded assassin, than a milkmaid!

Unless they'd let you have a cow. She'd be happy with a cow. A cow would make everything worthwhile. A cow had soft lips and gentle eyes and was much more kind, innocent, and gentle than the people around here. Cows had deep feelings and were holy, but people denied this with a sneer of contempt, saying *they* were the only ones who counted. Well, if "Thou shalt not kill" didn't mean cows too, then it was a base, base lie and a canard!

At least she had an idea who it was they wanted killed. Mr. Nielsen, the crabby old Swede who lived two houses down. The noise of Mr. Nielsen's mower always woke Dad up on his day off. It would be a crime of vengeance. She'd drop off a branch with lightning speed onto the mean neighbor's back, and strangle him with her bare hands. Or: an expert shot with a revolver, she'd gun him down. Or: paratropine. She'd read that a single drop in the bloodstream brings instantaneous death.

Or: ring his doorbell wearing a clever disguise while carrying a Colt Peacemaker. Or a six-shooter and a musket. But as this was a crime of vengeance, plain bare-handed strangling would be best.

"Ahoola," grunted the murderer, stretching her body to the full glory of its 46 inches. Yes, their jeers would soon be silenced. . . .

In a fever of expectation Jody Scott lay in bed until midnight. She felt calm enough to pass the time coloring a coloring book entitled *Lord Greystoke Grows Up in the Jungle,* and as always, our hero colored neatly, painstakingly, and beautifully; inside the lines, with her tongue poking out.

No sooner had the clock ceased striking than she scrambled out the window and slunk toward Mr. Nielsen's house.

She didn't cut through McAuliffe's yard next door but played it safe, circling around through fields of weeds behind the houses.

This block was at the very edge of the prairie. Chicago ended right at this spot. There were no more houses, only vacant lots, a willow grove, then the wide, grassy plains all the way to the Old West where the cowboys lived.

This was a long time ago, so you could see all the way to the Western Horizon; far, far out beyond the gas tank, a beloved landmark just this side of the drainage canal.

Behind every tuft lurked the ghost of a dead Indian. She was looking at one now. He'd been hanging around for 100 years, still wearing loincloth and moccasins and looking for his people. He didn't know they'd been wiped out to make space for the superior races from beyond the seas.

The moon was high and full.

No wind stirred.

After gliding through devious alleys across the worst part of Baghdad, the assassin reached her destination.

The coast was clear.

The tyrant was in his yard mowing the grass. Noisy varlet!, soon he would expiate his frolic in blood.

Stealthily, J.S. crept out on a maple branch in her stockinged feet. She'd be bawled out for that, so she stripped off the socks and tucked them into a cleft, then began inching out cautiously, barefoot, silent as a naked Indian.

Her sweat-streaked muscular body glistened in the moonlight.

Mr. Nielsen smoked a cigar, mowing the strip by the flowerbed, then began coming this way; slowly, slowly. . .

Our hero's silent form was poised against the moon. She must act quickly or her prey would be gone. The sun had long set. The night feeders were awakening in the bulrushes. Crickets chirped.

Mr. Nielsen was almost directly beneath the branch. He had no way of knowing that our hero was poised above, fingers curled for the kill. His head was bald and sweating. He was clad in bib overalls and a polka-dotted shirt. He was about the size of a linebacker, only fatter and a lot crabbier.

Once, the day after last Halloween, J.S. had crept to the Nielsen basement windows with a razor blade, being careful not to sit on the peonies. Our hero was scraping off the wax some older kids had scrawled there. (Last year, before all this happened, J.S. had been an eager bright-eyed idealist who loved flag and country and hated senseless vandalism.) But what had changed her? Mr. Nielsen rushed out and began yelling his head off, yowling like an enraged giant at the top of a beanstalk. He cursed her in broken English. J.S. was so terrified she dropped the blade and ran, mane standing on end, despising herself for such cowardice. Mr. Nielsen was an irresponsible varlet! Like all adults, he couldn't tell friend from foe.

Now: the mean neighbor was pulling out a handkerchief. He mopped his shiny pate. He threw away the cigar. It was a signal.

Fwap!, the blue-eyed killer fell upon the crabby Swede with a cry of savage triumph. It was a terrific leap. She was on him in a flash. The breath was knocked out of him. With lightning speed she strangled him with her bare hands. He had no chance against the young raven-haired Amazon. He gave a brief, bitter whimper, and slumped helpless. Stiff as a board. Rigor mortis had already set in.

No, on second thought she stabbed him with a Persian scimitar, in this manner: fastening the rope securely to the stout branch, J.S. descended all at once and plunged the hunting knife to the very hilt into Mr. Nielsen's heart. Blood squirted out. He flew backwards. He gave a shrill cry of mortal terror, then staggered and fell dead. Our hero not only killed the Viking, but ate of his flesh. No, on second thought she just killed him, for tribal laws forbade cannibalism.

Mr. Nielsen was cut down in the flower of his manhood.

J.S. dropped onto the Swede's round, fat shoulders. He gave a cry of terrible despair. She sent half a dozen smashing blows, "Ough! Ough!" backed by all the strength and weight of her steel-honed body. He bled like a stuck pig. He fell, speechless with surprise and chagrin.

"Now thou knowest!" the killer cried savagely.

She stood for a moment listening to the frogs croak. Then stepping over the body, she padded to the hose for a cooling draught.

There was no hurry. It would take 5000 U.S. Cavalry to find and flush her out. Cool, callous, indifferent, our hero stood in a thicket chewing a piece of jerky from her pack.

She was licking her bruised knuckles, smiling grimly, when . . .

Hujah!, she'd been spotted. By a varlet; a spy. It was Sue, following our hero around as usual, in a green bathing suit and pigtails, a towel around her shoulders with a picture of Betty Boop on it.

The snoopy kid shivered in the night air. She poked her tongue into the hole where the tooth had been, frowning.

Then suddenly, spotting the dead man sprawled at our hero's feet, she shrieked:

"I'll tell!"

Bam! Bam! Bam!

Would the killing never end? Once a man has dipped his fingers in blood, sooner or later he'll feel the urge to kill again. Jody Scott was forced to empty the six-shooter into her sister's small astonished body. The child crumpled. She fell, bleeding from every wound. She lay there without moving. It was awfully sad; Sue would have got a nickel, maybe a dime, from the Tooth Fairy tonight, but now . . . her chance was blasted forever.

Our hero sobbed heartbrokenly. And poor Mr. Nielsen lying there so round-shouldered, pudgy, and stupid. If he could have shut his mouth for ten seconds and listened, he'd have learned that the Recording Angel was not putting wax on his stupid windows, only taking it off.

J.S. stared morosely at the corpses sprawled in the moonlight. Then sighing, with a wave of the hand she brought them back to life. Sue and Mr. Nielsen jumped to their feet; they looked around, blinking, and were opening their mouths to yell and complain, but the killer had slipped away magically through the trees.

It would be great to bring the Indian back to life the same way, but he'd been shot dead by some upright citizen a hundred years ago.

Meanwhile our hero had learned an important lesson.

When they tell you to kill or not to kill, tell them to butt out.

When they try tricking you or saying "This is the law, you'd better obey it," just smile and walk away.

She spat between separated front teeth and swore a bloody oath: Don't listen to what they say.

Make up your own mind.

Otherwise, there's no honor in it.

THE LINGERING MINSTREL

Jessica Amanda Salmonson

Given that **The Tomoe Gozen Saga** *has been a markedly successful trio of books for Ace, commercial insight has it that a new Tale of Naipon would help sell the reader the present anthology. But I refuse. I want instead to introduce you to a fellow who may help convey the simple fact that I* do *write things that aren't Asian in their influences as well as* not *amazonian.*

I'm fond of this fellow and I plan a novel in which he is a key player if not protagonist and about the unusual city of Aispont not really glimpsed in this tale, but who can say what really will develop from plans and possibilities. I am susceptible to public pressure, however, and it would *be nice to hear someone ask something other than, "Are you going to write another book about Tomoe?" though I enjoy answering that question too.*

About me? I lived in a circus when I was a tadpole (a private jest, that, as I often wished I could get into the aquarium with a mirror-illusion called "Lady in the Fishbowl"). I was an infant transient whose pretty mother would send us begging door to door. I remember it clearly, though the family denies it now. We must've been charming little gypsies in the eyes of many, as "Don't play with those children!" was a phrase often heard from the mothers of children encountered on the way.

We were a family of thieves, but I was happy. By age seven the Department of Welfare stepped in, and I was placed with a brutal legal guardian and was never happy again. Not for more than twenty years anyway. Now things are fine, thanks to someone who is with me. But for a long time the only suitable phrase would be "This sad world!"—to quote a character in my novel **Thousand Shrine Warrior.**

IN SUCH TALES there is often a tavern, and in this tale, there was a tavern. It was called the Brass Ass, I know not why, for pictured on the signboard was a spoon, and not a donkey. I came upon it by night. A lucky vision it seemed to me, the forest having been so dark that my poor horse Elizabeth could not see her way, and went bumping us into trees.

I handed over the reins to a boy who took my speckled mare to the stable at the side of the tavern. As for myself, I headed for the door of the Brass Ass, attracted as I was by the smell of bison. Or it may have been braised ass; not that I would have been appalled to find out.

"Meat!" I said to the barkeep once inside. "And something for this dry spot in my throat." The barkeep pointed me toward a table at which three other gentlemen, using the term lightly, were sitting. It was a big table, and they did not find it hard to make room for me.

The air was thick and pungent with the cookfire in back and the smoking torches set in vertical braces. The floor was sawdust on tamped earth. There was quite a crowd, but the tavern's size could hold it.

An entertainment was planned. Some poor bloke was vaguely introduced by someone who mispronounced his name right off, and was not very convincing in telling how the evening's minstrel hailed from the famous Court of Aispont, where music is always at hand and always sweet. The laughing man who made this introduction undermined the chance of anyone's gullibility about this claim, for he winked outrageously at the audience as the lutenist climbed onto the stage.

A sadder looking fellow I have never seen. If he had played before a prince in Aispont, it must have been some while past. Although a courtly air was about him, it was somehow all askew. His hair was shot with gray, though he didn't look old enough for it; and he seemed a bit palsied, if not merely nervous before the grinning, rowdy audience.

I waited for my meat, which was long in coming, and watched the minstrel tune his instrument, which had a vast number of strings. Due to his slight problem of nerves, manifested in a shaking hand, he was quite slow in getting the strings in order. There were few women in the Brass Ass, and half those few were harlots. So there was no feminine check upon the mood of the men. The minstrel would be playing mostly for geezers, would-be mercenaries, and local farmers. I didn't envy him a bit.

Seeing he was already losing audience attention, he began to play although the lute was not quite perfectly tuned. He had a nice voice, and lost his nervous palsy as he sang. It wasn't a powerful voice, but a gentle one, unsuited to singing above the din of conversations. Only those of us near the stage could hear him well, not that the people in the other corners seemed to care if they heard him or not.

I began to think he was a court musician after all, not merely a lying braggart who had written a nice introduction for others to recite in jesting disbelief. His song was a pretty one of courtly love and honor. He seemed to believe what he was singing.

For this audience the song was a bit on the syrupy side. But the sorrow of his look and posture was so great that even these cruel men were kept from heckling. Instead, they talked more among themselves, as though he did not exist, and shouted only when they needed more to drink. Unheard, unnoticed, the minstrel plied his trade pitifully.

My own drink had come (the meat had not) and I sat with my three table partners, all larger men than myself, and I am not small. I tried to listen to the singer, half because I felt sorry for him, half as the lesser of two evils. It was better than listening to my tablemates jaw.

The meat came. It was rancid, but well-cooked, so I didn't think it would make me sick. I chewed it. And chewed it. The minstrel's eyes caught mine. He seemed aware that, by the third song, I was the only one still listening to him. He gave me a weak smile, but my mouth was full of gristle, so I could hardly smile back.

"What song would thee have, good traveler?" the minstrel asked. It took me a moment to realize he meant me. I swallowed too large a bite, but didn't quite choke myself. I replied,

"For this crowd, good minstrel, I should suggest a ditty such as 'To the Sword.'"

"But this crowd does not concern me, nor me them," said the minstrel. "What for you?"

The exchange was odd enough that the men around the tavern half turned their heads to listen.

"Why, then, I'd say another ballad, like the one you sang before."

"Have you no favorite, then?" he asked.

I felt very much on the spot. People were noticing me, and that made me uncomfortable. I'd rather eat in peace. "Why, I guess I've none," I said, feeling stupid indeed.

"In that case I shall rest from singing," he said, and got down from the small stage, leaving his lute. My three table-mates scooted nearer the wall, and the minstrel joined us. The folk around the tavern turned back to their private discussions, hardly concerned if the minstrel played or not, perhaps preferring he didn't.

He had gray eyes, that man. Sad ones, I should add. His hair, though shot with gray as I said before, was brown and quite long and naturally curled. He'd been lovely in his youth, I'd surmise. Now he had the look of a ferret hiding beneath a wig. There was a cloud about him, as gray as his eyes, and I had no desire to cope with some other man's melancholy, my own bouts with that illness being bad enough. But such sorrow was etched on his thin face that I could not rebuff his evident need of friendship for the evening.

"Some of these people came to hear you, I am sure," I said. "Just because I was too tongue-tied to think of any song, should you deny the rest?"

"They came because there's little else to do at night; there's no juggler or acrobat who is more interesting to ignore. I'm only an excuse for all of them to get sotted. I'm used to it by now. But you, good sir, nurse that one drink and shan't lose your wits at this rate, unlike these others. Do you know what you're eating?"

"Meat. Bison I should hope."

"Ah."

"It's rather a large portion," I said, catching his unspoken meaning. "Would you like a bit?"

"If you don't mind." He unsheathed a slender dagger, the

hilt mother-of-pearl. It was a mighty valuable article for a wandering lutenist. He stabbed my plate and whisked away rather a larger bite than I'd expected.

"The barkeep doesn't feed you for your songs?"

"A meal a day," he said. "It doesn't quite suffice. My name is Ernro, not Gorno as that lout announced. You?"

"Esben," I said, eating rather faster than I had prior to being helped.

"I know the name," said Ernro.

I stopped chewing long enough to say, "Is that so?"

"Esben Danesworth, is it not? I think we met once before. You wouldn't recall me, I'm sure. There was a scuffle with a smart aleck in a street of Aispont about two years ago. That thin sword of yours poked the fellow's breast and found his heart. I was his companion, who tried to keep him from picking a quarrel, to no avail, alas for him."

This worried me a bit. It could mean the minstrel meant revenge for his friend's sake and only pretended to need conversation.

"Forgive me for having forgotten your face," I said. "I do recall the event, though. Please believe me when I say I really have not dueled so many men that I've forgotten which ones died."

"I understand, good Esben. The man was a passing acquaintance, that was all. I met him only that night, much as I've just met you. I did not know him long enough to seek revenge on his behalf, if that is why your eyes went wide for a moment. But as I was singing a few moments ago, I noticed you, and was certain you were that same duelist. It was skillfully done, as you well know. I haven't forgotten the grace of your lunge. I've seen men die since then, but I'd not seen it up until that time. I'd been raised, virtually, at court, a daintier life than the one I've lived the last two years or so."

So he played at court, as he claimed. I offered him a wry smile and said, "As Satan cast from Heaven, eh? A grimmer world you've seen outside the halls of Aispont's palace."

"That much is so," he said, looking at his hand and the pearl-handled dagger in it. That look of sorrow intensified a moment. Then he tried to look less downcast as he said, "But as I was recounting, it was an impressive duel, the more so for its short duration. Your sword came forth and was deep into his breast in the blink of an eye. I think he died not knowing the fight had been engaged, though he'd been ready first. I talked of it for days afterward, I was so astounded. A few people knew who you were by my description—the black shock of hair, the expressive lips, and one eye larger than the other—and so I learned the name of Esben Danesworth, and have heard it a few times since as well. As a matter of fact I wanted to look you up when the occurrence was fresh, but couldn't think of a reasonable excuse. Now, with two years and many miles between the event and place, I find we meet at this crossroads tavern. Life is full of surprises."

"It is that," I allowed. I don't know how it was that he could eat and talk at the same time, but suddenly my plate was empty, and my stomach but half full. I sipped my mug of hot beer, glad that men think it uncouth to share one mug.

In the next moment, without warning, the minstrel Ernro lunged across the table at me, his greasy dagger aimed true for my heart. I rolled backward off the bench so that only my shirt was cut, the lacy part which I should afterward have to remove altogether. My beer soaked my pants in an embarrassing position. As I somersaulted from the bench, my dueling blade came forth without my hardly thinking about the deed. I came up on both feet upon the sawdust, sword slicing the leaping minstrel's thigh. He dropped his dagger, grabbed his wound, and exclaimed, "Not as good as that night, sir! One pierce to the heart is all it took!"

The incident had lasted the space of two heartbeats, but several men were witness and quick to approach the trouble. My tablemates volunteered in my behalf, "That singer started it, with no excuse at all!"

"It was nothing," I protested before anyone could lay hand to him. "A spat between friends, that's all. Please back off from us now."

I sheathed my weapon and helped the minstrel to his feet. I cleaned grease and sawdust from his dagger and put it in its leather for him. He limped badly, so I braced him as we went outside. My cut had been a deep one, and a barber should have to put some thread to it.

Outside I said with strained patience, "I saw the mark of melancholy upon your brow, man, but did not expect you to attempt suicide upon my very steel! In poor taste, I should say. There are cliffs and cold rivers to do the job for you, if you must."

"Forgive me," he said, unable to look me in the eyes. "I've left my instrument inside. Could you go back and get it for me?"

I left him leaning on a rail as I went into the Brass Ass to get his lute from the stage. Many eyes watched me. They would talk, certainly, without any notion what they were talking about. If the minstrel wished to play to the foul crowd some other night, I saw no reason for him to feel too embarrassed to do so. For tonight, though, the best thing was to get his leg stitched and see him to a room.

I went back out through the tavern doors and Ernro was not there. I followed the track of his blood a short ways, but he must have staunched the blood more successfully, for I lost the mark and could not see where he'd limped off to.

I looked for him the next morning. No one had seen him. Nor was anyone willing to hold his lute for him. I felt severely put upon and had no intention of dawdling in the town merely to return his property. I left a message at the tavern that I was on my way to Bretol, where a job awaited me unless I was too late for it. If no one came to claim the lute before my employment expired, I should then pawn it cheaply and treat myself to a whole plate of bison.

Such was my message.

Then with the lute tied to the saddle, Elizabeth and I set forth along the eastern road. There would be no more towns until I reached the mountain pass, and I expected to spend two nights camping beneath stars.

The first night at the side of a campfire, I started playing Ernro's lute to ease time before turning to my blankets. The instrument was very badly out of tune from bouncing on Elizabeth's flank much of the day. It suited my skill, however. I had fun with it, making many an unworthy sound, plucking one or a trio of strings here and there, tapping on the body of the instrument as though it were a drum. I sang "To the Sword" to myself quite loudly, though the accompaniment seemed to be a different tune altogether, if tune it was at all. My caterwauling echoed under the canopy of trees, and a wolf or wild dog answered in the distance.

Before I had my roll spread out for the night, I heard Elizabeth fussing and stamping. I went over to investigate. Beyond the circle of firelight stood Ernro the minstrel.

"Ho, good Ernro! So you heard my awful playing?" I held his instrument up by the neck. "It gives me a greater appreciation for your talents, seeing that I have none of my own."

I laughed. But Ernro did not reply. In fact, he didn't move at all.

"What ails you there? Won't you come to the warmth of my fire?"

How strange he looked in the darkness. I started toward him, thinking he couldn't move because he'd worn out his injured leg making it this far. As I approached, I saw that his hair and clothing were soaking wet. Then too I noticed his translucence.

"By the gods, Ernro!" I exclaimed. "You look like some ghost out of Hades!"

He nodded then, and I felt a shiver. He spoke, and his voice was quite unchanged from life. "You suggested the cold river yourself, my friend. Life is an awful thing, is it not? I was hoping to end my own. What makes me linger, do you think?"

What a look of extraordinary melancholy was on him! I cannot describe it. To see him made my body shake, not because I knew him for a ghost, but because the misery about him was a contagious thing and I did not wish to catch it.

"It often happens," I said, "that a man who takes his own life cannot rest. You shouldn't have courted such a notion! Now I suppose you'll wander this world forever. I pity you, dear minstrel; but do not ask succor of me now. It's too late for you. I was willing to help all I could last night, but what you've done cannot be reversed. Begone, therefore. I won't despise you, but I cannot urge your company."

"Yes, yes," he said. "I should be on my way."

He half turned from me, then looked back. He said,

"But where shall I go?"

"I cannot tell you that."

I hurried back to the light of my fire. Feeling that Ernro's ghost still lurked in the darkness, I kept the flames stoked until dawn, and that morning I was a weary mess. I half-slumbered in the saddle and somehow took a wrong bend or fork, ending up at a wide, blasted canyon which sustained no life. I could see far across the land. There were no steads, no inns, no burghs, no haze of smoke marking a settlement beyond far horizon. I should have to turn back, I knew, and find out where I went astray. But it would be dark soon, and I needed rest. I cursed my luck, fearing I would miss my chance at employment in Bretol.

It did not occur to me that the ghost might have been following. The moon had risen high into the sky when I awakened with a start and sat up in my roll. Elizabeth was gone. I never hobbled her, never needed to. My campfire was long out, and cold. I stood from the bedding, having slept fully clad, my sword beneath the cover with me.

Meaning to protect my property, assuming thieves were near, I moved toward the blasted stump against which leaned my saddle and the lute.

I whistled shrilly. Far away, Elizabeth replied in a soft whinny. She was not well sighted by night, and I did not think she'd go far, unless somebody led her.

Then I saw Ernro standing only a little ways off. His head was cocked to one side in a woebegone posture. He wasn't wet this time, and he seemed slightly more animated, especially about the shoulders.

"Have you caused this mischief?" I asked angrily. "Did you frighten off my mare?"

He looked at me with gray eyes moist and forlorn. "Would I do such a thing to a friend?"

"I will tell you this, dead minstrel, in case you haven't realized! A man's consciousness does not remain his own in death. Ghosts are always mischief; I know this to be true. You might have been a decent man in life, and injured by the pain of the world, and unwilling to keep living in it. But your spirit has thoughts of its own and will not let you off. You'll do bitter things, like to or not. But you've only been dead for two days and so should have a bit of control over what you do for a while yet. Do me this favor, then: Don't come near me again. Don't move from this place, in fact. There's a blasted valley down there just right for souls like you. Don't bother living men anymore!"

Saying this, I grabbed my bedding, saddle, and the lute, and went off in the direction of Elizabeth's snuffling, confused whinny. I saddled her and forced her to carry me, blind though the night made her, back the way we'd come. By dawn I realized that by traveling in darkness, I'd only gotten myself more lost than before.

I spent the whole morning and afternoon searching for a sign of civilization. There was not a single road. I was switched by branches as Elizabeth and I wove in and out of forested areas. Crossing a meadow, I was stung by a bee. I spent a lot of time cursing, I must say, for I was weary indeed, having had little sleep in two nights, and the third one approaching.

I did find a road at last. I followed it in an easterly direction, but had no idea where this particular road would lead. I passed no traveler, heard the axe of no forester, and passed no signpost or stead.

Before the sun was completely down, I happened on an abandoned house, its wooden shingles fallen away, part of the roof rotted through. It was shelter, though, and best of all, it had a functional hearth. I put Elizabeth in back, where a yard had gone to edible grass. In the house I started a healthy fire, the fallen shingles being fine kindling. Ere long, there were stars beyond the rafters.

There was only broken furniture, so I sat my saddle on a relatively sturdy portion of the floor and used it for a chair. I started plucking at the lute to entertain myself. Almost at once there stood Ernro in a shadowy corner of the ruinous structure. Only at that moment did I realize it was the lute he haunted.

Ernro had changed a lot since the night before. For one thing, he carried the smell of rot about him, the last three days having been warm ones. This was illusion only, for he was but a spirit, not putrescent flesh; but my nose could tell no difference. His left arm was twisted grotesquely, broken no doubt as rapids cast his drowning flesh against the rocks. One of his gray eyes was sealed behind a huge, red lid. The rest of him was bloated somewhat, as a corpse appears when fished from water.

"You're deteriorating, minstrel," I said. "You'd frighten the very devil as you are now. Can't you do something about it?"

He straightened his bent shoulder and arm, opened his eye, and in a few moments the swelling had gone from his body and he looked respectable.

"Much better, my sad friend. I told you, you would lose control sooner or later. How are you feeling just now?"

"Unhappy," he whispered, stepping nearer to me. I could see the wall behind him, on which a moldering remnant of tapestry yet hung. Some rubbish should have tripped him, but his foot passed through it.

"I seem to have figured this thing out," I said. "It's this lute you don't wish to leave behind which binds your spirit to the world. If I abandon it in this ruined house, I needn't be pestered by you again; or so I believe."

"It was not a special lute," he said, his tone so gloomy that it instilled within me a feeling of utter disheartenment.

"All the same, music was your life, was it not? It's hard to leave the things we love. What say you, dear Ernro, to my tossing this old lute into that fireplace yonder? Perhaps it would evaporate your ghost if I did so. I think it would be a kindness, don't you?"

As I said this, the ghost's visage became maniacal. I said quickly, "Control that look about you, Ernro! There's still enough human to you yet, I'm sure!"

But the maniacal look became more hideous still. I stood up from the saddle I'd been sitting astride, and edged my way toward the hearth. The ghost could not approach the fire. Knowing this, it began to howl. It was no longer Ernro so much as it was a raging abomination, festered, oozing, bleeding black blood and pus, yet unwilling to be destroyed.

Before I could throw the lute into the blaze, a whistling dart came through the hole in the ruined ceiling and cut across my wrist.

I dropped the lute, grabbing the injured backside of my hand. It was Ernro's pearl-handled dagger that swooped about the room. I drew my sword and batted the flying dagger as it dove at me a second time. As I leapt out of danger's way, my foot went through the lute and the crazed spirit's screaming became excruciating to my ears.

I dueled the flying dagger for some time, the hearth lighting the room weirdly, my own shadow leaping like a ghost. All the while I listened to the frantic screeching spirit.

It seemed to me the dagger became less threatening with each failed pass. At last it plummeted to the floorboards and lay there jerking and hopping, as though trying to make one more desperate lunge my way.

While the chance was at hand, I took up the broken lute, held together by its numerous strings, and tossed it into the maw of the fireplace. I turned to see how Ernro's ghost fared. The monstrous fellow writhed as though it were himself burning; but as his ugly visage melted away, it was no skull beneath, but the sad, prematurely aged, once beautiful face of gray-eyed Ernro as I'd met him first.

He sighed with familiar melancholy, but also with a note of

relief, and said to me in a voice grown calm,

"You've missed a couple splinters, Esben Danesworth, my good friend."

I looked where the lute had been smashed, and found indeed there were a couple splinters left.

"You've made me kill you after all," I said, taking the splinters toward the fire. It was hard to throw the last pieces within, hard to give the final blow to a man I hardly knew, certainly did not hate in any fashion.

"Don't hesitate," he said. "It was I who cast the final die, not you. You needn't feel guilty, nor pity me. My pain nears an end. But what of you, dark-haired Danesworth? You've a life yet to live; no doubt a long one. Who will pity you?"

"None needs to but myself," I said, and threw the splinters to the blaze. When I turned around, the ghost of Ernro was no more.

It was a year before I passed through Aispont again, that capital of a province near the sea, where Ernro said he'd first known of me. I asked around about a minstrel with that name, and learned a heart-wrenching tale of lost love, minor intrigue, and exile from the palace. It was not a unique story, to be sure, and to a degree it was boring. It put me thinking on the sorts of things that men will grieve for, and die for; and I hoped my own end would be less shameful, and for less foolish reasons.

THE HEAD OF SHEMESH THE ESHURIAN

Avram Davidson

Though born (1923) and educated in New York, Avram Davidson has been a traveler at the edges of the world, presently retired in the Pacific Northwest in the tiny town of Retsil. Very nearly the first time I met Avram, it was in a room-party at a science fiction convention into which he had trundled in order to suck gas from a balloon. Now you must realize that I've been reading this man's stories since I was a sticky-face kid. Avram is something of a Legended Giant even among professionals more jaded than I. So to see him suck gas from a balloon . . . well, my goodness, something *about that party certainly started me laughing.*

Avram stands among the finest modern writers of fantasy, science fiction, and mystery, winner of both the Edgar Award and the Hugo. He's a past editor of **The Magazine of Fantasy and Science Fiction;** *he drew together the lovely anthology* **Magic for Sale** *about very curious curiosity shops. Among his novels,* **The Phoenix and the Mirror** *is a noted modern fantasy classic. His wickedly civilized short stories have been collected into such fine volumes as* **Or All the Seas with Oysters, Strange Seas and Shores,** *and* **The Enquiries of Dr. Esterhazy.**

The hero Corydon was first encountered in one of Lin

Carter's **Flashing Swords** *anthologies, a tale considered by many to be the finest Lin ever acquired for that series. The present and long-awaited sequel will be particularly welcomed by discerning fans of adventure fantasy.*

"The Head of Shemesh the Eshurian" plays absurdity off pathos, self-serving nastiness off heroism, to bring us something not quite mocking, not really serious, and entirely convincing. The story transcends the gory trappings and characterizations found only within that strange subgenre of fantasy called Sword and Sorcery.

ONE DAY AT THE TIME when the sullen sun was veiled with mists behind the yellow sky, Corydon son of Corydon picked his way through plats of marsh grass which whipped against his muddy legs. He had indeed, or so it seemed, lost his pursuers: but also he had lost his way as well. Soon enough it would begin to be dark, and well enough he knew that from the beginning of the time when it begins to be dark until the time when it be dark indeed, is no great time. Woe that he was fleeing through the fens and lakes beyond the River of the Tarnavil. The girl had perhaps been rather young, but then, she had been rather willing too. Harsh and threatsome had been the cries her kinsmen had hurled after him, but rage does not quicken the legs as much as fear. Certainly it was far better to spend the night in the marsh muck, a prey to the small sharp flies, than to spend any part of the day or night being flayed and pegged; and yet somehow the approach of nightfall's forerunner, the twilight, and the keen whining of the fretful small sharp flies, did not incite Corydon to as much joy as one might think.

"A path," he muttered. "There was a path. Perhaps there will be a path again . . . do I but look." He stepped off at an angle, his foot sank into the squelch, he drew it out with one oath and observed its new-wrought nakedness with another. Swift was he about to plunge an arm up to the oxter in ooze in search, when he heard a voice say, from no great ways away, "Nay, now, but who is that approaching who swears after the manner of the Cartha Cabira, with a *By the brown crown!* and *The daemon take thy daughter! . . ?"*

The sound of a voice, any voice, made Corydon bethink him of his knife or sword; of turning with a swift and twisting motion and plunging himself at the man's knees and—But swift as thought, he recognized the voice as having nought in common with the coarse grottling howls that were the manner of the cot dwellers who had leaped after him as he rose and fled from the bed of sweetgrass in the forest hollow, the girl already beginning to pipe lies to cover herself: she having nought much else with which to make any cover, Corydon having tossed her single garment a good ways off. This voice was calm and free from force, and held but a touch of wonder in it.

So he turned slowly, and said softly, "The Cartha Cabira is a many days from here, nor is your own speech thereof, my sir." By the time he had said as much he was on his feet. And looking from the small man in the boat of reeds to his own newly naked foot, he could now think of nought else to say save, "I have lost one shoe. . . ."

"Throw the other after it," the reedboatman said promptly. "Leathern shoon be of no use hereabouts in any case."

Corydon kicked it off and away. It made but a slight plash. "Now do I indeed stand barefoot and supplicate before thee. Is there room for two in that scrannel craft? Know you the tavern by the harbor boom? Two steps down—"

"And two to the right. Step in steadily. Squat down slowly. Does Old Horn Head still overwater the sweet white wine?" The pole sped the boat along the reedy lane. Corydon faced the boatsman and ventured a wry smile. Said, "Aye. Hence those in the know prefer the red."

"And always did. True, I am not a Cabiraman. No more than you. But I have been there. As have you. Tis fellowship enough, in this wild place. As less by far would be." He raised his voice in a hoarse tenor and began the song called "Three Small Fish." Corydon, after a moment's memory, joined in.

The slough widened into a cove, the cove into a bay, the bay into a sound, the darkness came steadily, there were stars above, there was land ahead; he thought of those great fierce fish called the Mermen's Watchdogs, and he shuddered; he thought of the shag-legged foresters behind beyond-the-marsh, and he ceased shuddering. Said his host at the helm, "The life of a fisherman who salts and smokes roe for the twice-monthly markets is a free one, but as you may guess, mate, it is a lonely one. Tis halfway between last market and next, but there is wine in the jug and oil in the lamp, and if the bread be stale and hard, be sure it is not moldy; also there be mulberries in the bowl. Let us at any rate spend some several hours in singing old songs and seeking new tidings of old friends. And come mornlight, I will send you down at any place you pick within an hour of here. A bargain?"

Corydon said, "The bargain had been made as I stepped into your boat."

"My public name is Massilon. Mind your cramped legs as you step ashore."

The wine in the roe fisher's hut had not been overwatered—though it might perhaps have been the better for it if it had. The bread was medium-good stuff, of flour bolted but not sifted fine; stale it was indeed, but the wine softened it enough; besides, Corydon still had all his teeth. And if the oil were old and smelt ill, well, what the daemon?—a fisherman's hut is no city inn! They sang and they talked idly and they did in their ramblings find one friend in common—not Old Horn Head, who was no man's friend save his own—a rover of the rovers, one Gamminos. Massilon had known him on a coasting voyage to the Lesser Isles, and Corydon had known him in Another Place (one did not say the words, *the prison* quite so plainly as that, had one a decent respect for the Words and the Ways . . . and one who roved had better have). Corydon was not habituated to Another Place, but time and chance happeneth to us all.

If we rove.

And, it may be, even if we do not.

Well, and as another Word has it, "My friend's friend is my friend too."

And by and by, they slept.

"I would propose you," Massilon said, early in the foresun, "that we go fish-and-dish together, for there is roe enough for both hereabouts, the waters there have not been netted much before, the folk here have not that art, which I learned as a bare-breeched boy . . ."

Corydon let him ramble on, thinking of how he would soon in smooth and civil way decline the kindness.

". . . but there is too much chance that sooner or later you might meet up with yon pullet's parents as you sneezed about last night. So, no, I think it best thing I put you ashore on the countercoast, let your feet carry you off to safer sounds than this." He gestured towards the waters round about.

"I fear me you are right," Corydon said, sighing easily. "This way is not where I had hoped to go, but it is where I am—

"—going . . ."

Between the moment when his voice stopped and the moment when it continued, another boat had slid silently out from behind another island. ". . . I hope," he went on, after a moment. Massilon had seemed to shrink in upon himself. Corydon realized, perhaps rather late, that his host himself might have his own reasons for dwelling in a place so remote. "Who is yon craft?" he asked.

Massilon wiped a face too sweaty for the still-cool of the early hour. How many islands and islets there were hereabouts? Impossible to stay clear in wide waters. Impossible for a two-man craft, and a reedboat at that, valued for cheapness but never for speed, even to think of escaping a proper wooden bottom with six men at the oars. The fisher of roes essayed a reply, and his throat brought forth nought but a dry cluck. He swallowed, tried again. "They may be of no fret nor threat," he said. "Best we ply our way steady as she goes. Do we turn, certain they will follow in a flash. . . .Ah, who?" He cast a slant glance at the vessel swift approaching, wedge-front straight, oars adripadrip; again Corydon heard him swallow. "I think . . . I *think* it may be he who's called Shemesh the Eshurian. He holds, they say, rights and droits in all these waters: but as to what rights and as to which droits, ah me, some say one thing and some a second. . . .

"But none say much such as comforts me now, mate. . . ."

The wedge widened, the boat turned a broad side upon them. Looking down upon them was a man all brightavised in a helm that hid his face to the beard. "You there called Massilon," he said.

"Aye aye, Lord."

"You are to bring me two full packs of salt-smoked roes, the second market day from last."

A moment's silence. "We will settle the rest of it, then."

The voice was level. There was no threat. The voice stated facts.

"Aye."

"*You*. You are to come aboard. Now." The helmeted man turned away. Corydon had half begun to look and see who was meant. And then he realized that *he* was meant. Neither he nor Massilon wasted time on farewells. Corydon came aboard.

The ship (for in these waters in effect such it was for all that it was small) was a shipshape ship. Corydon saluted the guard. Then he waited to be told whatever it might be he was to be told. The message came by and by, in the form of a thumb cocked aft. Thither Corydon walked, steady and with short steps. A second sailor barely glanced up from his task of whipping rope's end, inclined his head toward the ladder. Corydon gave a look at the waters round about—here a fish splashed, there a covey of birds flew low and there another one flew high, aft an island looked green and fore an island looked black. Far-off, the blue-gray mountains. The air was clean. The wind kissed him lightly, and he felt it lightly, lightly, stir the hairs of his head. Corydon gave one more, briefer look all round about.

He had, he felt, never given a more appreciative look.

Then he went below.

It was between full daylight and darkdim down there. Shemesh the Eshurian (if that were he . . . whoever *he* was) sat facing him. His breastplate bore the Gorgonhead. He held his helmet, brightly polished, in his lap. Corydon was, had been, he himself noted, wrong in thinking that the helmet had covered most of the man's face, revealing only the lower part of his beard: the (as it were) beard was as much a part of the viziered helmet as its plume. The helm had not concealed the head. It had not needed to.

There was no head.

Corydon stood to attention. Said, "Sir."

The man seated before him let out his breath in a long sigh.

"This is well," he said, then. And, "This is very well. Usually those who see me—men, that is, for women I can after all receive in the darkness—usually they either bepiss themselves before fainting or beshit themselves before fainting. Of course, there are exceptions. Some faint before doing either one. So, what is your name, fellow? Corydon? Well. Corydon. Good.

"Deck, ahoy! Bring wine . . . and such. . . . Show me your sword."

He approved the sword. Corydon approved the wine. It had been watered just enough. The "and such" consisted of bread, cheese, fruits, small fish that had been boned and breaded and fried in the very best oil, and sweetmeats soaked in the honey syrup pressed from the reed suchari. There was another place for sitting, and Corydon had ventured to seat himself upon it as he ate.

Shemesh questioned him of this and that. Had Corydon been here? Had Corydon been there? Had Corydon fought in such and such a war? Had Corydon taken such and such a mystery? Participated in thus and so an ordeal? Had Corydon been in the Cartha Cabira? Ah. So. Corydon *had*. . . .

"Have you been in the Great Adyt of the Cartha Cabira?"

Corydon looked up from the wine bottle with a faint surprise. "Sir," he said. "No one has been in the Great Adyt."

"Ah," said Shemesh the Eshurian. "There you are wrong. *Some*one has."

Corydon had at that moment nothing in his mouth. Nevertheless, he swallowed. A tremendous thought came to him, a thought so bold that he made bold enough to voice it. "Has the Captain Shemesh the Eshurian been in it?"

"Yes."

No more than that. No more than *that?* Corydon's secret skin puckered. He slid a slight distance forward. "The captain *has?* Now, by the brown crown . . .! Oh, sir. Tell me. What is in it?"

Shemesh the Eshurian said, "My head is in it.

"You, Corydon, are to get it back," he said.

The vessel was heavy laden and it lumbered, but the lading was of green copperstone bound for the smelters, and copperstone does not stink, so Corydon counted his blessings: he had journeyed often enough with green hides or sheepfells, ill-cured fish, or other fragrant cargoes. Somewhat aft was seated another passenger, the white-shag geomancer even now slowly pulling out his beard as though—did he pull it long enough—it might give milk. This venerable scientist was of the school of the great Geat himself, as he had told Corydon (often) and would as sure as sunrise and sunset (often) tell him so again. But he was not yet ready to begin, so Corydon had his time to himself and to his thoughts.

What had possessed him to have agreed to such an insane mission? He asked himself this for perhaps the thousandth time. Earlier on there had seemed answers sufficient, such as: If I assent there will be safe-conduct for me through and past the land of the forest lopers who still raven for my life's gore, ill-sufficient though it be to undo the shedding of their daughter's maiden blood. And: I can always change my mind and slip away down there in Tarnabi town, at the river's mouth, and take passage for somewhere other than the Cartha Cabira. Or: The moneys that be given me as expense and charge by Shemesh the Eshurian, with these may I not embark upon another and a safer venture, though to be sure mine honor will constrain me to return it to him . . . some day . . .? Yes, I may.

And others, such as in detail now escaped his mind, squatting now as he was upon the salt-rimed deck of the creaky ship; though he had some recollections of having thought that, after all, he was Corydon son of Corydon, who had done this and done that, in the land of Scythia and the Land of Illiel and hither and thither: so why might he not do this as well?

(To port, some lengthy island came in sight, a-crouch upon the sea like some tawny lizard-orme: but he was in a sullen humor and bothered neither to reck nor ask its name.)

However, things had happened otherwise. Safe-conduct had he indeed into Tarnabi town, the city of the Tarnabi near the mouth of the river of that same name. No grottling forest folk could have got past the guards supplied by Shemesh—and indeed, they kept so close a watch and ward upon Corydon that scarce was he suffered to go aside and ease himself in privity. Was it to be believed that they kept aboard the copper ship until it stood down into the open sea, and went ashore with the pilot? It had had to be believed, for it was so. No chance at all had he to change his mind and slip away.

"Phaph! The daemon!" Corydon muttered now. "That any man should be so gross as to suspect me of an ill-conceit. Ah, well . . ."

But in his inmost ear an echo answered, ". . . *ill* . . . *ill* . . ."

And as the hireling guards of the suspicious Shemesh prepared to take water and return to land, Corydon mentioned a matter of great concern . . . at least, of a great concern to *him*. "Ahem. My masters. Guardsmen brave. I must raise a certain issue. Your lord and mine, the Captain Shemesh the Eshurian, gave me great assurances that he would guarantee me supply of cash for to meet necessary expense and charge. Surely you do not intend to leave without placing same into my hand?"

The guardsman in charge gave a sudden snort and slapped his hand to his brow. "Ah, yes, I had forgotten!"

Corydon, hope springing up afresh, said jovially, "Hahah, thou wouldst forget thy head, were it not . . ." His voice died away as he realized from their lowering, frowning glance that they savored not the jest. He cleared his throat. "Ahem. Tut-phut. Ah, the, ah, the, ah, *moneys*? Eh?"

A great purse was brought up from where it swung smack against the other's hip, and the man's great hand delved thereunto. But what he came up with was neither silver nor gold. "And what is this, this thing, what is it?" asked Corydon.

Said the guard chief, Grumbinus by name, "This is one half a talleystick. Arrived at the Cartha Cabira, present it unto Barshimshon the Shroff, whose bench is known to all, wherever he may move it. He will fit it unto the other half of the talleystick, and having that assurance, will pay into your hands a sum sufficient. *Fail not*. Now we go."

And go they went.

A recollection of boyhood . . . of everyman's boyhood, came now to Corydon: of stripping off his breechclout in the outermost antechamber of the public bath, to show himself before the lackluster gaze of the guardians, for were there so much as a single manhair upon him, perforce must he pay the charge for a man. A day there came, as come it must to all, when how proudly he had left his breechclout on and paid the charge before entering the regular disrobing room.

So. All that was long ago. Hair enough he had upon him now. A man, he had agreed to risk a man's risk. And with every league the ship made, the less his chances of retreat; the nearer grew, the greater grew, the risk. The risk, the risk! He bethought him of them now. Let alone the power of the Cartha Cabira as a power; (and a very great power it was); let alone the wrath of its people, so fierce to challenge and engage and punish an affront; let alone the sapient sly priests and *their* power—there was also the power implicit in the Great Temple itself!

And . . . there was not alone the immense question of how he was to get into the Great Adyt of the Great Temple, there was also the question of *how he was to get out*.

He moved his haunches restlessly, as though to gain a more comfortable, or a less uncomfortable, inch or two were to help his contemplation. The clean sea breezes which once he would eagerly have snuffed up, now were no more to him than the fusty odors of the olden schoolroom he had once been so eager to escape. No answers coming to him now of how he might avoid and escape the certain risk in the Cartha Cabira, he allowed his mind to dwell upon the certain pleasures of that splendid city: of its broad ways and bright gardens, its well-furnished and well-managed inns and taverns and cookshops and cunnyhouses, its merchant marts, its temples—

Nay! Of those he would not think.

Well. Of one of them he might now think. And so, of course, he had at once begun to think of it. Sacred to the goddess it was, and so were several hundreds of comely women, unto any one of whom he might, upon his choice, and after having made the proper offering of silver, be married with full ceremony and thus to enter upon all the rights and pleasures of marriage, for one whole week. After which, of course, the marriage contract lapsed and expired and the wife went back to her bridal bench in the temple yard, to await another spouse.

"Why, what am I then, but a sacred bull?" he muttered low. "Dedicate to be felled before the altar and hewn apart for sacrifice . . . the while I eat milky barley and be decked with garlands, and my horns a-gilded, and they bring unto me many a heifer and many a cow to cower at my pleasure and my lust: but my fate is predetermined and exact, and what awaits me in its hour but the felling hammer? And the knife."

And if he was at least a bit aware that this scene was not without its drama, and hence not even without its joyment, still and still . . .

Someone came now and sat before him. Corydon let the heavy forebodings roll on for another moment, a distilling from the some several drops of self-pity and self-esteem, before he looked to see who it was.

"Your Cartha Cabira, my son, hath, as is well known, a threble harbor port." Corydon's thought was, An it be well known, why need you know it me again? But being a douce young man, he did but make a face-show of great interest. Geomancers were prolix, almost by definition. Also it was his experience that it were well to suffer fools to ramble on over thrice-grazed ground, for it was sometimes the case that they said something which he had not known before and which it were well to know. In season a flower may blossom even on the blasted heath.

"Your Cartha Cabira hath a threble harbor port," the geomancer repeated. Corydon gave up hope of hearing anything new, but it was not worth the effort to move; he concentrated on the old man's face. The old man was the hairiest old man Corydon had ever seen. Beards grew from his ears. His eyebrows had eyebrows of their own, and his moustaches had moustaches—these last, to be sure, sprouted from his nose holes—and fortunate it was for his fellow voyagers that this old man was a cleanly old man. "Thus, in case of war and attack (the terms being after all semel and simul) it is possible to concentrate as be thought best your better ships in your central basin and to obstruct and blockade access thereunto by rowing, or as it might be, hauling by tow ropes your lesser vessels into your northern and your southern basins. Thus and in case of mimble mamble fimble famble bimble bumble a titty ta ta," the oldster nattered on; Corydon concealed a yawn. And he became slowly aware that something had after all been said that he had wished to hear, but the sense of which had passed by him. He frowned. The old man stopped.

"You disagree, then, my son," the old man questioned, "that in casting your tangent sejant for cadastral qualities, the fractions should be reduced to your nearest highest whole number and not your nearest lowest? If so, why?"

"Far from it, my father, of this I am totally persuaded by your logic inexorable; hem. But now, as you were saying: about the baths in the Great Temple . . .?"

The geomancer clearly had forgotten nothing. "Ah, yes. To be sure. And although the entire territory of your Great Temple is, I need to say, exempt from tax, and hence only its outer outlines need appear upon your cadastral maps"—here he doodled an outline upon the wax of his tablet—"still, hahah, geomancy is certainly no more constrained and limited to your cadastral than it is to your auspicious, your inauspicious, and your neutral frimble framble too too ta ta a himble humble," and he was off again.

Corydon waited till the geomancer paused to draw breath, then slid in at once, "The baths, then—"

"Ah, just so, so of course when it became needful to design and to lay out a new set of baths for to purify and ablute, lave, and in other words wash, and as one might say, ah, ah—"

"Bathe."

"Ah yes! Yes! Bathe! For your priests and priestesses, your acolytes, adepts, novices, your lustral libations, no wine without water, no piety without prayer, no offerings without washing, and so, therefore, ah, ah, and so therefore, ah—"

"Baths—"

"Ah yes! Yes! Your baths! And so when it was decided to erect new baths at your Great Temple of your Great City, for who does not know who is old enough to have to pay your two groats and a half a stiver minimal admission to your *pub*lic baths that, just as Cartha means City, so Cabira means Great, so when it was deemed necessary to erect new *sac*red baths therein and therefor, why, naturally we geomancers were selected to take new readings to allocate your locations, your directions, and all such matters your most essential . . ."

Corydon leaned forward, his face bearing an expression of so much awe, so much astonishment, that the old man first slowed down his eager flow of words, and next, paused altogether; looked at the young man and waited.

"You mean . . . you mean . . . that *you,* Doctor Dumdummus . . ."

The venerable nodded. "Yes, my boy. Seated here next to you, unworthy student of the students of your students of your Great Geat the Geomancer, D. Dumdummus Dumdaniel, laid out your formations and directions and outlines of your temple baths (new erections) in your Great Temple in your Cartha Cabira. . . . Yes . . ." And he nodded his hoary head so that his beard splayed out and lightly stroked Corydon's face.

Who now said: "But what an immense task! *How*— with all due respect and of reverence—*how* was it possible to perform such a tremendous task? And if I may say so, such a tremendously *dif*ficult task?"

"You *may* say so. It *was* difficult. It *was* tremendous. It *was* immense." And—with, of course, and inevitably, the assistance of many, many, *many* diagrams drawn upon his wax tablets with his brazen style—he proceeded to tell Corydon and to show Corydon and to explain to Corydon and to describe to Corydon, if not indeed more about the layout and the design of the innermost parts of the Great Temple than he, Corydon, cared to know, at least as much on the subject as Corydon could retain.

And more than this, of course, would be of no use at all.

At length even Dr. D. Dumdummus Dumdaniel felt that perhaps enough had been said upon the subject, for he fell somewhat silent and merely looked benignly upon Corydon. Who, feeling that his mouth had long enough been open in evident awe, now closed it. He would, of course, have opened it to express his thanks, but so dry twas that he was fane to leave it closed a moment more, at least. And then came the captain, who gestured portside to the distant but highly visible island which they had been passing for hours. "Menamnas," the captain said. "Menamnas, that's called. Coming this way, when as you sees Menamnas, 'Menamnas,' you may say to yourself. 'When Menamnas comes, the Cartha Cabira cannot be far ahead.' Aye." He patted his black-furred belly. "Aye. Not far at all . . ."

The customsmen paid scant attention to Corydon's little gear, and none at all to his person beyond a word and a gesture. He picked up his pack, this being all that the guardsmen of Shemesh the Eshurian had supplied him, this and the few items of clothing therein, and looked about him. Dumdummus the Geomancer he saw departing with a few several fellows of his craft, all walking with that peculiar manner and stance belonging thereto.The captain was busied with instructions as to his cargo, and the crewmen with their own tasks. The other two passengers, brothers by their look, and by their look, Adumians of the lesser sort, had never spoken to Corydon on the voyage, nor did they speak to him now. So—

—here he was in the Cartha Cabira again! And he was entirely on his own.

Well enough he knew the way out of the harbor, and that way made he now. He stopped only at the first shop, bought a small stoup of wine for the good of the house, added water, poured a small libation to the god, then sipped. Then he asked, "Landlord, and where does Bar Bar Shimshon the Shroff now keep his bench?"

The man thought a short moment, and said, "Last that I heard, he was keeping it between the Suffets' Chamber and the Sample House. May still *be*."

The Sample House was first, and thither all who come to the Cartha Cabira go to look and see what new wares (or, for that matter, what staples) are on display. But Corydon passed it by for the present. Sure enough, with the wall to his back, astraddle his bench on which were the grooves for his counting beads and a large supply of coinage both loose and piled, was Bar Bar Shimshon, his salty beard trimmed short, his eyes bent down, and his fingers sliding the beads up and down and now and then pausing to make a mark upon his tablet with his style. He looked up as Corydon stopped beside him. Corydon without a word handed over the tallystick.

"Ahah," said the shroff. He delved beneath his bench and

drew out a box, and from the box he took several bundles of tallysticks. These he examined and compared with the new one until he found one he liked. But it did not serve. He tried another, and then one more. "Ahah," he said. He held them side by side and raised his hand so that Corydon might see for himself.

Sure enough they matched: notch for notch, slot for slot, scratch for scratch. "Cut from one stick," Corydon said.

Said the shroff: "Ahah."

And he counted out upon a clear space on the bench a pile of copper, a heap of silver, and a few—a very few—pieces of gold. He made further calculations with his beads in their grooves, these he checked upon his fingers—tips and knuckles and joints—then he made some final assessments upon the clear side of his tablets. The result was that he slid some coppers off the bench and into his hand, where they rejoined the others on their pile, and added one more piece of silver. Then he counted these all once again. Then he looked up.

"Ahah?" he asked.

Corydon said, "Ahah." He opened his purse and himself counted them all before sliding them in. "Will you not have a glass of good wine with me, then, Master Shroff?" he asked.

The money changer allowed himself a brief and one-sided smile. "*Ah*ah," he said. And he waved his hand in a not unfriendly gesture. And he disposed of the two newly rejoined halves of the tallystick in a manner satisfactory to himself. And he returned to his countings and his calculations. But rise to have the glass of good wine with Corydon, this he did not do, nor show sign of doing.

So Corydon decided to have it by himself.

Over his second sip of the day—this time a much superior vintage, and the mixing water actually a preparation of fruit juices and spices—Corydon said to the tapster, "Bar Bar Shimshon the Shroff—hath he taken, do you know, an oath to drink no wine?"

"He drinks it well enough to home, either his own or those with whom he takes hospit," said the tapster, adding a trickle more of the best into Corydon's mixing bowl. "But no one has ever seen him partake in the open street or during time of work and commerce. And as for those in the shroffage who do, why perhaps their wits do not always stay full sharp. Sometimes they take a bad coin. And so, sometimes, they pass such out again. And as this becomes known, and sooner or later it does, why, what but that their custom dwindles and it may be they seek to make it up with sharp practice. And so before not long come the lictors of the Suffets, and they decry his name full loud, and they break his bench . . .

"... and he be lucky if they do not break his bones as well."

"Hmmm," said Corydon thoughtfully. He sipped the rest of his wine. And he sipped it more thoughtfully than usual.

There are those who say that the Great City is newer than the New City, and there are those who say that the New City is greater than the Great City. There are those also, for that matter, who refer to them as the City Great and the City New. But such fine points are finer than the fine sands that grain the beaches; so enough.

As Corydon strode along the Street of the Seven Stars, a smell the most savory assailed his nostrils, causing him to break step and consider whence it came, no great search: a few paces off the great street and into a smaller was a cleanly looking cookshop where goat was set out to roast, and from the looks of it, the task was almost done. Not only was Corydon tired of ship's biscuit and of pig's palate in pickle, but Corydon was indeed rather fond of goat, particularly that in between mutton-size and kid. The cookshopman was even now basting it with a look of pleasant concentration, and from the sight and smell of it, there lay in the basting sauce not only the rich juice and oil of the flesh itself, but such items as *onion*— a sovereign herb; *garlic,* which is not only tasty but an alexapharmic against more diseases and daemons than most men know the names of; atoms of the pungent shrub called *rosemarine;* berries of the *pepperplant* moiled in a mortar; and even as Corydon watched, the master cookman added a few squeezings of the small yellow fruit called "child of the citron," or *limoon*. Then the man looked up.

"Pardons the most innumerable, my sovereign sir," said he. "Be pleased to overlook my gross misbehavior in not having seen you sooner, and be seated upon this divan." Whilst speaking, he had set the basting brush back in its basin, and now he fluffed a cushion and flapped it back down. "After bringing you warm water with nard therein, to refresh both face and hands, may it not be that next—the while we wait the merest trifle of time for the flesh to finish roasting—I may bring the sir such a flatbread baked fresh, and softer than a maiden's paps, and sprinkled with sessamum seeds? Curds which need no more than the merest dewdrop of rosewater? A pigeon cooked with butter and farced with prune pudding? Or, or, and if none of these attracts the palate of my sir, there is a fine pot of plump scuttlefish in sauce of ink and mustard? A sallet of snails with lettuce, mints, and cress? Which of these items may I bring my lord? But say."

Corydon settled himself down upon the divan and looked from the kitchen to the great wide street with much content. "You may bring them all," he said. "And I would that you had six arms, that you might bring them all the sooner and at once." He added, "Bring also the wine jug and the water."

For the god has given many gifts, and of these, is not goodly food amongst all but the greatest?

There be temples aplenty in the Cartha Cabira (including, as is surely well known, one to Fingers Apollo, the patron of sneak thieves), and if not all be so extremely specialized—as for, to name another, the shrine of Baboon-Daemos, and to be precise, this consists of an angle in two walls that once, tradition says, sheltered a wax painting on a wooden board: tis equally incontestable that Baboon-Daemos is demigod of the Warrantchees and that no Warrantchees have ever dwelt in the Cartha Cabira, but legally the spot is a temple, and very small men are known to have used it to invoke the rights of sanctuary—if not all sacred spaces are so extremely specialized, yet none are of such general resort and purpose as the Great Temple itself. Here and here alone are taught the Tenets of the Dying Priest, including the Enclitic Paraphrastical, to wit: *That no god is all god, that each god is every god, that all gods are one god, and that perhaps the highest faith is to hold that faith which cannot be proven: such as that there is no god.*

This is, however, on the high and lofty plane of the abstract theoretical; on the plane pragmatic there is a shrine for every day of the year, an altar to every sign of the zodiac, images innumerable, and these last include the justly famed hermaphrodite image with a blank face: this be in case one wishes to offer prayer and petition to any god or goddess not otherwise imaged forth. And thither and roundabout be seen peoples from near and from far: Barbarfolk with pallid skin limned in blue designs, the Zizu all in scarlet and crimson and in rose and green (none of these colors being fast, the robes are dyed anew after each washing), the black Dimdoumi whose face flesh is raised in symmetric scars and whose earlobes are adrip with gold, the Rumans wrapped in strips of woolen cloth (haughty and proud be these last, though their habits are said to be filthy—else why need they so frequent bathe?), Tyriani in every shade of pourpre from red to lavender, and gross Adanim whose swoll ankles overfold their golden anklets. Here one sees the foul Rhybothēs from dread distances afar, of whom it is told (though who dare believe it) that however many brothers a family consist in, yet have they all but one and the same wife; and here one sees the Aravins whose beards are sticky with incense gum.

Here are seen those who shout aloud their prayers and those who pray in silence, and then there are the gant Isshkuri with long, long jaws: these recite their petitions and orisons in a level drumble, the language of which is not the daily language of the gant Isshkuri with long, long jaws but a secret, sacred cant, known (one must hope) not only to the gant Isshkuri (et cetera) but to their gods. And aside from all of these, and many many more, there are those who sell bread for the wayfarers and oil for the lamps, as well as fruits and flowers and other items of offering. And see Corydon walk amongst them all.

Several times a day for several days did he walk around and about the temple precincts. And then he gave a great nod, and then he returned to his inn.

About halfway between early morning and middle morning a young man was in the wood yard where the faggots of fuel for the fires are stored, and he had with him the rope and pad of the wood porters. Wood porters be bent beneath their loads so much that even when they are not laden down, they seldom look up. The costume of the wood porters consist of any clouths they care to wear, and over these and worn as a sort of cape a-down their bent backs is always a pad comprised of felt and sack; for on their backs they bear their burdens of wood, which they hold in place with a coil of rope.

Aside from their stoop and sweat and dustiness, their wood and pad, nothing distinguishes these porters from other men, for they be of no particular caste or countenance or color or size or shape: which is to say, they be of any.

So no one noticed Corydon.

He followed those porters whose ropes were slack and whose backs were empty; he followed them to the wood yard.

And thence, and bearing fuel, often he followed them to the fires. And thence, returning again. Often.

So soon as he had found himself a place apart, early on in his stay in the Cartha Cabira, he had set himself to set down all he remembered of the old geomancer's wamble and prattle; he set them down in wax newly smoothed, within the cheapest of tablets—*them* being, first, the general outlines of the area of the Great Temple. Then he scratched in what he knew of the ways and walks, the shrines and fanes: thus he covered much of the ground. But still, a blank place remained.

And blank it would have remained entirely—for beyond a certain limit the general did not go: hence, beyond this certain limit might not Corydon go—save that elder Doctor D. Dumdummus Dumdaniel had set down for him so specifically the outlines of the temple baths (new erections).

And so, having set down these upon his own tablet as he recalled them from the geomancer's, Corydon saw that not much much remained blank.

And so, logically it followed, and it had to follow logically, that within this blank the Great Adyt had to lie.

In part he took good care to reck whither he was going and whither he had gone; in part he rehearsed in his mind again and again the conversation that might well take place: as, perhaps, more or less, as so:

Dolt, what dost thou here?

At which would Corydon painfully straighten up an inch or two and look around with dumbstricken countenance.

Dizzard, the fires lie not this way nor that! Turn left, dimdome: Left, I say!

Or, as it might be, *right*.

And with a dull grunt and a small shake of his bent head, Corydon would comply. And so depart in safety and in peace —for who (so Corydon reasoned) would suspect a mere wood porter, filthy and streaked with runnels of dusty sweat a-bittled with bits of bark, who would suspect such of conspiring an illicit entry into the Great Adyt?

He hied him right, he hied him left, he wandered round about the mazy ways: ever he came out somewhere which was not at all where he wanted to be—some public place, some open way. Once it were in the shrine of the Great Goat, a-full to the walls with worshippers lustily making *Me'e'eh'eh'eahhh!* their heads reverently bowed down, with fingers fixed at temples to stimulate horns. Once,—nay, twice!—he found himself in the Fane of the Fay Fantina, where no one else was seen at all: save, first, an elderly woman with lips moving in pious prayer, and who had propped against the altar rail the simulacrum of an elder man a-stuck full-fill of thorns and pins; and second, an elderly man with lips moving in pious prayer, and who had propped against the altar rail the simulacrum of an elder woman a-stuck full-fill of pins and thorns.

More then, even, twice, he found himself somehow in the semicircular colonade where people are wont to take refuge from noonsun or (rarely) rain; he saw his feet taking him out onto the worn marble flags of the Great, the Median, the Lesser, and the Little Courts; he found himself in the Place of Public Healing, and in the House of the Brides—

—never did he find himself in the Great Adyt.

And remembering the adage about *All prayer and no play,* he after a while washed himself and put on cleanly clothes and betook himself a bride-for-a-week; the woman's name was Heramne, and, he asking what might please her, she looked at him with some surprise, as though this were a question she was not often asked; and said (after a moment) that she would like to take the sea airs upon a boat: he hired him a boat. Also for a week. The craft had seemed sturdy, but at the first swell began to fill with water. Corydon, with an oath or two, had delved for the leak and found it, and cut the rotten part clean and plugged it with a peg he swift whittled from a piece of the bench; direct, it gan to swell; the vessel leaked no more. "It would serve the boat liveryman right were I to . . ." he said, somewhat sullen, and finished not his words.

Circumspectly and circuitously he asked her of the Great Adyt. But she knew nothing of that at all, save the same legendry that know we all.

So to himself and not aloud, he said that the Great Adyt seemed safeguarded by the very reverse of a labyrinth: for the labyrinth served to draw one in and prevent one's finding the way out.

"Ah, this beautiful city!" said Corydon, lightly enough, politely enough; but sincerely enough, for that. He was not expecting what he heard next.

"I would that its beauty were lain in the dust and destroyed!" Heramne said, her lips in a rictus of hatred and wrath.

"Oh, you can't mean that—"

"I can!" she cried. "I can! I can!"

He said nothing, but gazed at her in perplexity and surprise.

Heramne took a few deep breaths and said nothing. Then she said, "I would gladly die to see this city die around about me. I would wish to be spared only long enough to see it burned, to see it harrowed, sacked, and burned. I would betroth myself to the daemon to see it plowed and sown with salt. Whenever I am sorrowful, whenever I am mad, I think of it as the abode of pelicans and hedgehogs: then I am renewed with joy. Did you think I was native here? Because its hateful accent comes swift and thick upon my tongue? I cannot help that. I hate that."

He knew, now. "Ah . . . You were a captive. . . ."

"Were? Still, I am."

He mused a moment. "You could come away with me," he suggested.

She flung up her head so that her hair danced in its thick-bound plaits, and she looked at him with what he thought was eager and hopeful assent; for a moment he thought so. "Come away with you? The Sea Suffets' fleets could not protect me to come away with you. I am a daughter of the goddess . . . as *they* say. It means that I am a slave of the goddess. It means that I am dedicate to be a prisoner in this city so long as I live. When I am no longer young enough to be rented out as wife-for-a-week, I shall serve as other servants serve, slave as other slaves slave. In my age, if I live till then, and many are my prayers that I may not—unless it be to see a sea of flames engulf this place—in my age I shall pick twigs with bleeding fingers, so that no wood be wasted in the temple fires. And when I shall be too feeble for that, even, when my fingers be too crippled even for that, or my eyes too blind: then they shall with great grace feed me with the leavings from the meals of those not yet quite so old; and as to what they themselves do eat, shall I tell?

"They eat the leavings from the meals of others yet. . . ."

How many men might have lain in her arms, here in the scented darkness, he did not know; and it may be that she did not know either. Had she received them, all of them, as she had him? Hardly, it was possible. He would miss her when their week were out. But on the morrow he must try his way again, somehow, somewhere.

Some recollections of the outcast Zaul of Zelb rose easy and ugly to Corydon's mind as he wandered the crooked lanes of Monkey Dell, as the bad quarter of the Cartha Cabira was called. Tripes seethed in stinking oil outside the filthy holes it almost seemed an abomination to call cookshops. Beggars blind and beggars maimed and beggars more diseased squatted thick as swollen flies and raised their voices in raucous sound intended to indicate that one should pretend this was music, but pretense will serve only so far. The effect was one of horror and menace alone. Now and then Corydon did toss a coin, the smallest ones he had. A break in the grotesquery of noise, a grunt, a squawk or squalling mew, served in place of thanks. Corydon kept his purse in his hand.

His left hand.

He kept his right hand on his knife.

There really would not have been room to swing a sword.

Here and there, from corner and from cornice, the swollen countenance of a gargoyle looked down and leered, thick tongue out a-jeer; and once a ghoul-woman accosted him: her stench-breath sufficient advertisement of what she was, it was hardly needful she should pluck aside her crusty robe to show her cubs clutching tight at each of her six dugs. He could but pass on: the ghoulfolk can take no money and they eat no bread; as for that which she wanted of him, he would perhaps not have died any death rather than supply it, but certain it was that there were a large number of deaths he indeed would choose instead.

Hags with painted noses winked and beckoned. Corydon was offered little boys, little girls, and dancing sheep. He was approached by pimps who pretended to be thieves and thieves who pretended to be pimps. Fairly prosperous-looking show-peepers with interesting deformities tempted him with brief flashing glimpses as he walked on. He walked on. A fat woman extremely naked came lumbering by at a lope, and after her, trotting at the crouch, a man of no distinctive look came following, in his hand a long stick with what seemed to be a nail at the end of it. Corydon stepped a bit aside as she ran flopping by, and at that moment the man, his face expressing only concentration the most extreme, lifted his stick and jabbed it into her back. She threw up her flab arms and disclosed her armpits, each spray of hair surrounded by a circle of red chafe marks, and gave two ululating hoots as she staggered on. Corydon could see flecks and smears of food on her thick tongue. The sagging flesh of her back showed speckles of blood in some places. And in some places the marks were scabbed over. And in some places there were scars.

Ware stood on small stalls and in small heaps before the hole-in-the-wall shops, ware such as finery and fruit, items such as are found for sale everywhere that there is anything offered for sale; save that here the fruit was rotting and the finery soiled. Filthy fat catamites, faces smeared with paint and ointment, winked and wiggled fingers at him as he passed on. He passed on. Now and then the alley he chanced to be in debouched into a wider street; and this wider street, though indeed the whole quarter smelled evil, stank of a most terrible stink and stench: for this was the dung street, and along it in the darkened hours the noisome carts and wagons of the nightmen rattled and rolled, and stained the ragged roadway with their spillage and slop.

What antic, if not indeed insane (and, perhaps, indeed insane) thought had possessed him to come hither, to the last extremity of the Cartha Cabira? And, whatever it was, could he not have followed it by promenading at the city's other extremity, where the villas and mansions of the greater merchants, the magnates, the emissaries, and the suffetic families dwelt; amidst broad ways lined with columns of marble, and with flowering trees, immense gardens, palaces, and private shrines? Certainly. If he were, indeed, exemplifying some klephtic conundrum, delphic in its interpretability, as it might be for instance *Who cannot go across, he must go around,* then why *here* and not *there?*

Finding answer neither to this latest riddle nor to his present quest, he, with a short sigh, half turned to retrace if not his exact steps at least his general way, and found himself gazing through an immense rent in the old outermost wall. (For generations the suffets had refused to repair it on this side, on the grounds that Monkey Dell was in any case indefensible, and perhaps an invading army might be anyway somewhat slowed in progress through it, if only by perverted curiosity or pestilence endemic.) Towards the utmost left the bare and lifeless sands stretched all around, dune beyond dune beyond dune, all the way (presumably) to the land of the Warrantchees, whose men wear beads, whose women wear beards, and whose king is a sacred baboon. Towards the uttermost right rolled the rock-splintered foam of the False Harbor, where not even so narrow a vessel as a plank-wide skiff might venture in safety; nor would any wish to. Here the sea beasts have their caves and hold their sullen sway. And none begrudge it them.

Also there as he looked, rising from the roll of rough ground, above the tumble of ruined tenements and half-broken hovels and chaos without name, were the massy bulks, stained with splotches of lichen and of substance less wholesome, of three structures roughly approximate in distance and in size.

The lepers' hostel.

The dung pit.

The charnel house.

Thither, as though thitherunto doomed, Corydon picked his way.

He soon enough lost it.

So often and to such degree had the ground sunk beneath the path, so much did it writhe and wind, that afore long Corydon had no longer any notion as to which noisome bulk was which. The lepers were not more silent than the dead. The charnel house did not stink worse than the dung pit. There was no sight nor sound of living form—no one touted, no one begged, no one pimped. He did not see so much as a mouse or a lizard. And—and this struck him as oddest of all—he did not even see or hear a fly. There were no longer lanes, nor were there alleys, but in between the stolid walls of stone and heaps of crumbled brick higher than his head, he half slid, half stumbled along in mere passages: round about, and round about and in and out, and round about. Up and down. And back and forth.

Thus it was that without warning and without transition, he found himself inside the Great Adyt.

Within, it did not at all look in any way as Corydon would have thought, had he had in any way thought what it might look like. Amazed, confounded as he was, he realized that he had never envisioned any semblance of it all. Whatever it was like, it was not like the rest of the Great Temple; it was not like any temple he had ever seen at all. For one, there were no images brightly painted: there were no images. No altar daubed with blood was there, neither any altar brightly scoured nor piled with flowers or fruits of offering: no altar was there. But, lying idly in one corner as though kicked aside for later removal, was what Corydon clearly recognized must be the head of Shemesh the Eshurian. Dust lay on the face and dust was upon the dark eyelids and the pallid lips, eyelids that now faintly blinked and lips that now slightly moved.

The light was neither bright nor dim, and came from some hidden source he could not locate. The ceiling was high. The ceiling was very high. After a moment in which his neck craned almost painfully, Corydon had to concede that he saw no ceiling; he saw no roof, either; neither could he discern any sky. Vertigo struck him and quickly he looked away, looked down.

It struck him now, and did nothing to decrease his vertigo, that neither could he discern any floor.

Nor anything beneath where the floor would be.

He felt, though, a smooth surface under his feet, his bare and suddenly sweating feet.

But of it he could see nothing.

In fact, as to the part of the immense chamber, if chamber it indeed was—and how came it, on the inside, to be so immense, when on its outside it was nothing of the sort? *There are questions to which the answer is known and questions to which the answer is not known and then there are questions to which the answer seems to be that there is no answer.* These words of the Dying Priest now rang in his ears, and rang even more loudly than the vertigo—in fact, as to that part of the immense chamber where he now stood, sweating and twitching and trembling, there seemed to be nothing at all save for those parts of two walls that emerged from indefinite distance to form a corner. And, lying in that corner, the head of Shemesh the Eshurian.

Afterwards (though not then) he bethought of the immense paradox that the Great Adyt of the Great Temple of the Cartha Cabira was not actually within the Great Temple . . . nor, for that matter, was it actually within the Cartha Cabira at all. And how this came to be, or when, or why, idea and answer had he none.

Ordinarily a head apart from its body would make a man who saw it feel less than well: but here, but now, but here and now the severed (if that were indeed the word) head seemed the sole familiar and reasonable item in sight. Corydon's dizziness died away.

Something else, however, gradually took its place.

Was there a whispering?

There was a whispering.

It came from nowhere and it came from everywhere. Almost, it seemed, he could make out words . . . phrases . . . entire sentences. But this was, of course, absurd.

A group of priests entered the Adyt, single file, and almost at the moment of entering broke line a step and scattered round about the room (if room it was). Corydon felt a moment of terror. Waited for them to see him, to cry aloud such cries as "Blasphemer!" or "Sacrilege!" and "Death by the Painful Penetrations!" But nothing of the sort happened. Some looked at him, as they might look at a sunbeam dancing with dust. Some frowned faintly, as though in the presence of a riddle, an escaped thought, a word both forgotten and on the tips of their tongues. Some smiled faintly, as though observing something mildly affectionous. One raised his eyebrows, only at once to let them fall. And some ignored him.

And one, chancing (it seemed like chance, for the man did not pause, let alone stop) to pass fairly near, said, "Ah, you have found." He did not say, Found *us;* he did not say, Found *your way;* neither nor said he, Found *it*— that is, the head. No. *Ah, you have found.*

All this was the matter of a moment, not more.

The manner of the priests was that of men about to perform a familiar task. In each one's girdle was a tablet and style. Some went this way and some went that. As they went, they seemed to listen. Some remained near enough for Corydon to observe them seeming to listen and to hark, and some vanished out of sight—that curious sight within the Adyt whereby distance was as it were rolled up, curtailed, made brief. Sometimes they stopped, two by two, or one would come over to another, listen a bit and shake his head yea or nay. Sometimes both would go on, or both remain. And after each indication that the signs of whatever it was they sought were favorable, each priest drew forth from girdle his tablet, and opening the wooden covers (inlaid with oliphant teeth sawed thin and speckles of gold) to the wax-filled sides inside, took up also his style and began to indite. And sometimes they muttered aloud, as secretaries may vocalize and repeat a message being copied down.

And so came Corydon to hear such things as: *The Suffet Bar Bar Barca hath purchased five oliphants whereas he hath leave to possess but two; what blow of state doth he conspire?* Or: *The Servants of the Queen-Bee of Heaven do ordain that henceforth her shrines shall be wrought of silver and not of gold alone, that more worshippers may afford them.* As: *Locust devour the barley in the Land of Uz.* Or: *Old Horn Head did promise me half-value on the purloined pearls and hath not given me a fifth, may the crab consume his cullions:* and much else.

Much, much else.

Presently it seemed to him that the whispering grew fainter, and then faint. The scribbling scribes of priests stooped and seemed to strain to hear; their writing went more slowly. And then the same numinous silence reigned throughout; the priests straightened up, those from afar came near; they bent their way towards a certain point, fell into line, and began to file forth. Again they glanced at Corydon, again there was no menace, nor indeed much interest in their glance.

In exceeding great haste, Corydon stripped off his engirdling sash and unfolded it. Within the wrinkled cloth he wrapped the head of Shemesh the Eshurian. And he followed after the departing priests.

Observing that none of them cast so much as one single glance behind, neither, so, did he.

He found himself in a passageway which was not the one by which he came. And then he emerged into a corridor beyond which he saw the Great Court. And none stopped him as he left.

It is easy enough to walk along with a human head wrapped under one's arm as though twere no more than a melon from the market. The Cartha Cabira is not, after all, a city of governance, as is Sorneum or Torg. Neither is it a city famed for its arts, as one might say is Valadin and, for that matter, Librasia. One does not go to it as one goes to Berenal, to see the games. The Cartha Cabira is a city of merchants and of merchantry and merchandise; this it is and almost this alone. And merchandise take a many muckle forms. And requires many a mickle cares. Hence in the Cartha Cabira, one finds no lack of good inns with good storages; for pay, to be sure. All is for pay in the Cartha Cabira. Any why, of course, should it be otherwise?

Hence Corydon felt no great concern when he approached the custos of the House of the Horse and said to him, "Well, and I have acquired yet another item which I do desire to store," and followed him into the stone building behind the inn. Corydon had, upon the way, obtained a chest of stout wood bound about with iron bonds and bands and into which he had deposited the article of his chief concern. And in a trice the custos had secured it to the post nearest Corydon's other baggage and had sealed it fast. A large man, this custos, and inclined to fat: but no weakly-looking one for all of that, and one who seemed not likely to affrighted be by any common fright.

Hence Corydon was more surprised than otherwise, not much later that night, as he sat discussing silently a beaker of one of the better vintages, to see the said custos (Tindario by name) approach him with chins a-wabble and his flush face all a-pale, and address him with these words, and no more: *"Get it out."*

Corydon followed after him without so much a shrug and out into the stone building out behind, where he severed the seals and took up his gear as the custos Tindario gestured him to do. "The scot and score?" asked Corydon.

But Tindario said no more than this: *"Get it out."*

This time, there being but the two of them present, Corydon allowed himself the shrug foreborn before. "Summon me a handcart," was his reply. Still, he thought best not to return yet to Heramne; so he sought and found another inn with a safe place to store one's goods and gear, this one being called Of the Lybyans and Two Green Geese. Here one may stow one's stuffs into small walled chambers—or, for that matter, large ones—with locked doors. And thus Corydon did, and afterwards he sat and sipped musingly before the firepot where dried camel droppings glowed. Presently he saw coming into the wine room the custos of this same inn (Of the Lybyans and Two Green Geese) a small man, but solidly made: he had been of a ruddy skin when Corydon last had seen him, but sundry several minutes ago, now his skin was muddy instead. And this one (Corydon thought his name was Numa) addressed him succinctly. *"Take it away."*

By the time he (Corydon) was in his third place of lodging

and of storage, it had come to his mind almost as a certain thing that the indifference of the priests had been mere simulation and that, aghast at his hardihood and sacrilege, they had secretly sent messengers after him to warn off the keepers of the three inns. He was confirmed in this supposition by his being addressed by a man both tall and thin and with naked arms, muscled as with ropes of wire and showing so many scars that no conclusion was possible other than that he was a retired gladiator (there were not many) who had taken employment in, as it were, private practice. Evidently he was the night man at this third inn (a-clept The Swan and the Eggs), for there had been a quite different one on duty what time Corydon had taken lodging and waring there. His name may be of no account, and if so, tis just as well, for Corydon never learned it.

This one spoke to him one single word, to wit, *"Remove."*

One does not argue with retired gladiators (there are not many).

By now Corydon was more than weary, so he did not either bargain or chaffer at the inordinate price asked him for a room by himself in the tavern which, for all it had no sign and hence no name, Corydon knew full well, it being the one by the tavern boom. "But that I ken your face and remember it well as that of an old and valued customer," said the patrone, "I would be constrained to demand of you six times as much, for who knows how many seeking lodging I must turn away, by reason of your engrossing all of my second-best room. The daemon! Is it a woman or a boy or—"

"Horn Head," Corydon said, "be still."

Corydon, who was not at all hungry but knew that hunger, though it may be put off for a while, yet it will always return, ate a few mouthfuls of what coarse victuals the tavern provided; and carrying his wine with him (it was the red), went up to the second-best bedroom and bolted the door. The plaster had once been bright and red, no doubt, but that must have been long ago: now it was a faded rose and, falling off in patches, exposed the bricks of the outer and the lathes of the inner walls. Bed places had been drawn on the floor, but the ragged pallets and little-better blankets lay at a careless angle. Corydon's gear—the pack, the leather casket, and the wooden chest—he piled together round about, and flung himself down for moody contemplation and (he hoped) for sleep. Sundry gross scratchings on the wall, he ignored.

Soon the last rays of light dwindled, and all was dark.

Perhaps he had fallen asleep, perhaps he only thought he had. For why should a mere whisper awaken him? A mere whisper in the sleeping rooms of a tavern was unusual only in that sleeping-room sounds were usually louder than whispers: snores, sobs, groans, grunts, roars, bellows. Corydon turned over and tugged the tatty blanket as close to his nose as the ranker than usual smell of it allowed.

"Help," said the whispering voice. "Help. Help. Help."

Perhaps, thought Corydon, someone was having a bad dream. Or, even, it was not impossible, perhaps someone was actually imprisoned in the next room. In either case it was no affair of his. Besides, the absurdity of it! Calling for help in a *whisper!* He rolled over and sought a cooler spot (or perhaps a warmer).

"Pssst! Pssst! Anybody there? Somebody? Hey. Pssst!"

With a sigh of annoyance, Corydon half sat up. "Cease this importunate susurration," he said. "I am a peaceful traveler on lawful business bound. If your supplications are not at once concluded, I shall have no choice but to contact the custos of this place and—"

"Help," the voice continued (it had continued during Corydon's comments). "Help. Pssst. Get me out of here. Hey. Pssst."

"Oh, by the brown crown! The daemon take thy daughter! Who are you, then—not that I much care, of course—and where are you?"

Yet, although Corydon plainly heard the small voice, the small voice had perhaps not plainly heard him, for it continued to whisper and to plead, without in the least stopping to answer his questions, how often repeated. And then came a slither, a bump, another bump, and a fall. It was right next to Corydon's bed. His groping hand disclosed that the chest had fallen down. He knelt, and grunting, more with annoyance than effort, picked it up and started to lift it back.

"Pssst," the same voice said. "Hey. Help. Get me out of here."

The voice sounded almost in his ear.

It was not, then, in the next room at all. It was right there. In the small chest.

Corydon thumped the chest in anger. "Imbecile head!" he said, his teeth clenched. "It is my entire attention to *get* you out of there! I have risked life and limb and time and toil entirely for that sole purpose. Merely remain quiet, and if you can manage, comatose. And we shall in no great time see that you are united to the torso of your rightful owner, videlicet the Captain Shemesh the Eshurian."

The chest moved and toppled in his arms, the head plainly rolling and bumping from side to side within it. "Pssst. Help," the voice said. "Hey. Get me out. Pssst."

There was a sound on the landing outside. A glimmer of light shone through a crack. A hand fumbled. And the door burst in.

To be sure, Corydon had bolted the door. But there had been a small panel above the bolt, closed with a pair of bent nails. He should have paid more attention to this, but truth to tell, what with annoyance, fatigue, and fear, he had hardly noticed. And now someone via a well-directed fist had simply knocked the panel out, bent nails and all, and slipped the bolt and entered, all before Corydon could even rise from his knees and reach for his sword.

Or vice versa.

"Oh, don't bother to move," a rougher voice said—so rough, in fact, that Corydon, with an inward sigh, perforce had to assume that the civil tone of it was assumed, and indeed, that its civility bordered upon sarcasm. "In fact, I must insist upon it. If your muscles cramp, let me know, and I'll loosen them for you—with *this*."

In the faint flickerlight of the single small oil cruse (almost at once set down), Corydon was able to observe that his unsought visitor was a man with large arms and a sword ("... this.") to match. Corydon did not move.

Behind, coming up the steps, was a slower footfall. The large man moved slowly to one side, not taking his eyes off Corydon at all. The newcomer was gant and stooped and covered with a cloak of rusty black, such—so one hears—as they wear in Berretinia, the Tin-bearing Islands off the coast of a far-off and northern sea. His head was bald and his chin- and cheek-flesh drooped: so that, withal, and the way he held his arms akimbo under his cloak, he looked like some bird of prey. "Where is it, then?" asked this one.

Corydon said no word. And waited. But the telltale head, for once, was still.

"Where is it, then?" asked Skinnybird again.

Corydon said, at length—Large-arms showing some small

signs of impatience, and not wishing that they should wax great—"I must advise you, sir, that I have neither jewels nor gold: and as for the few pieces of silver in my pouch, why, surely they are not worth your risking the wrath of the suffets over your taking them aforce."

"Taçhá!" said Skinnybird. "I care nought for your few pieces of silver. And much would the suffets care. However, much *would* the suffets care were they to know that you have purloined away the head of Shemesh the Eshurian."

And he cleared his throat and looked upon Corydon with dismal glance.

Corydon thought it best to address himself to this point. "I should advise your honor," he said, "that the said head I carried away with the sufference and assent of the holy priests who serve in the holy Adyt."

This defense in no way served to modify the desire of Skinnybird, who burst out, "Why think you the head was *there*, wittold fool? He wagered it. He lost. It was left there as a pledge. It was hypothecated unto me for a hundred measures of gold of imperial assay, and I therein did deposit it for safekeeping."

Corydon sighed a great sigh. "Well, master," he replied, "an hundred measures of gold of imperial assay was the reward and return the aforesaid Shemesh the Eshurian did promise unto me for returning unto him his head. And it beseems me now that he has been less than open and aboveboard with all of us, and therefore I would propose that we engage in a solemn league and covenant against him and—"

The proposal, however, was never completed, for Skinnybird had made a gesture with his raptorial hand: see now at once how Large-arms slashed his sword upon the corded box chest so that its cords fell severed, the sword at once returning to the ready, and the large one's large and reddened eyes returning to Corydon, on whom he was certainly determined to keep both watch and ward.

"Is it in here? I think it is in here. Shall we see if it is in here?" And Skinnybird did, with these muttered words as accompaniment, lift up the lid and stoop even farther, so as to look inside.

The head leaped forward and buried its teeth in the stooped man's throat. Large-arms gave a croak of alarm, and starting forward, stumbled and fell over the empty chest which had in the same moment dropped to the floor. Corydon dashed the lamp from its shelf, grabbed for his pack and his sword, and dashed down the steps, two and three at a time, not pausing even though he could plainly feel that someone was seizing hold of the hem of his tunic—doubtless with an intention to slow him down.

In the tiny courtyard Corydon, pausing a moment in the light of a small and guttering cresset in order to obtain a firmer grip on his gear; and simultaneously looking around to see who was holding onto the hem of his tunic, Corydon heard the plaintive voice of Skinnybird lamenting, "Mandar, thy great sword hath been the death of me"; and of Mandar (as, now that it was ceasing to be of matter, it appeared Large-arms was called) as he grunted, "Thou hast paid me, Master, by that deadly daggerstroke." If it was not that in the darkness and confusion each had slain the other, then what was it?

Corydon looked wildly all about—no one held him—and then, as he gazed neither right nor left nor fore nor aft but up and then down, he saw that clinging by its teeth to the hem of his garment was nought else but the head of Shemesh the Eshurian.

Corydon attempted in vain to disengage it. He then with one hand took his knife and cut loose the border cloth as he held the head by its hair with the other. He lifted it to the level of his eyes and said, "Thing, dost thou wot well the troubles thou are causing and hast already caused me?"

The head did not so much spit out the bit of cloth as allow it to drop from between its teeth. Its lids fluttered and its lips moved. Then, in a voice not above a whisper, it said, "Hey. Pssst. Help. Get me out of here."

Corydon replaced the knife, took up his sash, and bound the head with it so that the jaw could not open. Then he dumped the contents of his wallet or pack onto the dry spot in the courtyard, stuffed the head into the place thus made, stuffed his extra clothes back in and around, and tied it shut with a few more knots than usual. And so with his baggage under his arms, he went forth.

Two slutty lamps marked the premises of a late-staying merchant who, eyes as sharp as eyes in the Cartha Cabira needs must be, raised head and hands and asked, "Young master, pause a bit and tell me: How may I serve with thee, and with what items?"

Said Corydon: "With a new sash. And with tidings of a place for the night."

• • •

Walking along the western foreshore, Corydon saw an elder man, evidently no more than taking, as it were, the air: and after a moment during which he mused lightly that the man's face looked not unfamiliar, his eyes met the elder's. Who gave him a bow of light civility. Recognition came to both at the same time. Corydon performed a pro forma genuflection—that is, he did not indeed bow, but he slightly bowed his knees and spread forth his hands palms down, as though he were about to. As he did not indeed prostrate himself, the elder one could scarcely have raised him to his feet, but instead placed both his hands palms up and elevated them an inch or two.

"Tis more easy to find one's way hence and thence than in regard to a certain place where last we met," the priest observed. And it was that same priest who had commented, *Ah you have found.*

"Ah, mine uncle, indeed how true!"

"Shall you be long tarrying here? For if I am not in error, you be no resident."

"Indeed, mine uncle, how true. Ah, who knows? The future lies hidden behind the Mother's mantle ('the veil of Isis,' as others put it)."

"Ah, my nephew! How true indeed."

And after such polite patter, they gazed keenly at one another. Corydon realized that from this one he had nought to fear, and never had. So he made bold—he made very, very bold—and he said, "You do not feel vexed at all at having seen me in a certain place where you had seen me, then, mine uncle?"

"Not the slightest least. It were no concern of ours, we priests of the evening watch."

"Nor taken any objection to my having thence removed an object which need not be named?"

"Not the slightest least. It were no concern of ours, we priests of the evening watch."

And, both times, the priest had placed a certain small emphasis upon the word *ours*. Corydon caught this up. "Whose concern, then, might it be?"

"'Whose?' Ah, why, to be sure, of the priests of the morning watch."

A breeze came from off the waters and passed between the tamarisks and terebinths, mingled a moment with the roses and the lilies in the gardens opposite, returned to whence they came. But it was not the breezes that slightly lifted the short hairs upon Corydon's nape.

"Might they have resented me and my mission?"

The priest said but the one word, *"Might?"*

"And," and here Corydon swallowed, "and might they have, ah, taken steps?"

The elder sacerdoth informed him that such steps as might have been taken by the priests of the morning watch would have included following him in stealth whithersoever he would wander, until such time ("Be it by seven years sundered from now") as they would find him solitary, and alone. And further he said, then, not.

Corydon swallowed once again. "And would then . . . then . . . have done me a mischief?"

The elder priest gazed on him with some bemusement. "'A mischief . . .' And, O my nephew, would you call Deucalion's Flood 'a moisture'?"

"Why, then, it seems to me," Corydon cried, "that Shemesh the Eshurian hath been less than forthright in dealing with me to re-obtain for him his head; forasmuch he told me nought of such a peril. And, if fact," Corydon added, "it wonders me sore, if indeed," here his brow lowered, "he fully intended to pay me for my toils that hundred measures of gold of the imperial assay as promised me."

"Well," said the venerable, "he hath never paid to anyone any sum he hath promised, yet."

They parted civilly. Corydon went his way full fill with thought. Of choices. Of chances. Of risks. It was a while before he glanced to sea; meanwhile a heavy mist had gan to settle and to roll. He started. And he stopped. Such fogs came seldom. And they seldom went off soon. A new thought—or one almost new—came sudden to Corydon's mind, so sudden that his head snapped up and back. He stood for a second, stick-stock-still. And then he quickened his steps.

The fogs did not lift soon. And when they did, the woman, Heramne, gave a low, brief cry. Corydon let his breath out, sharp. And took it in. Sharp. Astern stood an immense array of ships. The winds bore to his and her ears the shout that rose as they were seen. At once signal flags went up from the main mast of what was clearly the suffet admiral's vessel. Drums began to beat their *tump-tump, tump-tump, tump-a-tump, tump*. Horns blared.

Thus: at once.

Almost at once, the ships began to spread out—at first like a triangle. Then like a fan. The right and left became wings. Then horns.

The advance was incredibly swift. Almost it might have been beautiful to see the complete coordination of every vessel and how each fitted into place and formation, to see the water sparkling as it fell from the oars.

Almost. For another moment Corydon watched, listened, fascinated: doomed. The fighting men were chanting something he could not make out, but he made out how they beat the flats of their swords and the hafts of their spears upon their burnished shields. Bows? Bowmen? Arrows? No, he saw none, in a flash realized that none would be used. It was not any intention that he and she should be killed.

Yet.

Something, he saw, being tossed abroad to spread out its folds. His stomach lurched as he realized that it was a net. She: one fish. He: another. (And how fish-silvery-pale her body had gleamed for him, only that morning. Only that moment.)

What he did next, he did not even remember doing. He had evidently opened his pack and tossed the wrinkled clothes to right and left. In his hand was the head of Shemesh the Eshurian. He had ripped his sash apart and off from it, and as he tore, thus he spoke: "Listen, thee. We are all of us in peril. We shall never get thee back to thy body of desire. Thee must get us out of here. Dost thou hear? *Act!*"

The head had blinked, and as its lips were moving, it may have been whispering as well. The lips lay a second still, then the lips puckered. The lips issued a shrill whistle. And then another. And then—

From whence had come that sudden wind? Those black clouds? That towering sea? How swift had changed that clamoring, triumphing chant into a broken and a discordant howling alarm? In less than a winking of the eyes, Corydon saw the sails of the fleet torn into slatters and tossed into the ravening teeth of the onslaught gale. The drums tried to beat a different tune, the horns fell discordant, then silent; signal flags slapped down, others were slapping up when the oars were seen to beat vainly upon seas that, often as not, now oftener than not, were not there on one side when the oars came down, and twice and thrice as great upon another side, rising and swamping rowers and decksmen alike. The formation had shattered like a painting upon a plate of glass some hand or shock dashes to the ground. Here a ship was on its beams' ends, here a ship had turned and was attempting to flee with the storm at its back, here a crew desperately unstepped a mast or hauled in sail, and there—and there! and *there!*—ship crashed into ship and into ship. . . .

But where the tiny cockle craft of Corydon and Heramne stood, see: all was calm.

They lay in each other's arms, hearts beating a slow-descending violence as great and exhausting as that of recent and remembered loving. Almost they had been murdered, both, in a passion of which they had been for the most part merely witnesses. Sweat-drenched hair and spray-splashed hair mingled. Voices murmured faint, but spoke no word. And, abaft, the head of Shemesh the Eshurian canted, propped at an angle against the sheltering pack; the eyes for once did not wink and blink, but now and then the tip of a tongue peeped out from between the lips and licked a bit at the salt as the spray dried upon the otherwise sere flesh.

Some have said that the River of the Tarnavil, like one other river, is turbid with gold. And others say that it is merely turbid. Certainly its stain marked upon the sea its proximity a good ways off before its mouth was sighted. A pilot came aboard by and by; they had lit a fire fore and a fire aft as a signal for him.

"What news in port?" Corydon asked by and by.

The pilot shrugged for answer; the Tarnavi are reputed as spare of speech as though words cost money. After a while he said, "The same as always has been. Taxes are up and trade is down." And he took his hand from the tiller and scratched his hither armpit. After a longer while yet, he said, "Odd news from the hinterland."

Corydon waited till it were couth for him to say, "Oh?"

"Have you been to the Lakes and Fens . . .?"

"Yes . . ."

"Some strange story thereabouts . . ."

"Ah . . ."

"Of a man which haven't got no head . . ."

"Oh . . ."

"Well . . ."

"Yes . . .?"

"Never put no stock in such, myself . . . But. Een past yestereen. There come to port from upriver a chap in festal armor, as you might say. (Let out another reef, mate. Let her luff; she'll fill. See? There.) Whacking great helmet had he, burnished bright. Puts up at that inn. What's that inn called. The Bull? The Blue? Not for such poor folk as me. Ah. The Blue Bull. Calls for wine, drinks it alone in chamber. Calls for food, eats it alone in chamber. Calls for women *and* for wine."

They went up with the tide by the great channel. By now the pilot had warmed to his tale and devoted his attentions to his off armpit. . . . "Well, to make matters short, at midmorning up goes the governor of the Blue Bull, to see is he staying or is he not. Finds him *dead a-bed*. And what thinks you? For he had no head! Well! Now, a man might think, sure someone hacked it off, as to why, who could maybe say? But there was no blood, mate! No, not a drop! And as to his neck stump, why and here be the hard part, but mate, I seen of it myself: the neck stump was as you might say, all smoothed over. Just a hole for where would be his wizzen.

"The governor, as wants not, naturally, to give his place no bad name, goes a-stealth to seek for the woman as was spoke of, a respectable wench as had been in his service for a might say two-year. Finds her in her own bit room. On the floor in front of her, the helmet of which has been said and by me to you described. And her? She is setting and she is staring. And she is rocking back and she is rocking forth. And she is what shall I say, she is crooning to herself. The helmet? They taken it away. The woman? Still she sets, last I heard. And still she rocks and still she croons. But not word does she say. What? Mad? I should suppose *so*. Wouldn't you be? Eh? The body? Why, mate, twas two day past. Certain that it has been proper burned by now, with incense, oil, and libation wine, and priests a-chanting ditties, like. Ah. See that smoke over there? Well. I shouldn't wonder, but . . .

"No. I shouldn't wonder.

"Small boat basin to larboard. Ready with your line."

"Well," said Corydon with a wide-sweeping gesture, "here is the less than great city of the Tarnavi. What would you do?"

Heramne bethought herself of an answer. "As my very great dream has come true—that I might escape from the

Cartha Cabira, for I was hateswept when I said that dearest dream was to see that place burned—and even so, to have seen its fleet destroyed was well enough to quench most my hate: it will be a generation before that loss will be made up. But I ramble, do I not?"

He took the small hand she held out to him, and so doing, said, "Ramble on."

She put her other hand to her face. After a moment more, said she, "I spoke of my daytime dreams. In my nighttime dreams often have I seen my own small city as though still alive and fair, not as it was when they attacked and took it but as it would be today: yet this is but a dream of a dream. What would I? Well. Thou hast asked. I would go to my own city's twin. By some strategem or payment immense, I know not which or if both, that one escaped engagement; and still it stands, so have I heard. There have I kin. And there I would go. Thou didst ask, What would you?"

He nodded, but he nodded slow. He would have gratified her wish and he would have told her so. But then next he would have to tell her—

At this moment up came someone leading two horses, laden with gear and store. The man looked familiar, in a moment Corydon recognized him as the pilotman. Who now said, "Mate, I would save thy life! A few several forestlopers have been seen lurking roundabout, and have been heard to say that they saw you from the shore as we came in, and that they have some while held grudge and threat against you and will carry out some device of vengeance under nightcover."

Corydon exclaimed, half drew his sword, let it fall back; looked here and looked there. To meet any of these, of whom he had long thought not of, in fair fight: he nothing feared this. But to fend off several under nightcover, with who knew what hireling crew at their back and beck . . . moreover, there was Heramne.

"Governance here be not as twas, tis slack, tis slack," the pilot moaned. "Else I would have tooken the report to the magnates and magistrates. Oh, how it would ruin me in reputation, were folks to tell, 'Ah, he brought in a boat and afore but a night or two, and what befell the twain aboard?' So. Thus is what I plans and offers. Take these two horse, and what food they has aboard of them is enow for several days. Take the southern gate and southern road as leads away to the plains and thence to the mountings—and in return and for my service and my pains, give me the little boat."

Corydon hesitated. Corydon held out his hand. "Adone," said he. A bargain perhaps not of the best, it was. But he had wanted an answer. And here one was.

"Adone," said he.

Vast and of unmeasurable extent, the plains before the mountains. In the yellow dusk see two of two legs upon two of four. They ride slowly. But they ride side by side. Sometimes they lean close and sigh. And sometimes they throw back their heads, and across the wide grassland their laughter rolls into the wider sky. "He thinks," says Corydon, "that, sure, I have treasure aboard. He has smelled the smell of confusion. He has put two and two together and gotten five and one-half. He has afrighted me off, he is sure, and the treasure left behind: I see all his thinking, now, though slow I was to see it then. Well! And what will he do, under nightcover? He will rip off the doorlet to the cubbyhold in the after part, for he espied it was nailed shut: most unusual. I can see him now. And having done it, he will pause a bit. And then he will hear something.

"And what will he hear?" Corydon asks. Again he reaches and takes her hand. And both of them together repeat the words: *"Hey. Pssst. Get me out of here. Help . . ."*

Vast the yellow sky at dusk time, and vast and free the wide-rolling plains beneath.

THE LION OF ELIRHOM'S ANGER

Michael Nicholas Richard

Michael Nicholas Richard, born 9 October 1955 in Saco, Maine, has lived the majority of his life in New Bern, North Carolina, and surrounding places. He says, "I am married to a patient woman named Sherri, who has put up with me for more than six years. I have a four-year-old daughter, Rhiannon, and an infant daughter, Maegen." Neat names.

When the poetically gorgeous tale of "The Lion of Elirhom's Anger" came to me, its author had but one previous short story sale under his belt, this to the little magazine **Space & Time** *published by Gordon Linzner, another heroic fantasy writer. So I barely missed making the singular discovery of a new and major talent all by myself (though, yes, the idea of editors "discovering" authors is ass-backwards). I cannot imagine that by the time* **Heroic Visions II** *is on the stands, Michael won't have sold a few more stories.*

I for one am very excited about the present tale and eager to see what its author produces in the future. Of the tale, Michael says, "The seed in my imagination which eventually became 'The Lion of Elirhom's Anger' was planted by Henri Rousseau's 'The Sleeping Gypsy.' Like anyone who has seen that painting, I wondered what in hell the lion was doing behind the sleeping man."

You're about to have Rousseau's visual riddle answered in a spectacular fashion.

TO BE FREE of the burning sand was good. Elirhom's dark face creased in a white smile, and his eyes glittered. The faint seawind was cool as it wove through his tunic and many-colored robes. Looking down upon the city, he was glad of the bustle that began in the bazaar and spilled along the tangled alleyways. He liked wealthy cities. Hefting the provision sack and pulling the straps to his lute over his back, he began the last stretch into the city.

The tidal marsh spread brown along the slender finger of seawater that cut through the desert. The jade waters failed at the point where the bones of the earth rose into bleached hills amidst the shifting sand. And there sat the city, with its awnings and market tents of bright colors set against the stark sand and hills.

No one paid him much heed, and seemed not to notice he had come drifting from the desert. All attention was drawn by three tall ships sailing along the inlet with early afternoon sun at their backs.

He decided against venturing too near the wharf because the pace was overly hectic for his trade. He opted instead for the shade of a wide silk awning, under which traded a very dour baker. The aroma of the waters drifted to Elirhom, and his eyes sparkled.

"I will play for you," he offered to the glum face beneath the sweat-stained turban. "People stop and listen, then smell your wares; then maybe they buy."

The baker looked over the cake-ladened board and sighed. "A full board means an empty purse. I have nothing with which to repay your services."

The accent was more difficult than Elirhom had expected, but he understood. From his sack he pulled a sandglass and turned it so the grains flowed into the empty globe. "If no one takes of your wares before the sand has emptied, then I gain nothing. If they do, then you give to me two cakes for each time the glass is turned."

The man's eyes narrowed into slits. It was a fair offer. Too fair to go without suspicion in the bazaar. The baker had the look of a man used to being cheated, and of cheating. Slowly he nodded.

Elirhom sat tailor fashion; his dark fingers strummed the lute to check the tune. He smiled to himself—this lute was always tuned. He began to play. It was a quick tune, darting like swift-winged desert birds. People heard, and slowly they began to find their way nearer the baker's awning.

Now he let the strings slow, and the music began to meander. This was a soft music. To this they would listen, thinking of the gentle moments in their lives. And the scent of the cakes would weave its own spell.

When the bottom globe was half full, Elirhom paused in his playing. Some of the people smiled, a few complimented his talents . . . and a good many laid ivory and copper coin on the baker's board in return for the aromatic cakes. Elirhom smiled and began to play again.

The upper globe was empty for the third time. Six cakes—he needed no more. The face beneath the turban was smiling now, for half his wares were gone. So was half the empty space in his coin sack. He looked up as Elirhom slung the lute over his shoulders.

"I am pleased that my music did well for you," he told the man. "Six cakes, however, is all I need."

"And half of what you'll get," snapped the baker, still smiling, but with glowering eyes.

"This is not as you agreed," replied Elirhom quietly. The baker, still smiling, took three cakes from the board and wrapped them in palm leaves. This bundle he thrust into Elirhom's hands.

"Get from here, desert scum. The guardsmen think unkindly of those who drift over the burning sands."

Elirhom looked for a moment at the cakes in his hands, even as the truth in the man's words settled upon him. He turned from the shade of the awning and stepped into the midafternoon heat.

He looked around the bazaar until his gaze fell on an old woman sitting beside a board of wineskins and earthenware flagons. She sat beneath a canopy which stood apart from any building. Most likely she, too, was a stranger—at least to this part of the city.

When he moved into the long cool shadow of the canopy,

Elirhom could see the old woman must be from the squalid desert end of the city. She wore no veil, and covered her head with only a thin gossamer scarf. Her face was contorted with a gap-toothed smile—until the look in his eyes told her he was not a patron.

"You're a dark one, eh?" she observed, with a voice easily maintaining her cronish image. "What do you want?"

"For you, I play . . . " offered Elirhom, explaining the sandglass to her. ". . . I will take a skin of wine?"

She laughed. "Would you? A goatskin, nothing larger."

Like a crescent moon in the night sky, Elirhom's smile appeared. Sitting again, he turned the sandglass and took the lute into his hands. The catquick music ran into the heat of the afternoon. It brought to people's minds the white glare of the sun, but was intriguing all the same. Then it parched their mouths and brought their thoughts around to the wine mistress's wares.

He scooped the sandglass back into his sack and turned the lute onto his back. He stood smiling again, because the old woman was happy with her business. She had not even noticed when the music had faded. Sensing his gaze, she looked up and then pushed a small earthenware carafe across the board toward him.

"A wineskin," Elirhom reminded her. "You agreed to one—an earthenware vessel is difficult to travel with."

"It holds nearly as much wine as a skin," replied the crone. "You cannot expect a goatskin for only a bit of music? Do you know how much ivory I must give for each goatskin?"

Elirhom was about to insist, when he followed her gaze across the square—to a red-turbaned guardsman. The musician's dark hand closed around the clay vessel, and he left the canopy of the wine mistress. It was confusing. Why were these merchants so niggardly? Almost it seemed to him that he espied a perverse contentment in their eyes as they cheated.

He wandered along the square, determined to exercise more caution in his next selection. A row of small, but neatly kept stalls seemed promising. Before he could reach them, however, he sensed a presence at his back. He turned to see two large, smirking men close behind him. Both men were dressed in torn and filthy robes. The seeming leader of the two wore a burnous, which draped over his shoulders and kept the hot sun off his neck. The second was bareheaded, and his face was framed by bushy unkempt hair and beard.

"Ow, this one's been burnt nearly black," chuckled the burnous wearer, nudging the other. With their long curving noses and sharp eyes, they looked like towering birds of prey. Each stood nearly a head taller than Elirhom, and moved menacingly.

"What do you have in the sack, desert man?" asked the bearded one.

Watching the two men, Elirhom laid the carafe and lute to one side. He held the sack open. "I will show you—"

The bearded one grabbed suddenly at the sack, and Elirhom felt the burnous wearer's hands on his arm. Although short and round-shouldered, Elirhom was gifted with powerful limbs. He shrugged off the grasping hands and jerked at the sack. The fabric was rent halfway down. His bedmat and a single copper coin dropped to the sand.

Elirhom slid his foot over the coin, but the bearded man's sandled foot ground down upon his. Elirhom shouted and struck out, but no one was there. The echoes of running feet reached past the pain ringing in his ears.

He looked up into a lean, stern face beneath a red turban. One hand rested on the pommel of a scimitar as the guardsman looked down upon the shorter man.

"What trouble are you rousing. You cannot come drifting into this realm like desert dust, irritating the merchants."

Elirhom shook his head. "Those two men attempted to . . . they took my provision sack."

"This is no place for you. It would be best for you to go back into the burning sands," said the guardsman.

Elirhom retrieved his lute and carafe. He lifted the coin and the bedmat from the sand—all this under the threatening eye of the guardsman. He then turned north, limping toward the seaward edge of the city.

The sun had settled on the horizon, the red glowing center of a tumult of rose, violet, and deep azure. The long shadows hastened the dark into the narrow streets. As the light was dimmed, the people began leaving the bazaar. Only a few stragglers passed by the dejected Elirhom.

Then he saw them. They glowed in the twilight air like stars brought to earth. A very tall man with white-streaked hair and beard stood near them. His robes of midnight blue were embroidered with hieroglyphic symbols.

A wizard, with arms folded, and weary eyes on Elirhom.

Each of the lights were the size of melons, and they drifted lazily around the gaunt form, but never ventured far. The dour gaze came to rest on the copper coin in Elirhom's fingers.

"For a copper you can take with you the light of the morning star," offered the wizard. With a slight motion of his hand, he caused one of the lights to drift near Elirhom.

The musician rubbed the edge of the coin with his forefinger. Twice cheated . . . the third time would be a charm, or the end of it. He laid the coin in the wizard's upturned palm.

Bony fingers closed over the copper, and the hand disappeared beneath the long robes. When the hand reemerged, the coin was gone, and the wizard pointed to the light. "It will follow you. It is yours."

And as Elirhom limped away, the light drifted along. He smiled as he watched its glowing form, even if he didn't know what he would do with a bit of the morning star. It followed him as he looked about for something to use as a walking stick. It followed him as he leaned slightly on the darkwood cane and left the city behind.

Along the edge of the tidal marsh he wandered. He was intrigued by the green waters glittering under a full moon. Yet as he moved away from the city, the wizard-light began to drift away, seeming attracted to the marsh.

Elirhom went to the softly glowing form, and it drifted even farther over the brown grass. Then his teeth shone in a moonlit smile. He should have known, and he waved his hand, as if to dismiss the luminescence.

"Your binding, I release," he said quietly. The light drifted low along the marsh. He glimpsed through the night haze the presence of other lights. They bobbed and drifted elusively, until he could no longer distinguish which had been his own.

Elirhom looked back toward the now distant city. He should have known better; light of the morning star, indeed. They were nothing more than unfortunate will-o'-wisps, enslaved by the charlatan wizard. What darkness lay secretly in the heart of a place so vulgar?

He came finally to a place where the sand and hills rolled up to the green water's edge. His hands unrolled the many-colored bedmat, and he sat upon it. The hills glowed beneath the moonlight, and the night had grown still. He pulled his lute into his hands, and he began to play.

His anger was in the cold edge of the music. It wove along the desert, drawing forth the burning gold strength. He watched it glittering beneath its own vague shadow-form—and he smiled. The music was allowed to fade.

The lute was set to one side as he lay down upon the mat and closed his eyes. The arms of dream awaited, and he slipped easily into their hold. He dreamed of his youth, of the most undeniably strong and fearsome thing he remembered. He dreamed of their tawny forms moving over the veldt. Even in his sleep his breath was stilled by the fear. But he watched them, absorbed their powerful though languid movements. One great head turned toward him in a golden swirl. The yellow-green eyes locked on his.

Elirhom had found what he sought. Nowhere in his mind could he dredge a more ferocious strength and cold courage. The shadow-strength of his music took form, all tawny gold with bright glaring eyes. It was through those eyes that Elirhom saw the world. It was with those eyes that his gaze went once again to the city.

The lion stood in an alley that cut down beside the baker's stall. Desert winds had swirled refuse into the twisted paths. Three ovens stood like clay beehives before a squalid mud-brick cottage. It appeared the ovens had been carefully built, but now showed the results of long neglect.

The ragged curtain across the outer door parted as the lion slipped into the interior of the dwelling. The darkness offered little hindrance to his eyes. Scanning the clutter of utensils and baking boards, the lion espied the baker, lying with his wife on a bedmat. The man was still clutching his coin sack with one hand, while the other rested beneath his cheek.

There was a shuffle from the opposite corner. The shaggy head turned to see one of three children sitting upright on a bedmat. It was a boy of no more than ten years. The lion saw itself reflected in the child's round dark eyes.

The moment hung in silence. Then the cat turned and slipped back through the curtain. The boy blinked once, as though waking from a dream, before lying back on the bed-mat.

The lion of Elirhom's anger moved with arrogance along the narrow ways of the city. Across the great deserted bazaar it walked. The tufted tail twitched, and the yellow-green eyes shone in the moonlight.

The red-turbaned guardsman slunk back into the shadows, drawing the wicked scimitar. But his moment of courage melted beneath the glare of the lion's eyes. Carefully, not daring to look away from the beast of dreams, the guardsman backed from the square.

Finally the man began to run. The sound of his sandals echoed in the night. Foolish with fear, he let go the scimitar and it clattered upon the stones. But the lion paid no heed. It moved away from the bazaar, wanting not the petty, fearful tendrils of the shadow—the lion would seek the shadow's heart.

In its darkness the city was uneasy. Wretched dreams made a tempest of sleep, and the cry of a woman or child would ofttimes drive like a shaft through the heart of the night. The scent of fear was borne on the night air. The sweat of fear dampened the brows of once brave men. And the golden dream of anger followed the shadows back toward their source.

The lion was now in that edge of the city that sprawled into the desert. The crumbling mud-brick houses gave way to tattered tents of hide and cloth. A dog began to bark, until it realized just what it was challenging.

Finally there stood a small cloth tent with a rack of wine vessels beside it. The old woman was sitting with her back against the earthenware flagons. Her chin was resting upon her chest as she slept, and a hardwood stave was in one hand. The glare of the great cat's eyes drove past the hold of sleep, and the crone stirred.

The woman's eyes widened at the vision before her, and she struggled to her feet. The stave was held defensively as she backed against the wine vessels.

"Get away from here," she hissed, with eyes tormented by the fear that some harm might come to her wares. It was a greedy courage that tightened her hands around the stave. And that same greed devoured her from within, until it alone burned with depraved fervor in her gaze. The darkness upon the spirit of this city had left nothing save a skeleton of her own soul.

It was with pity that the golden form turned into the shadows, leaving the wretched woman to defend that which would ultimately destroy her. In his sleep Elirhom directed it onward, seeking the fountain of the malevolent darkness, seeking the evil that devoured this city from within.

Following the scent of this evil, the lion passed the homes

of the wealthy merchants. The air was tense and suspicious, as the houses seemed to draw back from one another. Without the sun to shimmer upon their gilded facades, these structures seemed more like monuments to the dead than homes of the living. And the decay was not absent here, only hidden away, like a corpse arrayed with jewels.

Burning like the desert heat, the lion stood before the open gate of an estate somewhat beyond the city's reach. The garden was made barren by sand drifting over the roots of dead fig trees. Even the huge ebony door of the dwelling hung crookedly from its hinges. Into the shadows beyond, the lion disappeared.

It was Elirhom's eyes which saw the gaunt form in robes of midnight blue. Within the lonely dark of the great room, the charlaton wizard sat rigid. The gaze was locked into the depths of the darkness, so mesmerized that even the appearance of the lion could not draw them from it. So the lion's yellow-green eyes followed the gaze into the deepest shadow.

Beside the glittering waters the sleeping Elirhom grimaced. The glare of the lion's eyes pierced the shadowy cloak shrouding the bloated presence. Elirhom knew it: Ahl-ghul the devourer—he who is Lord of Avarice; djinn, god, and demon. He who sent the sirocco and whirling dustdevils to torment the lives of men.

The lion moved nearer the deep shadows. He sensed stale magicks hanging like cobwebs upon the tendrils of the demon's power. Once the wizard's magic had been more than illusion. Then he had stretched for more than he could hold, calling forth that which was beyond him. Now Ahl-ghul was the master.

The lion snarled and stepped into the deepest shadow, even to the feet of the djinn. Ahl-ghul glared at the beast, enraged by this challenge. The ruse was cast off and the shadows faded. As a fearsome and repugnant warrior the manifestation rose—eyes red with flame.

"This dream shall I devour," rolled the words, though the mouth had barely moved. A single ponderous step was taken, the shadow arms lifting.

The lion moved like the desert wind, sweeping past the wizard, who cringed now in the grasp of fear. The dark hands of Ahl-ghul reached for the streaking golden form, but were not nearly swift enough. Elirhom could feel the collision. He could feel the lion's claws—his claws—sink into the demon flesh. He tasted the blood as the dark neck was held in the lion's powerful jaws.

Ahl-ghul pulled the lion to itself, trying to crush the dream in the demonic grasp. But Elirhom's music had forged the strength of the earth's bones into the flesh of this beast. And into its spirit had been woven the fierceness of the summer sun. The tawny mane flowed as the lion tore the courage from the demon throat.

Anger and fear whelmed the dark soul of the demon. The flesh that bound its essence had never known pain. The hands sought desperately to cast off this clinging lion. Now did the demon fear for its very existence. It let go the warrior guise, becoming only vague shadowed flesh—seeking to be free of the lion's wrath. It struggled toward that dark hole in the wall of the world from which it had been summoned. But it would not be free of the flesh so long as it was held in the lion's grasp.

The earth trembled beneath their struggle. The walls of the room buckled and began to crumble. The wizard was released as the demon called all its power to itself. The man ran shrieking from the ruin of his home. And still the battle rumbled in the midst of the great cloud of dust and shadow.

There was another dark place awaiting the demon; a place it feared. But realizing it could not win free of the lion, Ahl-ghul manifested itself around the beast—determined to drag the lion with it in that long fall into the abyss. A perverse contentment lit the red eyes as it flung itself into the ultimate darkness.

Then those eyes widened in disbelief. With a long wailing shriek it fell, and it fell alone.

Elirhom's eyes opened. He had released the dream, but the tawny gold image danced before his gaze for a few moments more. He sat up, clearing his head with a deep breath of the cool sea air. He smiled.

The dream had not been Ahl-ghul's to hold, and it had faded from the demon's grasp even as Elirhom had released it from his own. The shadows lingered still, crouching in the corners of his mind. Again he breathed of the sea air, and reached for the lute.

The dark hands lifted the instrument as his eyes turned

toward the distant city. The healing of those wounds would be long, and that would be the task of another. With their greed the city had drawn the demon down upon itself, but could not have really deserved such a fate. Free now of the demon, perhaps they would deal fairly with strangers.

And Elirhom began to play a tune upon the lute—washing away the anger, and the last of the lingering shadows.

EAMMON'S BANSHEE

Gillian FitzGerald

A lot is said of this decade's influx of women to the adult fantasy industry (women always dominated juvenile fantasy), but what is rarely admitted is that almost all of it is drivel, as bad as the "adult" fantasy guys have written—shier of sadism perhaps, and gushing with a kind of romance previously relegated to the bodice-rippers, but no improvement as art. Now and then real genius pokes out of the morass, and Gillian FitzGerald, at the beginning of a promising writing career, is clearly among the brilliant exceptions.

Her first works have appeared in the award-winning anthology series **Elsewhere** *(a story reprinted in* **Year's Best Fantasy**), **The Magazine of Fantasy and Science Fiction,** *and* **Amazons II.** *She has been working for some while on an ambitious Irish novel about Silken Thomas, that I imagine will establish a reputation, if she'd only get it finished.*

Born 1949 in Connecticut of good Gaelic stock, she says, "I learned storytelling from my grandparents, who made up tales to keep me amused as a child. I learned of strong Irish women from that same grandmother, Anne O'Leary Connelly, who sprang straight from Juno and the Paycock *and all those wonderful O'Casey matriarchs." She has worked as a librar-*

ian, and presently teaches English in Florida. She's also involved with the Society of Creative Anachronists, whose slogan is "We wouldn't've been the serfs," har har, and she intends one day to be known as a "SCAdian" fighter, rather than just a warrior's lady.

She lives presently in the repugnantly named Niceville. Could I have invented that? Cross my heart it's true!

The following tale is further evidence that good fantasy is not merely escapist literature. Here is an especially poignant heroic vision.

THE BOYS FROM SOUTH ARMAGH were the only brigade in the Provisional IRA ever to number a banshee among its members, and at first the volunteers didn't know how to take the presence of a raven-haired woman in a white robe who showed a disconcerting tendency to appear out of nowhere. She was the stuff of legends, and they weren't certain that legends had any place in the dead-serious war they were fighting, though the Brits refused to admit they were fighting a war.

The first time she showed up was in front of a lorry Patsy MacBride had commandeered from the local bakery. He and Eammon O'Neill and Sean Coogan and Mick Farrell had planned to leave it parked in the middle of the Newry Road, where the Brit convoy would be sure to pass and would be forced to stop. When they stopped, they'd find a warm reception waiting for them, four Provos with rifles at the ready. If they didn't get an even dozen between them, there was need of more target practice—and what better targets to practice on than HRM's troops? They were driving down the road, nice and easy, with Patsy singing "Sean South from Gary Owen" a bit off-key, when suddenly there was a rush of air, and right in front of the windshield, floating on the night wind, hung a woman all in white, with hair black as night streaming around her pale face. She was beautiful, and she shouldn't have been there at all, not at all. Patsy slammed on the brakes as the pale woman opened her lovely mouth and emitted an earpiercing shriek.

Patsy stopped his tuneless muttering and asked wonderingly, "Now what in t'hell is that?"

"If I didn't know better, I'd say it's a feckin' banshee," said Sean. "The bloody Brits are turnin' our own stories against us now."

"That's the final insult, it is," growled Patsy, switching off the ignition and staring in horrified fascination at the apparition. He was a large heavy set man who spoke little and moved slowly, but he was the finest shot in County Armagh. "Eammon, lad, will you have a look at this?"

Eammon O'Neill, the OC, had leaned forward over the seat of the lorry when the wailing had begun. Now his black brows drew together and his mobile mouth thinned into a look of concern. "That's not the Brits, but a real banshee—I ought to know, she's my banshee, and if she's wailing, it's for a good reason. I'll bet there's a Saracen full of soldiers just around the bend, sitting waiting for us. Best to abandon the lorry and take to our heels."

"Your banshee? Eammon, what kind of superstitious nonsense are you talking?" Mick turned to stare at his commander.

O'Neill just looked at him, his thin face intent. "She's been my banshee as long as I can remember, and my family's forever. She's real, Mick, as real as you or me. I'll tell you the whole story once we're safe away, but for now, just get moving, and that's an order." He spoke the soft, unhurried English of Belfast, but even the natural music of his voice could not disguise the unmistakable note of command.

Sean and Patsy obeyed, and Eammon scrambled out after them, followed by Mick. It was not a moment too soon, because the banshee had attracted the attention of the English, and no sooner did they find some cover than the Saracen lumbered down the road, followed by a land rover filled with soldiers.

Even with the advantage of cover, they really hadn't much hope, and Eammon knew it. They were outnumbered, and the Brits had better weapons. The best they could hope for was to pick off a good number before they were taken, to go down fighting. Quietly, he gave his men their orders: take out as many as you can, then run for it, get away if possible.

It was a terrible night, that was, four young men, the oldest of them twenty-three, and nearly a score of English soldiers pouring over the fields in search of them. There was a constant barrage of gunfire, and it was not always possible to tell who was firing at whom. Out of nowhere came a heartrending cry, and the banshee appeared, floating in the blackness, her white robes ghostly in the moonlight. There was a startled yelp as the Brits caught sight of her right overhead, and Eammon fired rapidly in the direction of the sound, and saw two of them crumple. And that was the way the rest of the fight went. The banshee would vanish and appear, the Provos would fire at the spot beneath her, and another soldier or two would fall, until at last the officer in charge came to his senses and called a retreat. Four Provos were alive; less than half a dozen soldiers made it to the safety of the Saracen. They left the land rover behind, and Eammon appropriated it.

"Commandeering an official vehicle?" grinned Patsy.

"I'd call it a donation, wouldn't you?" He saw the banshee floating to the left of him, and smiled up at her. "Thank you, lady, you've done Ireland a good night's work."

When they were finally safe, Patsy kept at him until he told them about the banshee.

"There's not much to tell, really," he began. "I've seen her since I was a boy. I think the first time was when my uncle Willy died in the Border Campaign."

He grew up in the Short Strand, a Catholic enclave on the east bank of the River Lagan, surrounded on three sides by Unionist neighborhoods. He grew up with the sound of the Orangemen's Lambeg drums and his father's soft curses. His father was a carpenter, the only man in his neighborhood with a job; everyone else was on the dole. When Eammon was eight his father was killed in a fall, and Eammon and his mother went to live with Uncle Willy, a shopkeeper in Armagh.

Then came the stirrings of old discontent, and Willy, an old republican, rejoined the IRA.

The night that Willy was shot in a raid, Eammon was nine, still young enough to believe in ghosts and fairies and banshees, and he was afraid when he heard the terrible weeping outside the window. Since his room was on the third floor, he knew this was something out of the ordinary, and he flew to the window. He saw a beautiful lady in a long white dress, her long black hair flowing in the wind, and she was just hanging there, wringing her hands and wailing.

He dragged his mother over to see, and at that moment the lady began to keen, awful sounds that pierced the heart with their sadness.

His mother crossed herself and said, "It must be Willy.

He's the last man in the family except for you, and you're safe and well. Poor Ellen, what will she do with Willy gone? I remember she wailed like that when your father was killed . . ."

"Is she a banshee?" he asked. "Ma, is she?"

She told him yes, it was the banshee of the O'Neills, and he regarded the lady with renewed interest. He was still small enough that a banshee took precedence over his uncle's well-being, and he had not yet realized that his uncle was truly dead; besides, the banshee was outside the window, tearing the night with her keening. So he listened with great fascination as his mother told him the story of the family banshee for the first time.

Once, in the days when the Sidhe still walked the earth openly, there lived a woman of the Sidhe called Niamh the Sweet-voiced, for she had the most beautiful voice in all the kingdom of Ireland. She was as lovely as her voice, tall and white-skinned and black-haired, with eyes the color of summer skies and a mouth as red as rowan berries, but she was proud and cold of heart, caring for nothing but her music. Many lords of the Sidhe courted her, but none of them could win her. She treated them all with equal disinterest, even Cairbre, who was brother to Finvarra himself, the king of the Sidhe. Still, for all her cold heart, she might be singing in the raths right now if she had not shown some favor to a young harper, a mortal man camed Connla, of the family that would one day become this branch of the O'Neills. He was a gentle man, with a great talent for harping; not handsome, but pleasant of face, dark of eye and hair. He had no dream of winning Niamh's love, and asked nothing of her but the chance to sit near her and play for her as she sang, and this favor she granted willingly for the pleasure his music gave her.

To Cairbre, that fiery lord, this was the final insult. It had been hard enough to bear the fact that Niamh ignored him like all the others, telling him firmly to leave her in peace and bother her no more with talk of love, but to have a mortal permitted where he was forbidden to come was intolerable. As she sat singing with Connla one golden afternoon, his black eyes following her every move, Cairbre rode headlong into the clearing and challenged Connla to combat. The young man refused with grave politeness, pointing out that he was a musician, not a warrior, and that he had no quarrel with Cairbre in any case. This seemed to send Cairbre mad with anger, and he rode at Connla, hurled his spear, and it pierced the young harper to the heart. He died at Niamh's feet, his red blood staining her dress crimson. She rose without a word, went to Finvarra, and made her complaint to him.

Finvarra, golden-crowned upon his great throne, looked down upon his brother and gave judgment. "You make no denial of this crime, and for this reason you are banished from all the haunts of the Sidhe for two hundred years. Go forth from us, and do not return until I summon you." Cairbre bowed and left them. Finvarra watched his brother go, then turned cold eyes upon Niamh. "And what of your part in this, lady? Did you do nothing to stop my brother?"

"What could I have done to stay his hand? I am no warrior."

"My brother acted out of madness born of his love for you. A word from you would have been enough."

"I did not make your brother love me, or the harper either. I had no wish for their love. Many are the times I have sent Cairbre from me, but always he returned. I gave him no encouragement or false promises. I have done nothing wrong," she said calmly, lifting confident blue eyes to the king.

"You have nothing, and for that reason you are more guilty than my brother. I lay the harper's death at your feet. You care for nothing but your music, and though your voice is sweet, your song is as empty as your heart. You will sing no more until you understand love and grief in your own spirit. You will become the banshee of this harper's family, you will forecast the death of every man in the family, and the only sound you will utter is a wail, until the grief of the women of the line becomes your own. Until then you will wander the earth over, and be banished from the raths."

Niamh was too proud to protest, so she accepted her sentence mutely, her head held high. She spoke not a word, even when Finvarra ordered her to go with the procession that would bring Connla's body home to his parents. She walked silently behind the bier, and it all seemed a nightmare, for certainly this could not be happening to her; not to Niamh the Sweet-voiced, whose singing was the wonder of all Ireland?

When they reached the rath of his family, Cairbre banged at the gates and asked for the father of Connla the harper. A vigorous man of middle years, gray-haired but strong, came to the gate, a tall, still beautiful woman at his side.

"I am the father of Connla the harper. What do you want of me?"

"We bring you the body of your son, slain by my hand this day. For his death I am condemned to exile for two hundred years, at the order of Finvarra, king of the Sidhe."

"A light punishment, I fear, for two hundred years seems but a week to you who are ever-living. Why did you slay my son, who never did any man harm?" asked the woman, raising wise dark eyes to Cairbre's face.

"Oh, mother of Connla, I swear to you that he did no harm to me, but I was maddened for the love of this woman, Niamh."

Niamh came forward. She stared straight into the woman's eyes, and would not lower her gaze. She was not ashamed. She had done nothing, nothing, and Finvarra had condemned her wrongly.

She opened her mouth to make a calm denial, for what was Cairbre to she who could move him, but when she tried to speak, no words came forth, only a heart breaking, terrible wail, like the keening of women at a funeral. Then she knew that Finvarra's curse had borne bitter fruit, and she was indeed exiled from the raths forever, and condemned to watch the men of Connla's line die until the sorrow of their women became her own. But it never would, she vowed, and her keening turned into a horrible laughter, resounding with an awful joy, for the death of one more would only be the death of another enemy, for surely those who had brought her to such a fate were her enemies. . . .

"But she doesn't laugh now," said Patsy. "Not tonight, anyway, she didn't laugh."

"She's not laughed for centuries, the story goes. I think no one could watch so many deaths and so much grief and still laugh. Her keening's the saddest sound I ever hear. I'd like to make a song that would catch it, but my music's not good enough for that. Perhaps no man's could be." He lit his cigarette and puffed musingly, then smiled wryly. "So that's my banshee. What do you think of her?"

"If she gives us that kind of help, she's more good than most men," said Patsy.

"A banshee in the Provos . . . God help us if the stickies hear about it; they'll accuse us of enlisting ghosts next," said Sean.

There was more to the story that he could not tell them, for he did not know it himself. Oh, he knew that he had seen the banshee often from that first night. Her sad and lonely face, all the more beautiful for its sorrow, had haunted him, and he had discovered that he could see her even when there was no need for her presence. He only saw her out of the corner of his eye at first; then when he had worked up the courage to tell her that he was not afraid of her, that she was welcome, poor sad girl; then he saw her just looking silently at him out of those great blue eyes. They were ringed eyes, witch's eyes his mother called them, dark as midnight at the outside of the iris and shading to the silver gray of dawn around the pupil. He thought her eyes held all the sorrow of the world in them, and he worked hard to make her smile, but she never did.

What he could not know, for Niamh had no way of telling him, was what a wonder it seemed to her to be welcomed instead of cursed after all those centuries of loneliness. At first she had screamed a victory cry as another of her enemies went to his death, but she could not hold such hate in her heart for long, not when she saw how sorely they were missed by those who loved them. She went a little mad then, that she was condemned to such a terrible fate, and it did not help that all who looked upon her shrank from her in fear. For a woman who had known only love and admiration to be greeted with horror whenever she showed her face, was worse than death. Even the madness passed, at last, giving way to sorrow, and she began to share the sadness that men are born with. In all those long years only Eammon had looked upon her without fear, and so she was drawn to him, hovering about him protectively like a strange species of guardian angel.

When he left school to help out in the store, she hid away for a time, not wanting to force herself upon him, aware that what a lonely child might need might not be best for a young man. Still she could not keep herself away from him entirely, for he meant too much to her—the very center of her barren existence—and she would come to him when he was making music, singing and playing the guitar he had pinched pennies to buy. He would feel the caress of her presence like the brush of a lark's wing when he was singing in the village pubs, and he would smile and sing the better for the knowledge that she was listening.

The Troubles broke out again, but he went on with his life and tried not to think about it. He'd promised his mother to stay out of it, and he intended to keep that promise. Besides, there was a girl, Sheila Donnelly, and he hoped to marry her in a year or two. He watched as Patsy MacBride, his oldest friend, joined the newly formed Provisional IRA, while he and Sheila marched with the other civil rights supporters. But when he saw the film of Bloody Sunday and watched as thirteen unarmed people were murdered by the army, he wondered if Patsy wasn't right after all. A government that would shoot down its own people for no good reason could only be talked to at the point of a gun. So, like Patsy, he joined the Provos.

He told Sheila finally what he had done. She tried to talk him out of it, and when he would not be persuaded, she wanted to marry him then and there.

"You're going off to die for Ireland, the least you can do is make me your wife before you get yourself killed. Let me have that much, man," she told him.

But he held firm, kissed her one last time, and said goodbye. It felt as if he were cutting out his heart, and Niamh wept for him and for Sheila. Her soft sobs woke him.

"So you wanted me to marry her, did you, Niamh? Well, I wanted it too, but it's better this way for both of us. This way there'll be no one but my aunt to grieve for me if they get me, though I've no intention of dying if I can help it. The only woman in my life from now on will be you, girl, and that's that."

She stayed with him through all the fighting, but she never showed her face to anyone else till the night of the ambush, and then only because she could think of no other way to warn him of the danger. She had seen soldiers down the road, and she knew what it meant and did not want to lose Eammon. His life mattered to her, more than anything ever had except her music, and perhaps more than her singing once had. He was all she had, and she would not give him up easily, no, she would not. So with all her strength, and with all the memories of the long years alone, she screamed and saved them all.

From that night on she played a more active role, saving them on more than one occasion. One night Eammon and Patsy were picked up for questioning, and she appeared inside the police van and screamed right inside the ear of the driver, who ran into a parked car. Eammon launched himself at the door, kicked it open, and he and Patsy got clean away before the terrified driver could recover his wits. Another time she showed up while a loyalist squad were camping outside a pub waiting for Eammon so they could lob a bomb through the window. Her shriek made the bombers so nervous they dropped their bomb, which was made of old dynamite, and they blew themselves to kingdom come. The papers called it a car bomb and blamed it on the Provos.

Eammon was fast becoming a legend in republican circles. His daring exploits won him the esteem of his comrades, and having a banshee as a mascot did nothing to harm his growing reputation. His naturally merry disposition, quick to see the humor in a situation, helped to keep them going when it got tough, and he always kept a flute tucked away in his pocket to while away the long hours of waiting in safe houses. He seemed the complete hero, the perfect soldier. Only Niamh knew how much he hated the killing, how many nights he woke in a cold sweat, seeing the faces of the young British soldiers he had killed. They were never faceless enemies to him, and it cut him to the quick that they had to die. Then he thought of the kids on the Falls Road who might grow up without ever seeing their city not filled with Saracens and soldiers, for whom the only lullaby was the crash of sniper fire ringing through the night air—he thought of those kids and he hardened his heart.

He knew the day was coming when he'd be killed or captured. Provos didn't last long on the run. At twenty-six he was the old man of his unit. So many of them were only boys grown hard and old before their time, kids who had come to maturity on the barricades of the Falls and the Bogside, who should have been courting girls but who cradled an armalite in their arms instead. The Brits knew his name and feared him. So he was not surprised when they sent a squad of Special Air Services men after him, but he was flattered: the SAS was a crack British intelligence unit, and it was a testimony to his reputation that they had been sent to bring him in. They caught him alone in a rented room, but Niamh's warning scream brought him to wakefulness, so he was dressed and on his feet when they burst in. He had no gun, and no desire to spend the rest of his life in prison, so he made a break for it. Coolly, efficiently, they brought him down, and when he lay at the foot of the stairs in a pool of blood, the leader bent over him.

He was a tall man, gray-haired, with a look of the aristocrat about him and the coldest blue eyes Eammon had ever seen. Those icy eyes and that harsh-boned face would play a prominent role in his nightmares for years to come. The man bent over him and casually emptied his pistol into Eammon's leg. "That should hold you for a while, you Fenian bastard," he said, almost pleasantly.

They took him to Castlereagh, but the doctor ordered him moved to the hospital. First, though, they tried to force him to sign a confession that said he'd fired at them. They told him they had a gun that was found in his possession. He knew it would not have his fingerprints on it, and he refused to sign. The doctor insisted that he be treated, so they gave in and moved him to a hospital. He refused anesthesia when they took the bullets out of him. He had no intention of spilling his guts to them—if they wanted information, they'd have to break him, and he vowed they'd never do that.

He let them use a local anesthetic to dull the pain as they cut into his leg, but it could not eliminate the agony entirely. Through the dim haze of suffering, he saw Niamh floating over him, her white hands hovering about her mouth and her eyes seemed even sadder than ever to him.

They tried it all. He'd known what to expect. He'd heard the horror stories about the long hours of questioning, the beatings, the forced exercise, the brightly lit cells where time lost all meaning, the deprivation of food and sleep which rendered a man vulnerable. He'd known what was going to happen, but the theory was a far cry from the reality. Through it all he saw Niamh floating before him, tears streaming from her eyes, and he tried to nod reassuringly.

"I'm all right, girl," he whispered. "I'll make it." He was afraid she would scream again, and he didn't know what would happen if she did, only that it wouldn't help him.

They tried to force him to confess to a bombing, but he'd had nothing to do with it, and doubted that the Provos were responsible anyway: Sinn Fein had officially denied. They told him there were witnesses who would swear to it.

He managed to find enough moisture in his dry mouth to spit his contempt at them. The taller of the two RUC men hit him in the gut.

"You'll show respect for the law, you stupid Taig."

He had asked for a lawyer, but he never saw one the entire time he was in detention. At the end of the seven days they told him he'd confessed to membership in the Provisional IRA. They showed him a paper with his signature on it—it might have been his signature; it was too much of a scrawl to be certain. When he came before the judge, this was the major evidence against him, and the whole case hinged on whether or not he had been coerced into his confession. That he had confessed was never the issue. The outcome was never in doubt: the two RUC officers swore that they had witnessed his confession, and the judge found him guilty and sentenced him to ten years, the penalty for membership in the outlawed Irish Republican Army.

Ten years. Five if he got full remission for good behavior. He promised himself he would do whatever was necessary to survive in the cages of Long Kesh. He would not let them break him. He found the life grim, but not so terrible as he had feared, because he had political status. He wore his own clothes instead of a prison uniform, and was under the command of an IRA OC, who dealt with the prison officials. The ancient Nisson huts leaked when it rained, were hot as hell in summer and freezing in winter, but he was with his own people, and that counted for a lot. It made the harassment of the screws easier to bear.

They had access to some wood-working equipment, and with this Eammon was able to fashion a flute, which gave him back his music. He played whenever he could, and it helped to pass the endless hours. He taught his mates all the songs he knew, and learned some new ones from the more recent prisoners. There was a group trying to learn the Irish language, and he joined in eagerly. It was a matter of survival as well as pride: the Protestant screws didn't know Gaelic, and it was most convenient to speak a language they couldn't understand. The culture he had taken for granted became a lifetime in prison.

He heard that the English had revoked the political status and that one man had refused to wear the prison uniform, wrapping himself in a blanket instead. Others had joined him, and the blanket protest was begun. In the cages of Long Kesh, Eammon felt a stab of guilt. If he had stayed free, or been held on remand a few months longer, he would have shared their plight, and he didn't know if he had the strength of will to endure the life of a blanket man.

Through it all there was Niamh, the only comfort he had. His mother was dead, and his aunt wasn't well. The night Ellen died, Niamh came to him, and for the first time she wept silent tears at a death, instead of keening. He and Niamh kept the wake vigil for his aunt, and he played a lament that night, but it was not sad enough to capture the burden of sorrow in Niamh's eyes or in his heart. It was Niamh who got him through those long years, Niamh who had become the family he no longer had.

He was Niamh's whole world now, for nothing else bound her to earth. When he died the curse would be ended; there were no other men of his line left. She found she did not want the curse to end, because that would mean he was dead, and she could not bear the thought of him dying. She did not really understand what he was fighting for; she was of the Sidhe, and the small quarrels of men were beyond her. When he was taken, she was glad, because it meant he was safe, and though she knew how much Ireland meant to him, she cared more for him than for any cause, however just it might be. She needed him, and needed his music, for she had loved his music first, and through it begun to love him.

It was his music that decided his life for him. He could do Ireland no good as a soldier, and if the truth were told, he was weary of killing. He was glad. His fighting days were over, but he could reach into men's hearts with his music and awaken them to what was going on. The little wooden flute he carried could prove a more potent weapon than a rifle.

There were two other young men he'd met who shared his love of music, and he broached the idea to them, carefully at first. Dennis, who was blond and wiry, leaped to the idea like a fish after bait. He had a young wife, Maureen, and he'd promised her he'd give up active service once he was out, but his conscience had bothered him about it. This gave him a way to serve his country and keep his wife happy at the same time. Colum took some time persuading, for he'd planned to go back and do whatever needed doing. It took the pair of them to convince him that he might be more use to Ireland alive and singing than rotting in prison, for it was only a matter of months before the Brits had him under lock and key again. In the end Colum could not resist the lure of drumming again. Dennis had been a fair harpist, and had played the guitar as well. He promised that as soon as he was out, he'd practice till his fingers were raw. He was the first one out, then Colum, and finally Eammon breathed the fresh air of freedom and found it as heady as wine.

He headed straight for Belfast and his comrades. They called themselves the Tanists, for that was the old name for a chief's heir, and they believed that when this government finally fell, it was men like them who would inherit the reins of power. Dennis had gotten back his old skill at the guitar and harp, and Eammon found it came back to him pretty quickly. All three of them could sing, and Colum had gotten his cousin Declan, who played keyboards and pennywhistle, to join them. They played when they could, and had to subsist mostly on the dole and whatever money they could pick up from odd jobs, but after a while they began to make a name for themselves. It didn't hurt a bit that they were well-known in republican circles for their IRA exploits. Many a man came to hear them out of sympathy, but stayed for another set of songs because they were as good at music as they'd been at fighting. They had a break when a rep from a Dublin record company heard them, and they cut their first album. It sold slowly, but then one of Eammon's songs made it to the top of the charts in the south of Ireland, and they were on their way.

And then came the day when Eammon saw the SAS man who had shot him. He was coming out of a hotel where they had played the night before, making a final check on the equipment to make certain nothing had been left behind. The man passed him in the hall, and he recognized the angular face, and the eyes as frigid as the North Sea. Their eyes locked for a long moment, then Eammon wrenched his gaze away and walked on, as if nothing extraordinary had happened. For the first time in his life he was terrified. He did not know why the SAS officer was there, but he was afraid it had something to do with him. The Brits hated to leave an ex-Provo in peace; he decided they were probably setting him up. That it was the same SAS man could only mean a personal grudge on the man's part, and that boded no good. He'd not make it through another term in prison. He wouldn't be taken alive—he promised himself that. He couldn't face the existence of a blanket man.

When he got back to the van, he told the band what had happened and they agreed to make a run for the south as soon as the gig was finished that night; Maureen and the kids could come down later. If they were being watched, going about their business might well lull the Brits into thinking they knew nothing. The headlines in the paper that night did nothing to ease their nerves, however; a bomb had gone off in the very hotel they'd played at the previous night, killing three tourists. Now they knew what the SAS officer had been up to: setting up the Provos, for, of course, the bombing was pinned on them.

Somehow they got through the performance. As always Niamh hovered near, but tonight she seemed less sad and more nervous than usual.

"Don't wail now, Niamh, girl," Eammon told her, "not in the middle of a set. It'd never do." He thought that if banshees could smile, she would have then. "Just keep calm, lady. We'll be over the border in a few hours, and that will be the end of it. Once we're there, you can howl your head off, and I may well join you for sheer relief."

When they were finished, they loaded up the van with their equipment, and Eammon and Declan got into the back while Colum drove with Dennis to keep him awake in the front seat. They took the most direct route out of Belfast, to Lisburn, then south to Newry. But just outside Newry, in the early hours of the morning, they were stopped by a car in the middle of the road. When Eammon heard them stop, he began to sweat. This was what he'd feared. Someone had spotted them in Newry, had called ahead, and set this up. It would happen to them as it had happened to the Miami Showband, and they'd write it off as fighting between the extremists, or maybe find some way to pin it on the Provos—an execution of traitors.

It happened so quickly. The doors were yanked open, they opened fire, and Niamh began to scream and scream. He heard her even as the fire in his chest ripped through him and he lost consciousness.

There was little she could do, but when the killers piled back into their car, Niamh waited until they reached a crossroad and another car was coming, then shrieked with all her anger and pain, and the driver of the getaway car piled headlong into a tree. At least, she thought, they would not die unavenged.

Through the night she flew to the place where Eammon lay. He was bleeding badly but still alive, the only survivor. She knelt in the dirt, and her white robes grew crimson with his blood. What could she do? He still lived, but she was no healer, could do nothing for him. She began to tear her gown into strips and tried to staunch his wounds, but the blood oozed through her bandages in a steady trickle. If she could get him to a healer . . . In the raths there were healers, perhaps they would care for him, for the memory of her singing so many years ago.

She cradled him in her arms, and on the back of the rushing night wind she flew to the place where Finvarra had cast her forth. She looked down at Eammon's pale face, and longed to have a voice so that she could whisper something soothing to him, but she could only keen. She would save her mourning until her love was stolen from her by death, for now that she held him so tight in her arms, she knew him for her love. His eyes fluttered open, dark as Connla's had been, and he whispered, "Niamh, not yet, lady, but soon. Soon. Don't leave me, Niamh."

They reached the rath, and she set him down gently upon the grassy ground. She banged upon a door that to mortal eyes looked like a hillside, beat upon it until her white soft hands were red with her own blood, but there was no answer. Tears streamed down her cheeks, tears of fear and frustration. There was no other hope. In despair she opened her mouth to scream, but instead she sang, and her voice was clearer and purer than the song of the lark at evening. Her face was alight with the wonder of it, and Eammon stared at her.

At that moment the door in the hill opened, and Finvarra, golden-haired, golden-crowned, stood before her. "So you have come back to us at last, Niamh the Sweet-voiced, Lark of the Sidhe."

"No, my king, I have not come back," she told him. "Only have I come for aid for this man, whom I love."

Finvarra bent and laid a hand on Eammon's head. "There is no need to beg. We will aid him, for it is to him that we owe your return. Without him you would not have won back your voice."

"No, I would not," she said, and for a moment the old pride blazed in her face like a white-hot flame. "Have you forgotten the terms of your curse, my king? I would not sing again until the sorrow of the women of Connla's line became my own, and how could that be if I did not love as they loved? For all these centuries I have watched men die and their women grieve for them, and their grief is a part of me. I do not belong in the Halls of the Sidhe anymore, for I would sully your joy with the memory of this sadness. You have given me my love's life. If he will have me, I will become a mortal woman and spend my years singing at his side, and if he will not have me, then I will make my way alone among men."

"If I had known my curse would have such an ending, I would never have spoken it," Finvarra said.

"It is often so with curses, but they cannot be unsaid. Have I your blessing to go with him if he will have me?"

Eammon sat up and found to his astonishment that there was no pain, and no more bleeding. "Have you? My lady, you have been my life these seven years."

"Then we will sing together from now on," she told him, "with or without Finvarra's blessing."

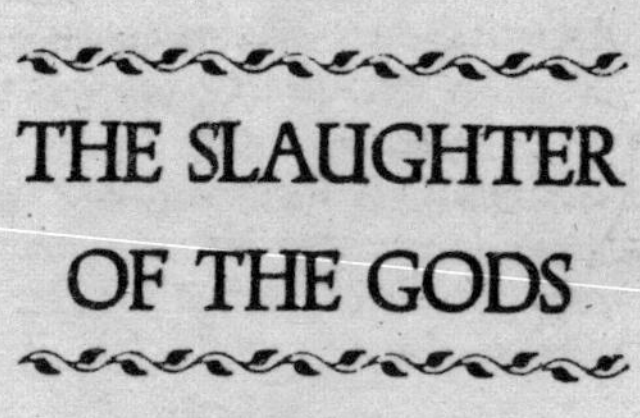

THE SLAUGHTER OF THE GODS

Manly Wade Wellman

Now I go about from time to time making a big stink about the tackiness of pulp fiction, imitated by modern writers. This criticism stems chiefly from the fact that it has been a dominant rather than merely contributory influence on today's heroic fantasy. It gets on my nerves. Heroic fantasy can *be great literature and* has *been great in the hands of Anatole France, Robert Louis Stevenson, and Gustave Flaubert. It gets on my nerves that every pip-squeak would-be writer of heroic fantasy only knows about Conan, and if they've delved* really *deep, Elak. Yes indeed, it gets my hackles up.*

But the truth is, I like *Conan and Elak and the whole school of barbarian schmoo. These stories are to literature what potato chips are to gourmet cooking. Potato chips are spiffy too.*

Having set a different standard for the **Heroic Visions** *series, I still feel terrifically justified in thinking it is essential to feature at least one good ol' pulp adventure. Not the dominant thread of any volume, but an integrated portion. And who could be better qualified to represent this popular aspect of heroic fantasy than Manly Wade Wellman, a true giant of the pulp era?*

Manly's Silver John novels for Doubleday have established

him as a major modern writer, but his career spans the length and breadth of modern fantasy's development, beginning in the l920s with **Weird Tales**. *Though born in Portuguese West Africa (1903), his ancestry dates to the Confederate south. His deep-south heritage is reflected in many of his finest writings.*

Kardios the Atlantean was originally devised with **Weird Tales** *in mind. Possibly because Conan and Elak were too similar, Kardios was rejected, unseen by the public until the advent of Andrew J. Offut's* **Swords Against Darkness** *series, where Kardios debuted long after his creation.*

The present tale was newly penned for **Heroic Visions II**, *to my great delight—and yours.*

SINCE KARDIOS, the last surviving Atlantean, had lost so many valiant friends and lovely ladies in the sudden awful drowning of his home island, he welcomed the comradeship of the fisher-captain Krarr and the crew of the square-sailed craft that put out on a sea he had never dreamed of. He dragged on nets and climbed masts with them, helping how he could. He was tall, tanned, wide-shouldered, black-maned, with the only shaven face aboard. He wore a sleeveless blue tunic, a leopard-skin kilt, a useful-looking sword in a copper-riveted sheath. His harp swung at his back. The whole company liked him.

"We're headed for a port called Sambarra with our fish, but it'll take a couple of days," said bearded Captain Krarr. "When you're off watch, play that harp and sing to us, and tell us what you've been up to."

Kardios played and sang tunefully, songs of his own making. They liked one that named tyrants and monsters he had met and killed:

> "I looked in their evil eyes and they crouched like cravens,
> I showed them my sword and they trembled and louted low;
> I gave their bones for food to the rats and ravens,
> And pray the gods for another and fiercer foe."

His story: Atlantis had sunk in the sea because Kardios had brought down a forgotten curse by kissing Queen Theona, and he had clung to wreckage for days of storm until, on a distant shore, he came among the giant Nephol tribe and killed a plaguing monster. Then wanderings, until he climbed the dizzy-tall Fufuna range, called the end of the world with only emptiness beyond; but beyond was more of the world, which maybe had no end.

"You've come a long, wearisome way," said Krarr, listening.

"It was too lively to be wearisome," said Kardios. "I found things to do, things to kill—even a god or so."

"Can gods be killed?" growled Krarr. "At Sambarra, gods walk around everywhere. Sambarra has no king, only gods. Of course, human subjects to serve them. Sing again."

Kardios strummed his harp and sang:

"Sambarra, Sambarra, by the sea,
What will you have to show to me?
Will it be wonderful, will it be wise,
Kindness or enmity, truth or lies?"

"I don't know how to answer that," confessed Krarr. "I just tie up to the merchant docks, sell my fish, and sail away again. But the men are bringing in another big netful. Let's go help."

They sailed the day away, and the night too, under a blazing moon. At sunset of the next day they entered Sambarra's rock-fenced harbor. Back from the docks stood blocky buildings of stone, rosy and blue and gray, with slender spires and square towers beyond. Among the houses hung a misty vapor. Krarr steered his craft to a pier, where his men made fast with cables around posts. Then Krarr stepped to the pier, and Kardios went with him.

There were merchants, richly cloaked and variously bearded, who came aboard to inspect the fish and make their offers. Krarr argued over prices. Kardios, on the pier, was aware of a babel of tuneful voices, and turned to look.

Half a dozen very attractive women with yellow and red and brown and black hair had come to the waterfront, all smiling and murmuring, and all dressed in garments that clung enticingly to splendid figures. Kardios smiled encouragingly at them.

"What a handsome stranger!" exclaimed a gorgeous blonde with amphora-curved hips and breasts like twin pleasure domes. "He wears a sword—he must be a hero."

"What's your name?" asked another woman, equally exciting of figure, and thunder-black as to her wavy hair.

"I'm Kardios," he said, strolling toward them. They gathered around him, smiling, bright-eyed.

"Kardios, Kardios," one repeated his name. "That means a heart. Is your heart warm, Kardios?"

"Always," he said to one with red hair as she cuddled a bare shoulder to his. "How hospitable you are."

"Come with us," she said, and they clustered to shepherd him toward a street that opened between high houses.

They came upon a smooth, violet-colored pavement. More houses looked down from either side. Kardios glanced back the way he had come, and the way he had come was no way at all. For what had been the head of the street was sealed away by yet another silent building, as if it had swung there like a gate.

"What—" he began to say, but nobody was there. The girls had vanished, like girls in a dream.

Something else was coming. Darkly it slouched along the violet pavement. Kardios had encountered many grotesque creatures, but this one demanded rapt, interested attention. It was as big as a cave bear, it moved on four many-jointed, knuckled legs, it was sootily shaggy all over. Its head, square as a box, had a face of a bilious green, eyes like pallid fire, a fanged mouth. It extended arms with claws like a nightmare lobster.

Kardios drew his long silvery-pale sword, made of metal from the stars and given him by the grateful Nephol tribe. He whipped it in the air. The creature paused and glared, then squattered toward him.

"Confident, aren't you?" Kardios addressed it, and as it shot a claw at him, he neatly slashed the claw from its arm. A piercing scream, and his attacker reared upright. Smoothly Kardios sped a lunge at the bald, soft-looking belly. His sword went deeply home, and he drew it upward as he cleared it. The misshapen body floundered down, kicking.

Behind it came another, this time tall and on two big slapping feet. Kardios hopped across the slackening body of his first attacker to face this second. Behind it scurried other abhorrent shapes.

"Here, you brave man!"

It was a woman's voice, rich and low, from the building next to him.

"Climb up here!"

From a high window dangled a rope woven of red and gold. Kardios darted his sword into its sheath, ran to the rope, and scrambled up it like a squirrel. He dived through the window into a circular room draped in many-colored hangings, decorated with characters he could not read. Its one piece of furniture was a great low couch with a gold-worked black spread, and upon this sat the woman who had invited him to climb.

From toes to throat she was draped in a robe of blue silk confined by a golden belt. Its folds snuggled to what were manifestly alluring curves. Her hair gleamed pale, almost like spun frost. Her oval, point-chinned face had dark blue eyes, just then fixed on Kardios, a short, straight nose with finely flared nostrils, and a red mouth like an appetizing fruit.

"Well," she said in her rich voice, "do you like what you see?"

"Very much," Kardios replied honestly. "Thanks for letting me come in."

"What's your name? Oh, I know—Kardios. You can call me Iltanie."

"A beautiful name. Who are you otherwise? I was told that Sambarra has no kings or queens, is ruled by gods."

"That's the truth. I happen to be a goddess—one of the seven ruling deities. No, six now—you killed one. I sent those pretty girls to bring you into town, on a whim. I called the gods to see what they might make of you. Mostly they paralyze humans by just scowling at them, but you killed the first one to come within reach."

Kardios lounged against the hangings. "How could I kill him if he was a god? Aren't gods immortal?"

Iltanie's smile was bewitching. "Gods die when their worship stops. Anyway, since you seem to have killed one, perhaps you're a god of some sort. How did you get to Sambarra?"

Kardios told of his survival of Atlantis, his wanderings over unknown lands, the perils he had met. He dwelt especially on the city of Nanyanya, and how he had been king there long enough to kill a so-called god called Tongbi, and how he had left Nanyanya a lovely queen called Yola. Iltanie kept smiling.

"You're going to be welcome here," she said when he had finished. "Dangerous—our human servants will cower away from you. And you're a very handsome man."

"And you're a very beautiful goddess."

She rose to her feet, a slim hand gathering her robe. "Goddess," she repeated. "Would you worship me?"

"Beauty is always worth worshipping," said Kardios.

"I think I know how to deal with you."

Iltanie let her robe fall all the way down to the golden belt. From the waist upward she was creamy-pink, abundant of breasts, smooth of flanks. Kardios had to stare. He had to say, "Magnificent!"

She unclasped the belt and dropped the robe the rest of the way. She stood in her symmetrically ample beauty, wearing nothing but a heavily jeweled collar. "Well?" she purred.

"Well, indeed," said Kardios. He had thrown down his cloak. On it he laid his harp, his sword and belt, doffed his tunic and kilt, and kicked off his shoes. He strode to Iltanie and they sat down together on the couch. She flung her arms around his neck, kissed him swimmingly, and sank down to receive him.

Kardios found her surpassingly adroit at lovemaking, and it was long before they finished with each other and sat up to study each other's nakedness. "That had to be done," said Iltanie. "You can call it a religious rite. Now I have you here, and you'll be useful."

"Useful? How?"

"With our human population, which obeys and does the work and serves the altars. You're human—very much—and you can help govern these people, direct them for me. They'll fear you and obey you. And I'll keep you happy." Her eyes twinkled. "Very happy indeed."

He shook his dark head. "I won't be staying. I'm going back across the world, to Nanyanya, where Queen Yola is waiting."

"But you love me!" she cried, almost an accusation. She caught her robe back around her. "You belong to me, I bought you!"

"We never made any formal sales agreement," he said, sliding into his clothes. "I belong to nobody. I'm too used to freedom to belong to you."

He took up his cloak and slung his harp. "Good-bye, Iltanie. You were so hospitable."

"And you're going?" she mocked. "Out the window? Look and see what's there in the street."

"Something ugly, naturally," said Kardios. "Or unnaturally. I'll leave by this door."

He opened it and stepped through, into the incomprehensible.

The hallway, if it was a hallway, was clouded with some sort of mist, pallid white and stirring. Kardios tried to walk into it—he was hampered, as though by fabric. He cursed under his breath, drew his sword and slashed at the stuff, made a space to step into, slashed again and again. He struggled to go through.

Behind him Iltanie seemed to sing words. The hampering whiteness vanished abruptly. He was in a long, long corridor that stretched to some sort of infinity. Its smooth floor was pale gray, like raw steel. Its walls looked sandy dun, and from them here and there opened black emptinesses, like caves. Toward Kardios waddled a dark, upright something with no head to see, only a mighty sprawl of tentacles. Kardios thought he had seen it in the street. More distant shapes came behind. Kardios moved confidently forward.

"Catch him!" Iltanie was crying, not soft-voiced now. "He's mine, I bought him!"

Kardios snatched a glance backward. Something was in the corridor there too, and not Iltanie. Where to Kardios's front moved ungainly, tentacled bulk, behind him crept lithe yellowness with the reddest of eyes, stale teeth in a gaping mouth, outstretched forelimbs armed with daggerlike talons.

"He's mine!" shrieked Iltanie again.

Both creatures charged, before and behind. They were almost upon Kardios when he flung himself low and scrambled clear, against a wall. There was a crash and clash of sound as the charging things slammed violently together, and Kardios heard both of them scream as he hurried to his feet and lifted his sword.

They clutched in a senseless, flurrying wrestle, neither knowing what was happening. Kardios sped a lightning thrust into the moss-shaggy back of one, whipped his blade in a whining circle and mowed away the tentacles of the other. The two bodies subsided in an unsightly heap, and Kardios moved swiftly past them. Three of Sambarra's gods in so short a time, not a bad beginning.

Iltanie screamed more orders. A shape whizzed above Kardios, flapping strange wings, and a claw ripped at his tunic. He stabbed upward, felt his point go home, heard a howl of agony, and fell back against the wall.

"Here," mumbled somebody from beside his foot. "In here."

A sort of trapdoor opened, low in the wall. Kardios did not stop to wonder, but flung himself down and dived in, head first. He landed in black darkness, on what felt like damp, coarse turf. A hand was on his shoulder.

"Come along, come away, they'll be after you."

He scrambled up again, in the dark. His companion held his elbow. "Come."

He touched a wall. It was of rough stone, and under his feet was the soggy floor. They approached to where Kardios could see a ruddy light ahead. It grew stronger as Kardios's companion brought him into a cave with splotchy pictures on the walls, centered with a pleasant fire in a pit. All around gathered people dressed in bright colors. Several were pretty girls. Kardios thought he recognized two who had shepherded him into his adventures.

"We're the human dwellers of Sambarra," said his guide. "The slaves of the gods."

He was a lean old man, with a beard as frosty as Iltanie's hair. He wore a trailing robe of coarse-spun brown. His eyes were wise and kind.

"Slaves?" repeated Kardios. "You're slaves? But the merchants I saw at the harbor, they looked prosperous."

"They're privileged, but they serve the gods by buying and selling. Seven deities rule Sambarra, and we obey."

"Not seven anymore," said Kardios. "I seemed to finish four of them, and that leaves only three. I doubt if they were gods."

"When you fought them, I had hope. That's why I brought you down here where we live."

"Here, Algru," said another man, holding out a scrap of white parchment. "They sent this down."

The old man called Algru took it and studied it. Kardios saw symbols on the parchment, symbols he could not read. Algru shuffled to an altarlike rock and picked up a rough earthen goblet. He held it out to Kardios. "A very special beer," he said.

Kardios took the goblet and tasted the beer. "Good," he said.

"Magic," said Algru, taking the goblet back. He shoved

the parchment in and brooded above it. Kardios saw the characters fading, dissolving. After a moment Algru fished the damp parchment out and drank the beer at one draught. "Now I know what they wrote there," he said. "They tell us, we must put you back among them or suffer."

"Don't worry, I'll go back among them," declared Kardios. "I've been killing them. Why not finish the job?"

"But they're all-powerful," protested Algru. "They can't be faced or denied."

"Nonsense, I've faced them," lectured Kardios. "Maybe you should have faced them long ago. They've frightened you, crushed you. How?"

"They came into Sambarra and made our fathers serve," said somebody else. "Made them work, raise crops, build for them, work for them. We've never known anything else."

"Because of fear," snapped Kardios. "I got free of fear some thousands of miles away. Now, I won't stop and listen to anymore. I'm going outside. I have a few more gods to kill."

"No earthly weapon—" began Algru.

"My sword isn't earthly," Kardios broke in. "It was forged from star metal."

He drew it and headed back along the rocky passage, his hand groping along the wall. He flung the trapdoor wide. In the corridor writhed a great dark shape that would have been a gigantic snake except for its many squat legs. It lifted its flat head at Kardios. Eyes glowed like sickly green jewels, jowls bulged to betoken poison sacs. It ran out a forked blue tongue, and stared.

"You're an ugly one too," Kardios greeted it. "Come on, if you're coming on."

The head launched at him. Fangs showed in the roof of the gaping mouth. Kardios flicked his sword and the keen edge reaped away the head, halfway down the neck. An agonized scramble and the body came against the head. Suddenly the head was back in place, an instantaneous healing. The snaky body trundled forward on its legs. Kardios decided on something.

"Come in, the door's open," he invited, and fell back in the dark passage. His foe writhed after him and darted its head again.

Kardios leaped high above the stroke, came down astride the wriggling body and slashed downward. He cut the thing in two and frantically kicked damp mud and debris between the two pieces. Kardios danced back, clear of it. Algru came behind him with a blazing torch.

"See!" cried Algru. "See!"

The severed halves strove, could not join with that clutter between them. They subsided. As Kardios and Algru watched, they went motionlessly limp.

"Dead," said Kardios. "I didn't let it make itself whole again. That makes five of your gods that proved they weren't gods after all. Now, let me get out there."

He slid himself into the corridor. Something waited there, but only for a moment. It spread murky, membranous wings, slid up into the air and fled. It was gone, up a chimneylike hollow in the ceiling, before Kardios could make out its shape.

"Sensible monster!" he jeered after it. "That's six gone, where's the seventh?"

The seventh was farther along the corridor, running uncouthly but swiftly. Kardios took a step, as if to pursue. The shape seemed to liquify, to stop being a shape, to go into a mist that rose too, that sought the ceiling hollow and vanished into it.

Kardios stood still and mopped his sweaty brow with his forearm. Algru was in the open with him. Others peered out and then slowly emerged in their turn.

"They fled from you," said Algru. "Fled from Sambarra. Kardios, you banished them. You're our ruler now, give us your commands."

Kardios laughed and shook his black-maned head.

"Don't you see?" he rallied Algru. "They weren't gods, not for a moment—only monsters, and they had to be faced. You're not slaves any more. Take over here, Algru. You act and talk like a sensible man. Maybe you and your people can make Sambarra amount to something."

Algru started to speak, but Kardios strode along the corridor, the way he had come. He had carried his harp all through this, and now he swept its strings and marched to his own music. He sang:

> "You called yourselves gods in Sambarra, you thought
> You were mighty and fearful and wise;
> But your rule in Sambarra is come unto naught,
> Sambarra is free of your lies. . . ."

Up ahead, a timid figure in a blue robe—Iltanie. He came to her, still fingering his harp.

"Now you'll kill me," she said, her voice dull at last.

"I'll kill nobody so beautiful," said Kardios. "But I advise you to get out of Sambarra."

Her blue eyes were on him, sad and weary. Her frosty hair drooped.

"Let me theorize about you," he said cheerfully. "You're a sorceress—you can live lifetimes, cast spells, all that. You picked up some unsightly monsters and came here and made the people think you were deities. But I came here and demonstrated the nature of reality, and your monster friends overreached themselves—tried to frighten me and couldn't."

She said nothing, only shook her head unhappily.

"As for you," Kardios went on, "trying to be a goddess is too rich for your blood. My friendly advice is to go ply your sorceress trade somewhere else. Maybe you've learned not to take men like me for granted."

Her robe drooped from a beautifully turned shoulder, perhaps on purpose.

"Kardios," she whispered, "you and I could have had such a good time together."

"We did have a good time together, a little while ago. I'll make a bargain with you. Let's both leave Sambarra."

"Agreed," she said, and walked slowly away.

Kardios went back to the room where they had made love, swung out of the window, and slid down the cord. The street was open to the sea again. On a dock, Krarr waved to him.

"Where have you been?" demanded Krarr sharply. "We've sold our fish—got good prices—and we want to sail with this coming tide."

"Sail where?" Kardios asked.

"Back to the coast where we found you, back to where the fishing's so good."

"Put me ashore there. I have it in mind to go back on my way through the world I've roamed. Go back to Nanyanya, where Queen Yola rules and perhaps wonders what's happened to me."

Krarr stroked his beard. "Just what did happen to you, in Sambarra?"

"I'll tell you when we're at sea. It's quite a tale, so get prepared to believe it."

COHEN THE CLAM-KILLER

Steven Bryan Bieler

Steven Bryan Bieler is a columnist for the **Jewish Transcript**, *a contributor to such publications as* **Asimov's** *and* **New Dimensions**, *and cute as the devil. At a recent fantasy/science fiction convention where Harlan Ellison was guest of honor, Harlan began to trumpet the extraordinary merits of Steve's writing, much to Steve's blushing embarrassment and wholehearted agreement. The young star on the horizon has now joined the ranks (and files) of Harlan's contributors to* **The Last Dangerous Visions** *(that Algis Budrys said should be called* At Last, Dangerous Visions *when it does finally appear), an anthology rumored to include the complete works of previously unknown authors prolific in their lifetimes.*

Surely I've license to write a silly introduction for a silly story.

I first heard Steve's "Cohen the Clam-Killer" when he read it to a gathering at a Seattle book store. The audience was rolling around on the floor slapping one another's thighs, and it wasn't even an orgy. Much later, remembering this funny commentary on heroic fantasy, I wrote and asked to see a copy of the manuscript, wondering if it would hold up without Steve's brilliant oral delivery. And as a matter of fact, it seemed to me that "Cohen the Clam-Killer" was primarily *a piece of writing, not merely a monologue for someone who could have been a stage comedian, if the graver folly of literature hadn't called to him more loudly.*

This piece is reprinted from the writing manual **Prelude to Pulp**, *available only from the author (who you may encounter at f/sf conventions, staggering about mumbling, "Harlan likes my stuff; Harlan likes my stuff") and has its first professional publication here.*

ONE EVENING MANY MILLIONS OF YEARS AGO, a family of prehistoric proto-people were sitting up late in the cave, munching on bones while watching the fire. In contemporary terms this is the equivalent of munching double-fudge brownies while watching Monday Night Football.

These proto-people had no furniture and no carpeting; they had no furniture polish and no upright vacuum cleaners. Archeologists today sneer with derision and refer to them as "primitive"; the proto-people, not the upright vacuum cleaners.

One of the family members, having finished his bone and not seeing anything in the fire that he cared to watch, decided to employ the new skill of speech, the rage throughout the Jurassic Period. He told the others about his day in the jungle, about the hunt, the heat, the lack of public rest rooms, and the saber-toothed tiger that got away. He opened his arms wide to indicate the size of the creature's fearsome teeth. One of his listeners, after thoughtful digestion of both this story and his bone, belched into the primordial darkness.

Thus did both fantasy fiction and literary criticism come into being.

Science fiction could not exist before the current technological era; could not exist before the advent of a future substantially different from the past. Fantasy required nothing more than writers and storytellers skilled in the concoction of literary whoppers. Ancient civilizations, possessing no more technological expertise than how to break rocks, invented a bureaucracy of deities in charge of everything from thunder to love to traffic at downtown intersections. This was fantasy fiction at its finest; at least, we hope it is fantasy! The Greek poet Homer, who regularly wrapped himself in bedsheets and once ran twenty-six miles to warn his countrymen that the

Persian army had parked in a tow-away zone, authored two fantasy best sellers, the *Iliad* and the *Odyssey*. It was two thousand years before the invention of copyright registration. Homer received no royalties, and today nobody knows his last name.

As with pagan theology, many fantasy classics were not intended by their authors to fall within the bounds of that genre. Among these are books that claim cooking is easy, and the instruction manuals to almost anything.

(An interesting variant of the fantasy story is the *fairy tale*, not to be confused with the Presidential press release. Like fantasy, the fairy tale deals in the supernatural; unlike fantasy, you cannot be licensed to write fairy tales unless there is something wrong with you. Whoever wrote *Little Red Riding Hood*, an example of good nutrition through the consumption of grandmothers, or *Goldilocks and the Three Bears*, an imaginative study of sexual attitudes in suburbia, was not playing with a full deck. Are *you* missing a few face cards? If affirmative, you can pick up your fairy tale license application at any office of the federal government.)

The literature of fantasy is alive and throbbing today. Bookstores bulge with fantasy novels abrim with words, sometimes one or two hundred different words, many of more than one syllable. Theaters screen fantasy films wherein dragons with no job skills gobble fair maidens and trample rose bushes while battling men and women armed with swords and dressed for aerobics. Someone is making real money from this make-believe. How does the perspiring writer cash in on the big-money world of fantasy fiction? How do you go about writing a fantasy novel? Let us consider the structure and function of one representative work, *Cohen the Clam-Killer*.

The basic fantasy novel begins with a hero, or if you are so inclined, a heroine. Sadie Cohen is just such a person. As dictated by fantasy tradition, she is a barbarian, a dealer in sudden death, and an accountant. She lives in an unspecified century that closely resembles Europe after the decline and fall of the Roman Empire but before the book of the same name. It is a time of powerful kings and queens, evil dukes, treacherous wizards, ferocious forest creatures, and simple peasants whose only desires are for a good harvest and the installation of cable television.

Once you have your heroine, you must send her on an epic

quest. There is something out there that must be taken away from whoever owns it at the moment; it can be a weapon, a ring, a tap-dancing buffalo, or enough premium ale to float Camelot. Whatever it is, it is enchanted, guaranteeing good luck and absolute power for its owner. The wielder of the enchanted buffalo never has trouble finding a seat on the subway. If accompanied by the buffalo, he gets all the seats he wants. In *Cohen the Clam-Killer,* Sadie is sent by her accounting firm to audit the books of Thurman, the Baron Berman, who is behind in his castle payments. The Baron is the holder of the Perpetual Cash Machine Card, which never jams in the slot, and from which he draws both his dark powers and drafts on his checking account. Sadie rides to meet him aboard a unicorn with five-speed transmission, dressed to aerobicize and equipped with sword, longbow, and twelve-function calculator.

The bulk of the book now looms ahead, like a dragon between you and the refrigerator. It is not the successful termination of the adventure that is important; readers know that Sadie will succeed, that she will nag the Baron into paying all funds owed and/or repossess the Card, and if that isn't what happens, nobody is going to buy another book with that author's name on it.

The quest itself is all that matters. You must have the necessary ingredients: the hero or heroine; a muscle-flexing wrecking crew with all the subtlety of the National Guard on maneuvers in your living room; the merciless villain, defaulting on promissory notes and running up a fortune in debt-servicing charges; feudal Europe, with some name changes and a primeval forest thrown in; and interesting subsidiary characters who must hold the stage while the big shots are sleeping off all that beer they drank in Camelot.

Thus it is vital, as the book progresses, or regresses, that your heroine find allies on her journey. These allies come in all shapes and sizes; they can be illiterate peasants, magical beasts of the field, unemployed magicians, or almost anybody with time on their hands. In *Cohen the Clam-Killer* Sadie is befriended by Moshe the Frog, Cabala the Wizard, three French hens, two turtle doves, and a radio newscaster who does voice-overs during battle scenes. The frog and the newscaster alternately provide the romantic interest.

The villain has his allies as well. The Baron Berman is

defended on the field by his thoroughly reprehensible thugs, Vinny and Rocco Lefkowitz, and their army of vampire clams.

From here it is best to let the interplay of these titanic forces decide the course of the quest; whether the story will fill three books, or, if sales figures warrant, sixteen.

The successful fantasy author often thinks of those prehistoric bone-munchers, staring into their fire and wishing they could change the channel. They laid the foundation for that author's success; and when archeologists sneer and compare cave dwellers unfavorably with the Three Stooges, that author smiles knowingly and counts his royalties.

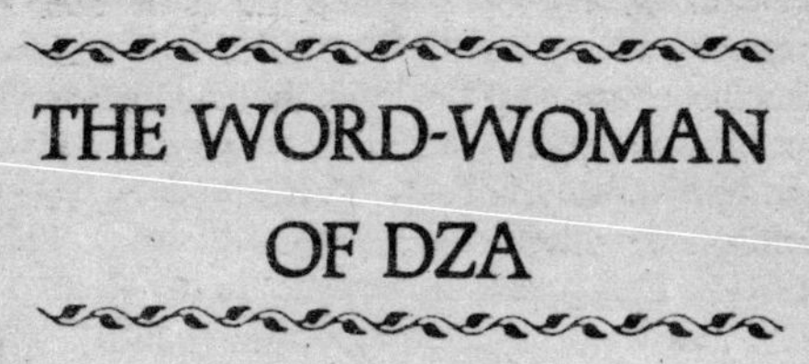

THE WORD-WOMAN OF DZA

Grania Davis

Grania Davis, though born in Milwaukee, Wisconsin, in 1943, is a west coast transplant, a Northern Californian at heart. Her novels have included **Dr. Grass** *(1978),* **The Great Perpendicular Path** *(1980),* **The Rainbow Annals** *(1980), and* **Moonbird** *(1984), this latter based on Balinese legend.*

Her short stories have appeared in **Amazing Stories, The Magazine of Fantasy and Science Fiction, Universe, Orbit, Cassandra Rising,** *and* **Interfaces,** *among others. She says, "I rarely write about other planets, because I'm endlessly fascinated by the shifting wonders of this one." She lived among Tibetan refugees in India, which inspired* **The Rainbow Annals** *and other tales of Dza, one of which was "The Nun and the Demon" in the first volume of* **Heroic Visions.** *"The Word-Woman of Dza" is, as the title makes obvious, another in this series, as unique from her other Dza tales as the whole series is unique among fantasy literature.*

The word-woman is as marvelous a heroine as we are liable to encounter, in this anthology or any other, and I feel honored to present her to a fortunate audience.

THE SECLUDED HIGHLAND VALLEY OF DZA was a land of intense silence. Hidden from the bustling world by the surrounding embrace of vast snow peaks, eerie music was created by the landscape itself: the crackle of glaciers, the growl of thunderstorms, and the haunting cries of birds drifting across the deep turquoise sky. The burbling creeks of clear melted ice, lined with old willows and gnarled apricot trees, snaked across the grassy valley floor with a wistful song.

The people of Dza respected the calm silence of their land, and enjoyed their spacious isolation. Thus they were regarded as taciturn (and rather dull) by the lowlanders, who loved to amuse themselves with chatter and gossip, songs and mysterious stories. The Dza folk took pleasure in the strange music of their valley, and went about their business softly. The King's soldiers quietly guarded the Tibetan border from their royal stone fortress. The monks and nuns in their caves silently performed their endless meditations. The villagers herded their furry yaks and grew upland barley on terraced fields, and all was peaceful in the highland valley of Dza.

Only the children broke the hush with their playful laughter. Their elders in the sprawling family compounds of mud bricks elaborately carved wooden beams, smiled indulgently, watching them romp and tumble on the hillsides. The little ones were like birds. They needed to chatter and sing as their exploring minds darted and flew about. They would discover the deep satisfactions of silence as they grew older. Meanwhile their mirth added a certain lilt to the natural music of the landscape.

In Dza one girl is customarily married to several brothers. As she grows older, she becomes the matriarch of an extended family network. The lowlanders snigger over such polyandrous arrangements, and wonder how the Dza maidens can satisfy an entire household of brothers. But the Dza folk know that this keeps the family intact and avoids the inheritance squabbles that divide the lowlanders. A proud woman of Dza is adorned with turquoise and coral beads, and is treated with consideration by her several husbands. Her children will have no rivals in the family, so they will live peacefully together and never feel lonely.

In such a large family compound at the edge of a small creekside village lived a young girl, Drolma, with elongated black eyes and high ruddy cheeks, who was unusually quiet, even for Dza. She spoke rarely, and whole days would pass between her sparse words.

"Perhaps she's simple," remarked her concerned mother and several fathers in the sprawling, yak-herding family. "Perhaps Drolma can't learn normal speech or live normally. She may need an uncomplicated, sheltered life as a shepherd or a nun."

Yet Drolma didn't seem stupid. She was unusually quick at games with the other children. And the odd truth was that when she chose to speak, her words had the effect of prophecy. When Drolma said *rainbow*, a glowing prism would soon arc across the dark blue sky. If Drolma said *hail*, the people rushed anxiously inside, fearful of the bright stones that would soon pound down upon their village—and destroy the tender crops.

For a long time her bustling family, and the creekside village of herders, farmers, and traders, refused to acknowledge anything special about Drolma. They weren't fond of magical tales, like the lowlanders. They preferred the orderly and natural cycle of events. Crops grew when and where they were planted. People were born, lived, and died. It's true that invisible spirits inhabited every rock, tree, and river of Dza. But they could be placated with ritual offerings of yak butter and barley dough. It's true that strange things sometimes happened, but they seemed random.

The people of Dza felt no need to invent demons and fairies to explain each shift in the weather (like the lowlanders). Rain fell when thick clouds gathered—not because the thunder gods dueled. But unseasonable rain also occurred when Drolma spoke the word "rain." Even if the sky were clear, within hours dark thunderheads would obscure the bright sun and cold drops would batter the surprised villagers.

"How did she know it was going to rain?" asked her mother and several fathers. "Did Drolma sense the rain—or did her words *create* it?"

One strange morning Drolma suddenly frowned and said, "Bandits." The villagers were frightened, for mounted gangs of roving raiders were a menace in those days. These nomad hordes had no homes or villages to tend. They grew no crops. They rode their horses bareback across the grassy steppes and through the mountain passes, pausing only to attack and pillage, rob and burn along their erratic way. These verminous bands were perpetually hungry. They wanted food and horses, gold and jewels from the villagers' storage chests—and they wanted women.

The King's soldiers, who guarded the Tibetan border passes from the massive stone fortress, were poorly armed and unprepared. They passed their time with hunting and dice games, archery tournaments and sports. It would be easy for an armed and mounted gang of wild nomads to overwhelm the good-natured soldiers of Dza and race through the valley, robbing and raping, burning and killing as they went.

Yet there were no bandits in sight on this quiet, sunny day. One simple girl had said one simple word. Surely there was no cause for undue alarm. The villagers downstream would laugh and tease if everyone geared up for battle because of one simple word spoken by a child—and no bandits appeared.

"Think I'll sharpen my knives today," said one of Drolma's fathers, shrugging, trying to look unconcerned. "They've gone a bit dull."

"Good idea." Her mother nodded. "The scythes could use sharpening too."

"Mine too," said a neighbor thoughtfully. "My knives and scythes could use a new edge—harvest is near. Maybe we'll mend the broken gatepost too."

Soon all the villagers around Drolma's family compound set to work, quickly but quietly, deftly but almost nonchalantly, to arm themselves and fortify the village—just in case that simple child's simple word were true. Blades were honed to a glittering edge. Gaps in mud walls were swiftly and silently mended. They donned stiff yak-leather tunics and caps, and selected knives and scythes to defend themselves and their village. Only Drolma did nothing. She wandered around the kitchen courtyard, eating dried apricots and absently humming.

Before noon the dust clouds appeared, as the ominous mounted troop of armed brigands in greasy black leather armor raced along the narrow hillside pathway between terraced barley fields, towards the isolated village. Mothers grabbed their small children, set the growling mastiffs outside the compound walls, and locked their sturdy gates. The people fearfully sharpened and resharpened their blades, knowing they were no match for a fully armed gang.

Then Drolma slipped out a small side gate, still humming, and wandered out to the rutted roadway. Her worried family tried to shout and call her back inside. The raiders would devour her young body. Drolma looked back at them and smiled. Then she lifted a thin arm, pointed a finger at the approaching horde—and said, "Fall!"

At that moment the earth shook and a large section of the dusty roadway collapsed with a deep roar. The bandits and their screaming horses rolled and slid down the hillside, and were crushed by a pursuing avalanche of tumbling boulders.

Earthquakes and avalanches are common in the mountain regions, yet finally even the stolid villagers had to admit that there was something special about Drolma. Her mother and several fathers decided to consult with Pama, the old shamaness who dwelled nearby. Pama lived in a shabby yak-hair tent hidden in a grove of birch trees that grew alongside the lucent creek. As Drolma and her family approached, they could hear the grimy old woman in the threadbare woolen robe singing an ancient epic, as she stirred a rusty stewpot full of wild roots and herbs over an open fire outside her tent. The shamaness was rumored to be nearly two hundred years old. When Pama saw them, her leathery face crinkled into a gaping smile.

"You've brought the word-woman to Pama," she crowed.

"Word-woman?" asked Drolma's mother.

"Yes," said Pama, gently stroking Drolma's sleek black hair and pinching her round cheeks. "All the spirits in the valley are buzzing like flies with excitement. No word-woman has appeared in Dza for many generations. Her words are powerful."

"What kind of power?" asked one of Drolma's fathers.

"The power of—words!" chortled the old shamaness, scratching at her woolen robe. She began humming and mumbling to herself as she sorted through a grubby collection of dried herbs in a leather pouch and placed a few leaves and twigs in a tiny felt bag.

"I don't understand," said her mother. "Did Drolma's words anticipate the bandits and the avalanche—or did her words *cause* them?"

"Pama is no philosopher," said the old woman, sealing the felt bag with melted wax. "Pama merely talks with the spirits and prepares soothing, healing herbs. Only the wise ones, the lamas, can answer such complicated questions. Pama can only give the young word-woman this amulet—to keep her words pure." The shamaness pounded rhythmically on a small bone drum and sang an archaic chant. She moved her gnarled hands in skilled, complex gestures, and hung the little felt bag around Drolma's neck with a grubby yak-leather thong. Then she returned to her stewpot and her ancient epic. Like any other woman of Dza, Pama saw no reason to continue speaking when she had nothing more to say.

The villagers wanted to know more about their word-woman, and only the wise lamas could satisfy their questions. So a delegation of gruff village leaders dug into leather and brass storage chests for their best woolen robes and turquoise ornaments, and led Drolma to the great monastery in the grassy foothills, about a day's journey from their village.

They were all very impressed by the massive complex built of whitewashed stucco and gleaming blue tile, with ornately carved, painted wooden beams, and vast courtyards.

Drolma's face brightened and she spoke one word, "Gold."

"The girl has an eye for finery," laughed the village headman, dressed in his best gray felt robe and boots, and carrying his feathered ceremonial staff.

When they entered the great incense-scented hall of the monastery, they saw that Drolma spoke truly. For upon the huge altar were countless icons and images of gods, demons, and wise ones of the finest gold, set with shimmering jewels. The villagers were dazzled.

"Gold," smiled Drolma. Rarely had she spoken so often.

The lamas lived in a network of damp caves which honeycombed the foothills. The abbess's cave was spacious and decorated with the comforts of a noble's house. Thick, colorful carpets held in warmth and the rare scent of sandlewood. A pot of rich buttered tea bubbled merrily on a carved bronze, yak-chip brazier. Colorful religious banners, painted images, and valuable icons were everywhere. The abbess was a serene gray-haired woman seated on a low, carpeted couch and robed in heavy yellow silk brocade. With a kindly smile, she motioned Drolma to come closer.

"Madam," said the village headman, nervously fingering the silver and turquoise reliquary that hung around his neck. "Whatever this girl says comes to pass, and we'd be most grateful if you could explain why."

"Why?" laughed the abbess. "There are infinite possibilities within the simple word *why*. We must debate the philosophical nuances of this question."

So the abbess summoned the wisest lamas, yogis, and yoginis from endless meditative retreat in their silent caves.

Soon the monastic assembly was gathered in the luxurious chamber, with gaunt and pasty high-cheeked faces, long wispy beards and top knots, and musty crimson wool robes scented with mildew.

"The question," said the abbess, "is whether our young guest predicts events—or creates them."

A hoarse buzz rose from the assembly as they broke their vows of silence and solitude to debate this complex issue. They discussed the profound implications, split fine doctrinal hairs, and quoted ancient texts. Finally the lamas, yogis, and yoginis reached the following conclusion: The young word-woman neither predicts nor causes the events. Neither word nor event are truly real; they arise simultaneously from the infinite swirling void to evoke the illusion of reality.

The village leaders looked confused. They'd never heard so many words in their lives—and they didn't understand half of them. They gruffly thanked the abbess and the wise ones, finished their salty buttered tea and barley dumplings, and led young Drolma away.

As they trekked silently across the high, grassy plateau to their village, Drolma suddenly stopped. Her black eyes flashed as she pointed with her outstretched finger to a distant snow peak, and said loudly and clearly, "Gold!"

"I don't care if it's real or an illusion," guffawed the head-man. "Lead me to the gold, child. Show me where it is!"

The village leaders were excited. Everyone knew that the surrounding peaks contained rich deposits of gold—enough to make all the villagers wealthy. But finding the gold was a difficult and dangerous task—unless they had a clever young word-woman to guide them.

"Gold!" laughed Drolma, leading the eager villagers up into the craggy, barren snow peaks where only eagles fly and leopards tread. Now she had spoken a word of tremendous power, which sends feverish highlanders and lowlanders off on hazardous quests.

But even with a guide their journey proved perilous. Drolma scampered between thickets of wild rhododendron and bamboo, following a pathway cut by a small brook up through the snowy forested foothills, and into the steep rocky slopes above the treeline where the frigid air was thin and the sky the color of lapis lazuli.

In the uncharted mountains there were few sounds except the keening wind and the cries of solitary birds. Even the prowling snow leopards do not climb above the tree line, and no hunter, herder or mendicant of Dza had ever explored these slopes.

Lured by their eagerness for gold, the stolid band of villagers followed Drolma through the twining maze of steep canyons. Treacherous footholds in crumbling gravel set off small avalanches that loosened boulders, so the whole world seemed to be tumbling around them. Sudden storms drenched them with sleet, and their provisions soon ran short. The villagers panted in the thin air and backtracked countless times, picking their way along icy, narrow ledges that easily collapsed under their weight. Even these sturdy highlanders began to fear for their lives, yet the desire for gold led them on.

Late the next afternoon, they descended into a remote alpine glade filled with a profusion of orange and yellow poppies, brilliantly illuminated by the violet rays of the setting sun. The place looked inviting, and the exhausted band sank down to rest and revive themselves with the last of their cold tea and barley flour.

But the young word-woman of Dza went wild. "Gold!" Drolma whooped, romping and capering among the lush and magnificent poppies—which did have a golden tinge in the sunset. "Gold!" laughed Drolma as she frolicked about.

"Where's the gold, child?" asked the village headman wearily.

"Here," said Drolma, with a happy face.

"Do you think she meant them flowers?" asked one of the villagers gruffly.

"Could be," said the headman with a taciturn nod.

Had Drolma's words foretold the glade of golden poppies—or created them? Or were both words and gilded poppies an illusion, arising simultaneously from the swirling void?

The silent Dza folk were too stiff and weary for such questions. They watched their young word-woman play merrily among her pure, golden flowers while they rested for a day. Then with benevolent chagrin they followed her home, to their poor but peaceful village in the quiet highland valley of Dza.

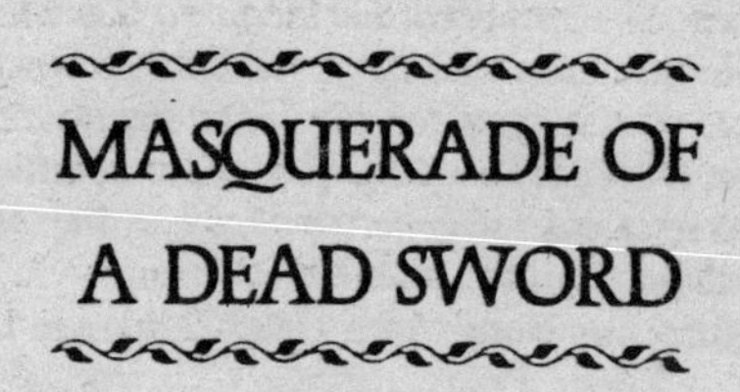

MASQUERADE OF A DEAD SWORD

Thomas Ligotti

I first encountered the work of Thomas Ligotti in the macabre-surrealist journal **Grimoire** *edited by Thomas Wiloch. I wrote at once to Karl Edward Wagner suggesting in particular one story for* **Year's Best Horror**. *Karl lacked the good sense to listen to me. Another respected magazine of weird surrealism is* **Nyctalops** *from Silver Scarab Press, where I again encountered Tom's work. Other specialty publications to feature his stories are* **Fantasy Tales** *and* **Dark Horizons** *in England, and eventually the new* **Fantasy & Terror** *edited by myself and published by Richard H. Fawcett in Connecticut. I outline this so that you'll know generally how Monsieur Ligotti has been creating a fierce stir among the fanatic devotees of horror literature. But his voice is perhaps* too *original for instant recognition among the typical editor or anthologist of horror fiction, a field where conservatism invariably translates* artistic *as being* pretentious *and where even a microscopic moment of the experimental creates paroxysms of disdain. You see, Thomas Ligotti is not a fellow whose chief inspiration can be seen to be the dreary horror of the pulp era. He tempers this inspiration with an easy comprehension of the gloomier aspects of the German expressionism and French symbolism* *long before "the pulps" degraded fiction to the level of comic book scripting.*

As indicated, Thomas writes mainly horror, and horror of a kind not sleazy, stupid, or boring enough for most horror publishers. I had detected, however, a very dark sort of romanticism that would adapt nicely to the kind of heroic fantasy that, to me, is what great heroic fantasy is all about. Ah! If only I could convince this horror author to try his hand at heroic fantasy! Did I convince him? The proof is before your eyes right now—Monsieur Ligotti's debut to the "general" public, the newsstand buyer as opposed to the fanatics who already know him from the little magazines.

His first collection **Songs of a Dead Dreamer** *is forthcoming from Silver Scarab Press, Albuquerque, New Mexico.*

When the world uncovers some dark disguise,
Embrace the darkness with averted eyes

—Psalms of the Silent

I. Faliol's Rescue

No doubt the confusions of carnival night were to blame, in some measure, for many unforeseen incidents. Every violation of routine order was being perpetrated by the carousing mob, their cries of celebration providing the upper voices to a strange droning pedal point which seemed to be sustained by the night itself. Having tentatively declared their town an enemy of silence, the citizens of Soldori took to the streets: there they conspired against solitude and, to accompanying gyrations of squealing abandon, sabotaged monotony. Even the duke, a cautious man and one not normally given to those gaudy agendas of his counterparts in Lynnese or Daranzella, was now holding an extravagant masquerade, if only as a strategic concession to the little patch of world under his rule. Of all the inhabitants of the Three Towns, the subjects of the Duke of Soldori—occasionally to the duke's own dismay—were the most loving of amusement. In every quarter of this principality frolicking celebrants combed the night for a new paradise, and were as likely to find it in a blood match as in a song. All seemed anxious, even frantic to follow blindly the entire spectrum of diversion, to dawdle about the lines between pain and pleasure, to obscure their vision of both past and future.

So perhaps three well-drunk and boar-faced men seated in the alcove of a roisterous hostelry could be excused for not recognizing Faliol, whose colors were always red and black. But this man who had just entered the thickish gloom of that house was attired in a craze of colors, none of them construed to a pointed effect. One might have described this outfit as motley gone mad. Indeed, perhaps what lay beneath this fool's patchwork were the familiar blacks and reds that no other of the Three Towns—neither those who were dandies, nor those who were sword-whores (however golden were their hearts), nor even those who, like Faliol himself, were both—would have dared to parody. But these near notorious colors were now buried deep within a rainbow of rags tied about the man's arms, legs, and at every other point of his person, seeming to hold him together like torn strips hurriedly applied to the storm-fractured joists of a sagging roof. Before he had closed the door of that cavelike room behind him, the draft rushing in from the street made his ragged livery come alive like a mass of tattered flags flapping in a calamitous wind.

But even had he not been cast as a tatterdemalian, there was still so much else about Faliol that was unlike his former self. His sword, a startling length of blade to be pulled along by this ragman, bobbed about at his left side, unbuckled because buckleless. His dagger, whose sheath bore a mirror of polished metal (which now seemed a relic of more dandified days), was strung loosely behind his left shoulder, as if it could fall at any moment. And his hair was trimmed monkishly close to the scalp, leaving little reminder of gloriously hirsute days. But possibly the greatest alteration, the greatest problem and mystery of Folial's travesty of his own image, was the presence on his face of a pair of simple . . . spectacles. And owing that the glass of these spectacles was unevenly blemished, as though murky currents flowed within their brittle surface, the eyes behind them were obscured.

Still, there remained any number of signs by which a discerning scrutiny could have identified the celebrated Faliol. For as he moved toward a seat adjacent to the alcove where the booming-voiced trio was ensconsed, he moved with a scornful, somehow involuntary sureness of which no reversals of fate could completely unburden him. And his boots, though their fine black leather had gone gray with the dust of roads that a zealous equestrian such as Faliol would never have trod, still jangled with a few of those once innumerable silver links from which dangled small, agate-eyed medallions, ones exactly like that larger and onyx-eyed medallion which in other days hung from a silver chain around his lean throat. The significance of this particular ornament was such that Faliol—though often questioned, but never twice by the same inquisitor—avoided revelations.

Now, however, no medallion of any kind was displayed upon Faliol's chest; and where he had lost or renounced the inkish eye of onyx, he had acquired two eyes of shadowed glass. Each lens of the spectacles reflected, like twin moons, the glow of the lantern above the place where Faliol seated himself. As if unaware that he was not settled in some cloistered cell of lucubration, he removed from somewhere within his shredded clothes a small book having the words *Psalms of the Silent* written in raised letters upon its soft, worn cover. And the cover was black, while the letters were the red of fallen leaves.

"Faliol, a scholar?" someone whispered in the crowded depths of the room, while another added: "And a scholar of his own grief, so I've heard."

Faliol unfixed the tiny silver clasp and opened the book somewhere toward its middle, where a thin strip of red velvet cloth, one the same shade as the letters upon the cover of the book, marked his place. And if there had been a miniature mirror bound in place of the book's left-hand leaf, Faliol could have seen three thuggish men gazing mutely, not to say thoughtfully, in his direction. Moreover if there had been a second mirror seat at the same angle of the book's right-hand leaf, he could also have noticed a fourth pair of eyes spying on him from the other side of the hostelry's engrimed windowpanes.

But there were only long, stern-looking letters written—to be precise handwritten, in Faliol's own hand—upon the opposing leaves of his book. Thus Faliol could not have seen either of these parties who, for reasons separate or similar, were observing him. He saw only two pale pages elegantly dappled by the words of somber verses. Then a shadow passed across these pages, and another, and another.

The three men were standing evenly spaced before Faliol, though he continued to read as if they were not present. He read until the lantern above was extinguished, its stump of tallow snuffed out by the middleman's hugely knuckled stumps of flesh. Clasping his book closed, Faliol replaced it within the rags around his heart and sat perfectly still. The three men seemed to watch in a trance of hilarity at this slowly and solemnly executed sequence of actions. The face at the windowpanes merely pressed closer to witness what, in its view, was a soundless scene.

Some harsh words appeared to be addressed to the man in rags and spectacles. The first of the three standing men splashed some ale in the seated man's face, as did the second man from his enormous tankard. Then more ale—this time expectorated—was received by the victim as the third man's contribution to what became quite a lengthy series of petty torments. But Faliol remained silent and as motionless as possible, an attitude of mind and body that seemed only to provoke further the carnival-mad souls of the three Soldorians. As the moments passed, the men waxed more cruel and their torments more inventive. Finally they jostled a bloody-mouthed Faliol out of his seat, two of them pinioned him against the planks of the wall, someone snatched his spectacles . . .

Two blue eyes were suddenly revealed: they firmly clenched themselves closed, then reopened as if bursting out of black depths and into the light. Faliol's mouth stretched wide to let out a perfectly silent scream or one beyond human hearing—the scream of a mute under torture. But very soon his features relaxed, while his ragged chest began pumping up and down with an even rhythm.

The one who had taken Faliol's spectacles had turned away, and his clumsy fingers were fiddling with delicate silver stems, fumbling with two shadowy lenses—as though shadows were sealed within them—that were more precious than he knew. Thus amused and diverted, he did not perceive that Faliol was terrifying both of his companions out of their wits, that they had loosened their grasp on him, and that he had drawn his dagger from its shoulder sheath.

"Where are you go—" he started to shout at his loutish comrades, as they ran bleeding from the hostelry's horror. Then he turned about-face to feel Faliol's sword against his greasy leather doublet. He saw, he must have seen, that the blade was unclean but very sharp; and he must have felt it scrape playfully against the chain-mail vest concealed beneath his doublet's sorry cover. Soon Faliol was lowering his blade until it reached the spot where the mail vest's protection no longer protected. "Now put them on, that you might see," he quietly instructed the giant with the pair of tiny toy spectacles. "Put . . . them . . . on," he said in a calm, dead voice.

The giant, his lip-licking tongue visibly parched, obeyed the command.

Everyone in the room leaned to see the giant in dark spectacles, and so did the well-groomed face at the hostelry window. Most of the men laughed—drunkenly and anonymously—but a few remained silent, if they did not in fact become silent, at this sight. "And a scholar of the wildest folly too," someone whispered. Faliol himself grinned like a demon, his eyes widening at his work. After a few moments he returned his sword to its sheath, and even so the giant held his transfixed position. Faliol put away his dagger, and the giant did not budge a hair. Frozen, paralytic, he stood with arms hanging limp and thick at his enormous flanks, slightly trembling. The giant's face was extraordinarily pale, his grizzled cheeks like two mounds of snow that had been sown with ashes. Above them, circles of glass gleamed like two dark moons.

All laughter had ceased by now, and many turned away. The giant's meaty lips were opening and closing, very slowly and very much in the manner of a dying fish gasping in the dry air. But the giant, having worn Faliol's own eyes, was not dying in his body: only his mind was a corpse. "The wildest folly," whispered the same voice.

Gently, almost contritely, Faliol removed the spectacles from the face of the grotesque idol, though he waited until he was outside the hostelry's latest horror before replacing them on his own.

"Sir," called a voice from the shadows of the street. Faliol paused, but only as if considering the atmosphere of the night and not necessarily in response to an unknown accoster. "Please allow me to identify myself with the name Streldone. My messenger spoke with you in Lynnese? Good, that is a blessing. Here is my coach, so that we need not talk in all this confusion," he said, gesturing toward the jerking shadows of that carnival night. And when the coach began moving down streets on the circumference of the festivities, this expensively attired man—though he was still only a youth—continued to speak to a silent Faliol.

"I was informed that you had arrived in Soldori not long ago, and have been following you since, waiting for a discreet moment to approach you. Of course you were aware of my presence," he said, pausing to scan Faliol's expressionless face. "Well, but this is all something I know nothing about. In any event, how unfortunate that you were forced to reveal yourself back in that sty of a drinking house. But I suppose you couldn't allow yourself to undergo much more of that treatment merely for the sake of anonymity. No harm done, I'm sure."

"And I am sure," Faliol replied in a monotone, "that three very sad men would disagree with you."

The young man laughed briefly at what he understood to be a witticism. "In any event, their kind will have their throats wrapped in the red cord sooner or later. The duke is quite severe when it comes to the lawlessness of others. Which brings me to what I require of you tonight, assuming that we need not bargain over the terms my messenger proposed to you in Lynnese. Very well," said Streldone, though obviously he had been prepared to haggle. But he left no pause that might have been filled with the second thoughts of this hired sword, who looked and acted more like one of the clockwork automatons that performed their mechanical routines high above the town square of Soldori. Thus with a slow turn of his head and a set movement of his hand, Faliol received the jeweled pouch containing one-half the total sum of his payment. Streldone promised that the other portion would follow upon the accomplishment of the night's work, as he now portrayed its reasons and aims.

It seemed there was a young woman of a noble and wealthy family, a young woman whom Streldone loved and who loved him in return. At least she loved him to the point of accepting his proposal of marriage and cleaving to his vision of their future as two who would be one. But there was also another, a man who called himself, or who was called, Wynge. Streldone referred to him thereafter as the Sorcerer, by way of further severing his adversary from the dignity of an authentic name. As Streldone explained the situation, the Sorcerer had appropriated the young woman for himself. This unnatural feat was achieved, Streldone hated to say, not only with the compliance of the young woman's father, but also through the powerful offices of the Duke of Soldori himself. Both men, according to Streldone, had been persuaded to this deed by the

Sorcerer's promise to supply them, by means of alchemical transmutations of base metals into gold and silver, with an unending source of riches to finance their wars and other undertakings of ambition. Without bothering to embellish the point, Streldone explained that he and his beloved, in their present state of separation, were two of the most wretched beings in all the world and two of the most deserving of assistance in their struggle to be reunited. And tonight Faliol must help untangle them from the taut, controlling strings of the Sorcerer and his compatriots in evil.

"Do I have your attention, sir?" Streldone abruptly asked.

Faliol vouchsafed his understanding of the matter by repeating word for word Streldone's account of his plight.

"Well, I am glad to know that your wits really are in order, however distracted you may seem. In any event, tonight the Sorcerer is attending the duke's masquerade at the palace. She will be with him. Help me steal her back so that we may both escape from Soldori, and I will fill the empty part of that pouch."

Faliol asked if Streldone had possessed the foresight to have brought along a pair of costumes to enable their entrance to the masquerade. Streldone, somewhat vainly, produced from the shadows of the coach two such costumes, one that was appropriate to a knight of the old days and the other that of a court jester of the same period. Faliol reached out for the wildly patterned costume with the jeering mask.

"But I am afraid," said Streldone, "that I intended that costume for myself. The other is more suited to allow your sword—"

"No sword will be needed," Faliol assured his nervous companion. "This will be everything," he added, holding the hook-nosed fool's face opposite his own.

They were now traveling in the direction of the palace, and Soldori's carnival began to thicken about the wheels of Streldone's coach. Gazing upon the nocturnal confusion, Faliol's eyes were as dark and swirled with shadows as the raving night itself.

II. The Story of the Spectacles

His eyes fixed and clouded as a blind man's, the mage sat before a small circular table upon which a single wax taper burned in its plain silver stick. Illuminated by that modest flame, the surface of the table was spread with inlaid designs composed of both esoteric symbols and representations of natural objects, a constellation of shapes that reduced essential forces of spiritual and material existence to a few rather picturesque patterns. But the mage was not occupied with these. He was simply listening to someone who was raving in the shadows of that most secret chamber. The hour was late and the night was without a moon: the narrow window behind the beardless, pallid face of the mage was a solid sheet of blackness gleaming in the candlelight. Every so often someone would move before this window, his hands running through his thick dark hair as he spoke, or tried to speak. Occasionally he would move toward the candleflame, and a glimpse could be caught of his fine attire in blacks and reds, his shining blue eyes, his fevered face. Calmly the mage listened to the man's wild speech.

"Not if I have become mad but of what my madness consists is the knowledge I seek from you. And please understand that I have no hopes, only a searing curiosity to riddle the corpse of my dead soul. To the question were there not deeds in my past life that one might deem mad, I would be obliged to answer—Yes, countless deeds, countless mad games of flesh and steel. Having confessed that, I would also avow that these were *sanctioned* provocations of chaos, known in some form to the body of the world, and even blessed by it, if the truth be spoken. But I have provoked another thing, a new madness which arrives from a world that is on the wrong side of light, a madness that is unsanctioned and without the seal of our natural selves. It is a forbidden madness, a saboteur from outside the body of known laws. And as you know, I have been the subject of its sabotage.

"Since the madness began working its destruction, I have become an adept of every horror that can be thought, or sensed or dreamed. In my very dreams—have I told you about them?—there are scenes of slaughter without purpose, without constraint, and without end. In fleeing them, I have crept through dense forests where each tree is a crudely formed pike, upon each of which a more crudely formed head has been fixed. And each head wears a face, the same face, one that would forever blind the eyes that saw it anywhere but in a dream. These heads follow my movements not with eyes of their own, but with shadows that move within empty sockets. Sometimes the heads speak as I pass through their hideous ranks, telling me of their ancient impalements in a manner I cannot bear to hear. But I cannot prevent hearing their words, and I listen until I have learned the history, the horrible secrets of each brutal head . . . and the voices from their ragged mouths, so clear, so precise to my ears, that every word is a bright flash in my dreaming brain, a brilliant new coin minted for the treasure houses of hell. At the end of my mad dream the heads will make an effort to . . . laugh, creating a blasphemous babble which echoes throughout that terrible forest. And when I awaken I find myself standing on some hillside where I have never been, and for a moment the night continues to reverberate with fading laughter.

"But did I say that I awoke? If I did, then that is only one more madness among many. For to awaken, as I once understood this miracle, means to reinherit a world of laws that for a time were lost, to rise into the light of waking as one falls into the darkness of dream. And it is this feeling itself that, for me, is lost. There is no sense of breaking through the envelope of sleep, that delicate membrane which excludes merely a single universe while containing countless more. Not the faintest breath, not the smallest stitch of the slightest seam divides these dreams, these visions. For when that one leaves off, this one begins, each giving way to the other like a labyrinth of connected rooms which will never lead to freedom beyond their strange walls. And for all that I can know, I am even now the inhabitant of such a room, and at any moment you—I beg forgiveness, wise man—you may begin to disembowel weeping children before my eyes and smear their entrails upon the floor so that in them you may read my future, a future without escape from those heads, that hillside, and from what comes after.

"There is a citadel in which I am a prisoner and that holds within it a type of school, a school of torture. Ceremonial stranglers, their palms grooved by the red cord, stalk the corridors of the citadel or lie snoring in its shadows, dreaming of perfect throats. Apprentice artists of mayhem curse softly as their mutilated canvasses prematurely expire of their elegant lacerations. And somewhere the supreme inquisitor waits as I am dragged across crude, incredibly crude floors and am presented to his rolling, witless eyes. Then my arms, my legs, everything shackled and screaming to die before the Torture of the Question—"

"Enough," said the mage without raising his voice.

"Enough," the madman repeated. "And so have I said numberless times. But there is no end, there is no hope. And this endless, hopeless torment inspires me to the single ambition of turning its power on others, even to dream of turning it on all. To see the world drown in the oceans of my agony is the only vision that now brings me any relief from this madness, from this madness that is *not of this world*."

"Though neither is it of any other world," said the mage in the same quiet voice.

"But I have also had visions of butchering the angels," replied the madman, as if to argue the absolute hopelessness of his mania.

"You have envisioned precisely what you believe you have not envisioned. But how could you have known this, when it is the nature of what you have seen—this anima mundi of the oldest philosophers and alchemists—to deceive and to pose as the soul of another world, not the soul of the world we know? There is only one world and one soul of that world, which appears in beauty or in boredom or in madness according to how deeply anima mundi has revealed itself to you. It is something that is not there when you look, and there again when you look away. Having the aspects of every god or demon ever conceived, it nonetheless keeps itself beyond conception."

"Though you speak of it as you would any being."

"There is no other or truer way. Like god or demon, it is all of ourselves and no one of ourselves. But no further words now," finished the mage.

He then instructed the mad dreamer to seat himself at the table of arcane designs and to wait there with eyes calmly closed. And for what remained of that moonless night, the mage worked secretly in another part of his house, returning to the wretched dreamer just before dawn. In one of his hands was the product of his labors: a pair of strangely darkened spectacles.

"Do not open your unhappy eyes, my friend, but listen to my words. I know the visions you have known, for they are the visions I was born to know. There are eyes within our eyes, and when these others open, all becomes confusion and horror. The meaning of my long life has been to seize and settle these visions, until my natural eyes themselves have altered in accordance with them. Now, for what reasons I cannot say, anima mundi has revealed itself to you in its most brutal aspect; which is to say, its secret face. Thus your life will never again be as you have known it. All the pleasures of the past are now defiled, all your hopes violated beyond hope. There are things that only madmen fear because only madmen may truly conceive of them. Your world is presently black with the scars of madness, but you must make it blacker still in order to find any soundness or peace. You have seen both too much and not enough. Through the shadow-fogged lenses of these spectacles you will be blinded so that you may see with greater sight. Through their darkly clouded glass the lesser madnesses of anima mundi will diffuse into the infinite, all-permeating vision of things in which madness is the sole substance, and thereby becomes absent and meaningless for its very ubiquity and absolute meaning. But what would murder another man's mind will bring yours peace, while making you a puppet of peace rather than its prince.

"Henceforth, all things will be in your eyes a distant play of shadows that fretfully strive to impersonate something real, ghosts that clamor to pass themselves as flesh, masks that desperately flit about to conceal the stillness of the void behind them—henceforth, all things will be reduced in your eyes to their inconsequential essence. And all that once shined for you—the steel, the stars, the eyes of another—will lose its luster and take its place among the other shadows. All will be dulled in the power of your vision, which will give you to see that the greatest power, the only power, is to care for nothing.

"Please know that this is the only way I may help you, for my life has taught me that no single soul may be restored where there is no hope of restoring the soul of the world itself. One final word: you must never be without these spectacles, or your furies will return to you. There, now you may open your eyes."

Faliol sat very still for some time. At first he did not notice that one of the mage's own eyes was closed, covered by a sagging eyelid. When at last he saw this and perceived the sacrifice, he said, "And how may I serve you, wise man?"

In the window behind the two seated figures, the dull light of dawn was grappling with the darkness of the past night, with the shadows that seemed almost to be clinging to the window's glass or were sealed within it.

III. Anima Mundi

While the revelers in the streets of Soldori remedied their discontents by throwing off the everyday face of orthodoxy, those attending the masquerade at the duke's palace found their deliverance by donning other faces, other bodies, and perhaps other souls. The anonymity of that night—no unmasking was expected to be held—enabled a multitude of sins against taste, from the most subtle to the most grotesque indiscretions. The society of the court had transformed itself into a race of gods or monsters, competing at once with the brightest and highest of stars and the strangest of the world's lower creatures. Many would undoubtedly spend the succeeding days or weeks in darkened rooms behind closed doors, so that the effects their disguises had wrought on their bodies might be known to none. For a few rare souls this, by necessity, would be their last appearance in the eyes of the court before a final seclusion. All were quite clearly arrayed as if something unparalleled, and possibly conclusive, was to occur that night. Musicians played in several of the palace's most sumptuous and shimmering halls, glittering glasses were filled by fountains of bizarrely colored wine, and masters swarmed about like living gargoyles freed from the cathedral's stone. All, or nearly all, were straining for some unheard of antic, suffering the pleasures of expectancy.

But as the hours passed, hopes dissolved. The duke—in essence a simple man, even a dull one—took no initiative to unloose the abundant possibilities of the masquerade; and, as if secretly aware of these perilous directions, he restrained the efforts of others to pursue them, to digress from the night's steadily unwinding course. No coaxing could sway him: he allowed several odd witticisms to pass unacknowledged and feigned, if it was not so in fact, that certain dubious suggestions and proposals were obscure to his mind. Unnourished by any source in the duke's own nature, every attempt at innovation curled at its colorful edges and died. The initial strangeness of the masked gathering went stale; voices began to sound as though they were transacting business of some tedious sort, and even the sight of a jester—albeit one with darkness within the eyes of his mask—offered no special merriment to this sullen assembly.

Accompanying the jester, who moved in no lively manner, was a knight out of armor, dressed in radiant blues and golds, a crusader's cross proudly upon his chest and a white silk mast of blandly noble expression covering his face. The odd duo progressed from room to dazzling, crowded room of the palace, as if they were negotiating a thick wood in search of something or someone. The knight appeared nervous, his hand too obviously ready to go for the sword at his side, his head patrolling with skittish alertness the bizarre world around him. The jester, on the other hand, was altogether more composed and methodical, and with excellent reason: he knew as the knight did not, that their purpose was not a difficult one, especially as they would enjoy the complicity of Wynge himself, whom the knight had called the Sorcerer and whom the jester addressed as a wise man mage. Had Faliol not been invited to Soldori by a certain messenger who served two masters? And was not Wynge eager to release himself from the unhappy girl who was only a pawn in her father's and the duke's game of power? Once she was out of the scene, these two men, both emulous of a god's glory, would lose the link by which they attached themselves to the mage, whose retorts and formulas they mistakenly believed would provide them with magical riches. Under the present circumstances the knight might easily regain his beloved, and the jester would finally make good a debt, settling the price he owed for a pair of spectacles.

The two characters paused at the hugely arched entrance to the last and most intimate of the masquerade's many rooms. Pulling at the knight's golden sleeve, the jester angled his pointed, sneering muzzle toward a costumed pair in the far corner. These distant figures were impersonating two monarchs of the old days, a king and queen in ancient robes and stoles and many-horned crowns.

"How can you be sure that they are the ones?" whispered the knight to the buffoon at his side.

"Boldly approach and take her hand. You will be sure, but say nothing until you have let yourselves back through these rooms and to freedom."

"But the Sorcerer," objected the knight. "He could have us both executed."

"All is safe. While I engage him as the king's jester, you will make off with the queen. Trust that what I tell you is true."

"I do trust you," said the knight, as he surreptitiously stuffed a jeweled pouch twice the size of the first into the belt of the jester.

The two characters separated and merged with the murmuring crowd. A few moments later the jester arrived first at their destination. From a distance he seemed to speak a few words into the king's ear, and then suddenly leaped back to play the fool before him, wheeling about wildly. The knight bowed before the queen and then without ostentation led her away to other rooms. Although her masked face smothered all expression, the manner in which she placed her hand upon his appeared to reveal her knowledge of the knight's identity. After they had gone, the jester ceased his antics and approached the stern and statuelike king.

"I shall watch the duke's men around us, who may have been watching you, wise man."

"And I shall see that our two little babes find their way through forest," replied the mock monarch, who abruptly strode off.

But that was not part of your design, thought Faliol. And neither was the pseudo-king's playful voice that of the solemn mage. The dark eyes of the jester's mask followed the movements of the imposter, until he passed through the hugely arched entrance and became lost in the dreamlike throng of the next room. Faliol had just started in pursuit when a strange commotion in some distant part of the palace swiftly conveyed its anxieties and rumors through all the rooms of the masquerade.

But now that something unheard of had finally occurred, it seemed neither to delight nor relieve any of those same souls who had wished for some unique happening on that carnival night.

The disturbance originated in the centermost room of that labyrinth of rooms composing the arena of the masquerade. To the surrounding as well as the peripheral rooms, including the one in which Faliol was now caught by the crushing crowd, there first travelled sounds of sudden amusement. These were quickly transformed, however, into ambiguous outbursts of surprise, even shock. Finally the uproar took on the character of intense horror—all voices in alarm and confusion, all movements alarmed and confused. Word passed rapidly, though less and less reliably, from mouth to mouth, room to room. Something terrible had happened, something that had begun, or was initially perceived, as a fabulous hoax. No one knew exactly how it was possible, but there suddenly appeared in the midst of the most populated room some outlandish display: two gruesome figures whose costumes went far beyond anything previously displayed at the masque. Someone said they were most closely akin to giant leeches or worms, for they did not walk upright but writhed along the floor. Another had heard that the creatures possessed countless tiny legs, and thus more properly resembled centipedes of some type. Still others contributed further characteristics—many-taloned claws, reptilian tails, near-human faces—which made up the composition of the fantastic beasts. But whatever may have been the initial reaction to these presumably artificial creatures—at some point they inspired the crowd with unreasoning panic. And however the subsequent actions may have transpired, the consequence was that these bizarre intruders were hacked and torn and trampled beyond recognition by the frenzied, nightmarish gathering.

Tragically, once the massacre was accomplished, it was not the slaughtered remains of two uncanny monsters that the masqueraders—their masks removed—now looked down upon. Instead it was two of their own—a knight and queen of the old day—whose blood now trickled across the intricate designs of the palace floor. Their two bodies, once separated, were now all but indistinguishable.

Throwing off his jester's face, Faliol worked himself near enough to the scene to confirm the horror with his own shaded eyes, merely to confirm it. For the image delivered to his mind immediately took its place among the seamless and unending flow of hellish eidola that constituted anima mundi, that monotonous tapestry of the terrible constantly unfurling itself before his vision in unaffecting tones of shadowy gray. Thus the appalling tableau he now witnessed was neither more nor less sinister in his sight than any other the world might show him.

"Look again, Fa-fa-faliol," said a voice behind him, as a forceful boot propelled him within inches of the carnage.

But why was everything painted so brilliantly now, when a moment ago it seemed so dull, so unspectacular? Why did every piece of severed flesh quiver with color? And even more vividly than their red-smeared forms did the horrible fates of these unhappy beings affect Faliol's mind and feelings. He had been hired to save them and he could do . . . nothing. His thoughts were now careening wildly through crimson corridors within him, madly seeking solutions but falling at every turn into blind corners and flailing hopelessly against something immovable, impossible. He pressed the heels of his hands to the sockets of his eyes, hoping to blacken the radiant scene. But everything remained invincibly there before those omniscient eyes—everything save the spectacles.

Now the duke's voice broke into the brief lull of the dazed and incredulous assembly. It shouted orders, demanded answers. It proclaimed the ruler's prophetic misgivings concerning the masquerade and its dangers: he had long known that something of this nature might occur, and had done what he could to prevent its coming to pass. On the spot he outlawed all future occasions of this kind and called for arrests and interrogations, the Torture of the Question to be liberally implemented. Exodus was instantaneous—the palace became a chaos of fleeing freaks.

"Faliol!" called a voice that sounded too clear within all the confusion to have its origin outside his own mind. "I have what you're looking for. They're with me now, right here in my hand, not lost forever."

When Faliol turned around, he saw the masked king standing some distance away, unmolested by the frantic mob. The king's hand was holding out the spectacles, as if they were the dangling head of a conquered foe. Fighting his way toward the unknown persecutor, Faliol continued to remain several steps behind him as he was led by this demon through all the rooms where the masquerade once flourished, and then deeper into the palace. At the end of a long silent corridor, the gaudy, flapping train of a royal robe disappeared into a doorway. Faliol followed the fluttering bait and at last entered a dim chamber with a single window, before which stood the mummer in a sparkling silk mask. The spectacles were still held by the velvet fingers of a tightly gloved hand. Watching as the dark lenses flashed in the candlelight, Faliol's eyes burned as much with questions as with madness.

"Where is the mage?" he demanded.

"The mage is no more. Quickly, what else?"

"Who are you?"

"Wasted question, you know who I am. What else?"

"What are you?"

"Another one like the other. Say I'm a sorcerer, very well?"

"And you killed the mage as you did the others."

"The others? How could you have not heard that rattling pantomime, all those swords and swift feet? Didn't you hear that there was a pair of leviathan leeches, or something in that way, menacing the guests? True, I had a hand in the illusion, but my hand contained no gouging blade. A shambles, you saw it with your own eyes."

"In their fate you saw your own future. Even a sorcerer may be killed."

"Agreed, even a sorcerer with three eyes, or two eyes, or one."

"Who are you to have destroyed the mage?"

"In fact he destroyed himself—an heroic act, I'm sure—some days ago. And he did it before *my* eyes, as if in spite. As for myself, I confess that I'm disappointed to be so far beneath your recognition. We have met previously, please remember. But it was many years past, and I suppose you became forgetful as well as dim-sighted once you put those pieces of glass over your eyes. You see why the mage had to be stopped. He ruined you as a madman, as *my* madman.

"But you might recall that you had another career before the madness took you, did you not? Buh-buh-brave Faliol. Don't you remember how you were made that way? Don't you wish to remember that you were merely Faliol the dandy before we met on the road that day? It was I—in my role as a genuine charm seller—who outfitted you with that onyx-eyed amulet which you once wore around your neck, and which made you the skillful mercenary you once were. That you loved to be.

"And how everyone else loved you that way: to see a weakling transformed into a man of strength and of steel is the stuff of public comment, of legend, of the crowd's *amusement*. And how much more do they love to witness the reverse of this magical process: to see the mighty laid low, the lord of the sword made mad. This was the little drama I had planned. You were supposed to be *my* madman, Faliol, not the placid fool of that magician—a real lost soul of torments in red and black, not a pathetic monk chanting silent psalms in pale breaths. Don't you understand? It was that Wynge, or whatever his name was, who ruined you, who undid all my schemes for your tragic and colorful history. Because of him I had to change my plans and chase you down to this place. Blame him, if anyone, for the slaughter of those innocents and for what you are about to suffer. You know my ways, we are not strangers."

"No, demon horror, we are not. You are indeed the foul thing the wise man described to me, all the dark powers we cannot understand, but can only hate."

"Powers? At least the magician spoke of me as a being, a person like everyone but not quite like anyone. I honor him for his precise vision, as far as it went. But you're wrong to contend that no one understands me; and as for hating the one who stands before you—nothing, in truth, could be further from truth. Listen, do you hear those brawling voices in the streets beyond the window? Those are not voices filled with hate. In fact they could not possibly hold a greater love for me. And reciprocally I love them, every one of them: all I do is for them. Did you think that my business was the exceptional destinies of heroes and magicians, of kings and queens, saints and sinners, of all the so-called great? Such extravagant freaks come and go, they are puppets who dance before the eternal eyes of my true children. Only in these multitudes do I live, and through their eyes I see my own glory."

"You see but your own foulness."

"No, the foulness is yours alone to see, Faliol. You see what, for them, truly does not exist. This is a privileged doom reserved for creatures such as yourself. A type of consolation."

"You have said enough."

"Only because you wish my saying to go on, because you fear what will happen when I end my speech. But I haven't said what I came here to say, or rather to ask. You know the question, don't deny it, Faliol. The one you dreamed in those dreams that were not dreams. The Torture of the Question you dreaded to hear asked, and dreaded more to have answered."

"Demon!"

"What is the face of the soul of the world?"

"It is only a dead face, a face that is not a face."

"No, Faliol, it is *this* face," said the masked figure as it peeled away its mask. "But why have you hidden your eyes that way, Faliol? And why have you fallen to your knees? Don't you appreciate the vision I've shown you? Could you ever have imagined that your life would lead you into the presence of such a sight? Your spectacles cannot save you now, now that you have seen. They are only so much glinting glass—there, listen to how they crunch into smaller and smaller fragments upon the fine, cool marble of the floor. No more spectacles, no more magic, no more magician. And I think, too, no more Faliol. Can you understand what I'm telling you now, jester? Well, what have you got to say? Nothing? How black your madness must be to make you so rude a buffoon. How black. But see, even though you cannot, how I've provided these escorts to show you the way back to the carnival, which is where a fool belongs. And be sure that you make my favorite little children laugh, or I will punish you. Yes, I can still punish you, Faliol. A living man can always be punished, so remember to be good. I will be watching. I am always watching. Farewell, then, fool."

A glazen-eyed guard on either side of him, Faliol was dragged from the duke's palace and given to the crowd which still rioted in the streets of Soldori. And the crowd embraced the mad, sightless jester, hoisting his jingling form upon their shoulders and shaking him like a toy as they carried him along. In its scheme to strangle silence forever, Soldori's unruled populace bellowed a robust refrain to Faliol's sickly moans. And his blind eyes gazed up at an onyx-black night they could not see, which his vanished mind could no longer comprehend.

But there must have been some moment, however brief, in which Faliol regained his old enlightenment and which allowed him to accomplish such a crucial and triumphant action. Was it solely by his own sleeping strength, fleetingly aroused, that he attained his greatest prize? If not, then what power could have enabled his trembling hands to reach so deeply into those haggard sockets, and with a gesture brave and sure, dig out the awful seeds of his suffering? In any event, the deed was done, and done well. For as Faliol perished, his face was flushed with a crimson glory.

And the crowd fell silent, and a new kind of confusion spread among them—these always watching heads—when it was found that what they were bearing through the streets of Soldori was only Faliol's victorious corpse.